"Hard to resist. . . . The writing is so urbane and civilized it makes almost every other proctitioner sound thick and unimaginative. Mr. Pearce has something very individual to offer. May he thrive."

❀

"Great characters, exotic setting, intrigue, danger, and an intricate plot."

❀

"Written in a fascinating lighthearted vein with a hooded villain hovering nearby . . . will have you caught up in an old-time frenzy of finding out what is going on."

❀

"An entertaining and lively tale, enhanced with considerable insight to the time period and the problems of foreign occupation. . . . This is a book not to be missed."

MICHAEL PEARCE grew up in the (then) Anglo-Egyptian Sudan, among the political and cultural tensions he draws on for his Mamur Zapt books. He returned there later to teach and retains a human rights interest in the area.

THE MAMUR ZAPT
AND THE MEN BEHIND

A SUSPENSE TALE OF OLD CAIRO
MICHAEL PEARCE

THE MYSTERIOUS PRESS

Published by Warner Books

A Time Warner Company

Enjoy lively book discussions online with CompuServe. To become a member of CompuServe call 1-800-848-8199 and ask for the Time Warner Trade Publishing forum. (Current members GO:TWEP.)

First published in the United Kingdom by William Collins
Sons & Company, Ltd.

MYSTERIOUS PRESS EDITION

Cover design by Jackie Merri Meyer
Cover illustration by Harry Bliss

The Mysterious Press name and logo are registered trademarks
of Warner Books, Inc.

 Mysterious Press books are published by
Warner Books, Inc.
1271 Avenue of the Americas
New York, NY 10020

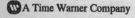 A Time Warner Company

Printed in the United States of America

Originally published in hardcover by The Mysterious Press.
First Printed in Paperback: December, 1994

10 9 8 7 6 5 4 3 2 1

CHAPTER ONE

Riding home from work on the back of his donkey one lunchtime, Fairclough of the Customs Department was shot at by two men. The shots were fired from a distance and missed, and the only damage from the incident resulted when the frightened donkey careered into a fruit stall nearby and deposited both fruit and Fairclough on top of the stall holder, who, since it was lunchtime, was sleeping peacefully under the stall.

Fairclough held court afterwards in the bar of the Sporting Club, which was where Owen caught up with him.

"It was ghastly," he declared, drinking deeply from his tumbler. "There were squashed tomatoes everywhere. Mind you, they saved my life. It looked like blood, you see. All over him, all over me. They must have thought they'd got me."

"What I can't understand," said someone else at the bar, "is why anyone would want to get you anyway. I mean, let's face it, Fairclough, you're not exactly important, and although everyone else in the Department regards you as a bit of a pig, I wouldn't have said that feeling ran high enough for them to want to kill you."

"Perhaps there's a woman in the case," suggested someone.

Fairclough, who was a lifelong bachelor, snorted and peered into his tumbler.

"Unlikely," said someone else. "The only female he lets get anywhere near him is that damned donkey of his."

"Perhaps it's an animal lover. After all, it *is* a very small donkey and a very large Fairclough. Perhaps after years of witnessing this unequal combat somebody has decided to take sides."

"Miss Crispley, perhaps?" suggested someone.

There was a general laugh. Then someone noticed Owen.

"Hello," he said. "On the job already? I see you're starting in a sensible place. The bar. We've got a suspect for you. Miss Crispley, of the Mission."

"Thank you," said Owen. "Or shall I begin with the donkey?"

•   •   •

Beyond what he had told everyone in the bar, Fairclough had little information to give. He always rode home for lunch on his little donkey and he always went that way. Both he and his donkey were creatures of habit. Yes, that would have made it easy for anyone who wanted to attack him.

"Though why in the hell anyone should want to do that," he said, aggrieved, "I haven't the faintest idea."

"You're Customs, aren't you?"

"What's that got to do with it?" said Fairclough touchily.

Customs was one of the lowest ranking Departments and its members were sensitive on the issue.

"I wondered if it could be a question of wanting to settle old scores?"

"Look," said Fairclough, rosy with heat and indignation and, no doubt, drink, "all I am is a bookkeeper. A high-level one perhaps, but basically that's all I am. The returns come in from the ports and I put them together in a way that makes sense to Finance. It's more complicated than it sounds but when you get down to it, that's all it is. I have nothing," said Fairclough with emphasis, "absolutely nothing to do with the front end of the business. Smugglers are just a row of figures to me. And that," said Fairclough, "is the way I'd like them to stay."

"There's been no recent row of figures of any particular significance?"

"Not to do with smuggling, no. From the point of view of Finance, yes. There always is. But even those bastards haven't got around to sending out shooting parties. Yet."

"If it's not work it could be personal."

"Something in my personal life, you mean?" Fairclough reflected, then shook his head. "Try as I might, I can't find anything I've done bad enough for anyone to want to shoot me."

"Women?"

"No," said Fairclough shortly.

"Others?"

Owen was trying to find a way of referring to any other preferences Fairclough might have.

"Bridge," said Fairclough.

"What?" said Owen, startled.

"Bridge. I play a lot of bridge. And, of course, feelings sometimes run high. But," said Fairclough, weighing the matter, "not as high as that."

"Oh, good."

Fairclough went on thinking.

"No," he said at last, shaking his head. "No, I can't say that anything comes to mind."

"Well, if it does, you'll let me know, won't you?"

"You bet I will," said Fairclough. "I don't want those bastards trying again."

Owen could get little more out of him. He hadn't even seen the men who had fired the shots. That piece of information had come from a passing water-carrier, who had seen two men step out from behind a stationary arabeah, fire the shots and then duck back in again. It had all happened so quickly that the water-carrier had barely had time to notice anything. He wasn't even sure whether the men were dressed in Western-style clothes or in galabeahs.

"I just heard the bangs," said Fairclough, "and then the bloody donkey was bucking all over the place."

He cast a longing glance in the direction of the bar.

Owen took the hint.

"OK," he said. "Thanks."

Fairclough got up. At the last minute he was reluctant to go.

"It's a funny business, isn't it?" he said. "Why would anyone want to kill me?"

"It might simply be a mistake, of course."

"Mistaken identity, you mean?"

"Maybe."

Fairclough brightened.

"That could be it," he said. "That could well be it."

Privately Owen doubted whether it was possible to mistake Fairclough for anyone else. The image of a second pink man in the habit of riding home on a donkey rose unbidden to his mind. He put it down firmly.

Even Fairclough, after a moment, began to have his doubts.

"I don't think it could be that, you know," he said worriedly.

"Why not?"

"I think they knew what they were doing."

"What makes you say that?"

Fairclough hesitated. "You'll probably think I'm being fanciful," he said. "But—I think that recently I've been followed."

"Followed?"

"Someone behind me. I've never seen anyone, mind. I've just sensed it. There's a sort of feeling you have." He looked at Owen. "You probably think I've been imagining things."

"No," said Owen. "No, I don't."

"I thought that myself—thought I was imagining it. So I took no notice. Told myself not to be so bloody daft. But then, this shooting . . ." His voice tailed away.

"It's not so daft," said Owen. "It makes sense for them to do their homework."

"But then—you see, that means they knew what they were doing. Knew it was me, I mean."

"Not necessarily."

"And then," said Fairclough, taking no notice, "this following business—"

"Yes?"

"There have been other cases, haven't there? Recently, I mean. There's been a lot of talk."

"I wouldn't believe everything you hear."

"You see, that would explain it. The shooting, I mean. It might not be anything to do with me. Not personally, I mean. If it was—well, you know."

"No," said Owen, "I don't."

"If it was something to do with, well, the present, well—situation."

"There's no evidence of that," said Owen, "no evidence at all."

•   •   •

"I had to reassure the poor little devil," he explained.

"Yes," said Garvin doubtfully. "The trouble is we actually want them to be a bit scared, don't we? So that they'll take precautions."

Garvin was Commandant of the Cairo Police, a big man in every sense: big in terms of physical presence—he towered over Owen, who was himself a six-footer, big in reputation with the Egyptians—he had been in the country a long time and was known in the underworld to have a special eye, big in standing with the Consul-General.

They were at the Consul-General's now. It was a reception for a delegation of businessmen newly out from London to which the Consul-General seemed to be attaching a lot of importance. Owen could see him now at the far end of the room deep in conversation with two of its members, both perspiring profoundly in their dark suits.

At any rate no one would be able to say he wasn't talking to Englishmen, Owen thought. The current joke in the bar ran something like this: "Have you been to one of the CG's receptions lately?"—"Oh no. You see, I'm not an Egyptian."

Gorst, the man who had recently replaced Cromer as Consul-General, was deeply unpopular with the expatriate British community. Although he had in fact served in Egypt before and was familiar with the country and its ways, he was something of a new broom, put in by the new Liberal Government in London specifically to liberalize the British regime in Egypt and to improve relations with the Khedive, Egypt's hereditary ruler.

Cromer had in fact been the man who had ruled Egypt and for thirty years successive Khedives and their Prime Ministers had been forced to submit to his iron will. His regime had been by no means a bad one. Under him Egypt's desperate economic problems, which had brought the British to Egypt in the first place to make sure they recovered their loans, had been largely resolved and he had introduced many much-needed reforms.

But after thirty years the Egyptians were beginning to feel that they would like to solve their problems themselves. The new Liberal Government in London was more sympathetic to nationalism than the previous Conservative Government had been, and Cromer's heavy-handed approach had not commended itself. One of their first acts had been to replace him.

Anyone following Cromer would have had a difficult time. Gorst, with his new brief and new ways of doing things, soon ran into trouble. He was thought to be too pliable, too soft, too keen on the Egyptians. Personally, Owen thought he was all right. It was just that, new in the job, he lacked Cromer's certainty, with the result that scruple and circumspection was easily misinterpreted as weakness.

As now.

There was something of a political crisis. The old Government had fallen. With all its faults it had been a good one. Its leader, however, had been a Copt. In a country where the bulk of the population was Muslim, a Christian Prime Minister could be only a temporary phenomenon.

So Patros had fallen. But who was going to take his place? Among the veteran politicians the jockeying was intense. Factions at Court combined and recombined, lobbied and blocked. The Khedive could not make up his mind—had not been able to make up his mind for six weeks now.

"Can't you get the stupid idiot to get a move on?" Owen had complained earlier in the evening to one of the Consul-General's aides.

"We're trying to. The trouble is we can only suggest. He's the one who has to actually make the appointment. It's his big moment and he's savoring every instant of it."

"Well, it's making things bloody difficult."

Because as the days went by it wasn't only the tame politicians at Court who began to maneuver. In the political vacuum created by the interregnum other political forces began to stir.

For the first time there was an openly Nationalist Party, small yet but growing in support, growing fast enough to alarm the other political groupings, which began to take on a protective nationalist coloring too.

And beyond them were other groups, less orthodox and less open: fundamentalist groups, bitterly resenting the imposition of a Christian as Prime Minister and determined to prevent it happening again; revolutionary groups eager to throw off hereditary class rule, the rule of the Pashas, as well as the alien rule of the British; the extremist political "clubs" and the secret "societies." Cairo in 1909 was a hotbed for such groups; and in the growing political tension they saw their opportunity.

Incidents began to occur. Hitherto peaceful demonstrations spilled over into violence. Stones were thrown. Bystanders attacked. Vehicles belonging to foreigners were damaged. There came the occasional report of a shop, usually belonging to a Copt, being broken into and set on fire.

There was a more sinister development. One or two senior people reported that on their way to and from work they had been followed. Nothing more than that. Just followed. But in the increasingly jumpy atmosphere that was enough.

Reports of followings flooded in, not just from the British but also from senior Egyptians. In the bar it was muttered that things were getting out of hand. The Consul-General should do something. He was as weak as water. Thank goodness the Army was standing by.

And now had come the thing Owen had been waiting for and fearing: the first shots.

"It might be nothing to do with it," said Garvin. "Why would they pick on Fairclough? There are much more obvious targets."

"They're usually guarded."

"Only people like the CG and the Khedive. One or two of the Ministers. You don't have to go as far down as Fairclough. Any Adviser would do."

All the big Ministries had a British "Adviser" at the top of them, looking over the Minister's shoulder. It was one of the ways in which Cromer had consolidated his power.

"The clubs don't always think like that. From their point of view any Britisher would do."

"They'd have to have some reason for choosing him. What reason could there be for choosing Fairclough? Political, that is."

"Or any other. The nearest I've got to a reason so far is enmity at bridge."

Garvin laughed and tilted his glass in the direction of a passing waiter. One of the advantages of this being a reception for a European delegation was that alcoholic drinks were being served.

"I don't think it will be that. And I don't think it will turn out in the end to be political either. Go on digging and you'll find something else." There was a touch of condescension in Garvin's voice.

"Even if you're right on this, you won't be right for long," Owen insisted. "Things are hotting up. It's only a question of time. Can't we get the Khedive to get a move on?"

"I'll pass on your views to the CG," said Garvin and drifted away.

Putting Owen in his place.

•   •   •

The next day as Owen was walking home he had a distinct feeling that he was being followed.

He told himself that he was a fool, that he was imagining things. But the feeling persisted. He stopped beside a drinking fountain and as the water played into his cupped hands covertly looked behind him. He could see no one. There was only the long, dusty street of the Sharia Masr el Atika, completely deserted in the noonday sun. Nevertheless, the feeling persisted.

It was, actually, not uncommon for Owen to be followed. There would often be someone who wanted to have a word with him, to present a petition, make a complaint or lay information against somebody who was too shy to enter the imposing offices at the Bab el Khalk where Owen worked, preferring to wait until they could approach him in the time-honored manner of the East, face to face, in public, in space which was common and where neither was at a disadvantage.

But this was not like that. Anyone like that would walk just a few paces behind so that the great one would become aware of their presence and when he was so minded turn and address them. But there was no comforting shuffle behind him, just the empty street. And yet the feeling that he was being followed burned into his shoulder blades.

An old woman was sitting in the dust under the trees, guarding a huge heap of oranges. She was an old friend of Owen's and he always greeted her, usually stopping to purchase a few oranges to make a drink with. The oranges were large and green and gave off a pungent smell.

"You're a strange man," she said today.

"Why, mother?"

"It's a strange man who has two shadows."

Owen thanked her for the warning, bought his oranges and went on.

He left the trees behind him and was walking now between old Mameluke houses. Their walls rose directly from the street in a steep unbroken line until high overhead a row of corbels allowed the first floor to project out over the heads of the passers-by. Higher still, heavily latticed oriel windows carried the harem rooms, where the women lived, a further two feet over the street.

At ground level, though, there was only the high, unbroken line of the wall and the occasional heavy, studded door barred against strangers. All the doors seemed shut. There seemed no escape from the street except that far ahead he could see a break in the line of the houses.

He suddenly felt an intense prickly sensation behind his shoulders.

Just ahead of him he could see a door which was not properly shut. He slowed down, hesitating.

The prickly feeling suddenly became overwhelming. He pushed at the door and then, as it swung back, leaped through it.

The door crashed back against an inside wall and then swung out again. As it closed he jammed his shoulder behind it and held it shut until he could pull the heavy wooden bolts across.

Then, sweating and feeling rather foolish, he stood looking into the inner courtyard.

At this time of day, with the sun directly overhead and the walls offering no shadow, it was, of course, deserted. Along one side, though, was a *takhtabosh*, a long recess with a carved wooden roof supported in front by pillars, which gave it a cool, cloisterlike effect. This was where superior servants might be expected to sit and Owen was slightly relieved to see nobody there.

He walked down the *takhtabosh* to the other end. As he had hoped, there was a smaller door leading out on to a street beyond. It was one of the oldest tricks in the game in Cairo for a thief pursued by the police to dash in at one door and then immediately out at the other while the police were still requesting permission to enter by the first. Owen had often been thwarted by it himself.

The street beyond was a small back street in which there was nothing but one or two donkeys, hobbled and left to doze. The sand here was worn so fine that it was almost silvery and reflected the sun unbearably into his eyes.

Again Owen hesitated. It would be easy now to slip away through the side streets. But the Mamur Zapt, Head of Cairo's Secret Police, ought to be of sterner stuff. Reluctantly he turned left and went back parallel with the way he had come.

After a little way a narrow alley ran back between the houses. He leaped straight across it and braced himself against the opposite wall. Nothing happened. The alleyway was empty.

He began to walk deliberately along it, noting in passing anything which might offer protection, but keeping his eyes steadily on the daylight at the other end of the alleyway. If anyone looked into the alley he would see them first and the second or two it would give him, while their eyes got used to the darkness, would be all that he would have to get out of their line of fire.

He himself was unarmed; a situation which, he told himself fervently, he would remedy as speedily as possible, if he ever got out of this.

The light at the other end of the alleyway came nearer. He found himself sweating profusely.

It was getting so close now that if anyone appeared, his best chance was to jump them. He tensed himself in readiness.

He was at the entrance into the alleyway now. Directly ahead was the broad thoroughfare of the Masr el Atika.

For a moment he listened and then cautiously, very cautiously, he stuck his head out and looked up and down the street. At first it seemed deserted. But then, at the very far end, he thought he saw, just for an instant, two men. He had time to notice only that they were in European-style shirts and trousers, and then they were gone.

CHAPTER TWO

Is this the way," demanded the note, "that the Khedive's servants should be treated?"

Privately, Owen suspected it was. However, as the note had come from the Khedive himself he thought it politic to reply soothingly, deploring the insult offered to the Khedive and the injury suffered by his servants, and assuring His Highness that he would do all he could to track down the malefactors.

"You'd better go, too," said Nikos, the Mamur Zapt's Official Clerk. "It won't do any good but it will look better that way."

So Owen betook himself to the Khedive's afflicted servant, Ali Osman Pasha. The previous day, on his way home from an audience with the Khedive, Ali Osman had been set upon by a mob. His arabeah had been overturned and he himself desperately injured. If his driver had not been able to sound the alarm, he would undoubtedly have been killed. He was now at home recovering from his wounds.

Owen walked in past the guardian eunuchs, named according to custom after flowers or precious stones, across the courtyard, his feet crunching in the gravel, and into the reception room, the *mandar'ah*, with its sunken marble floor and fountain playing. There was a dais at the back with large feather and silk cushions, on which a man was lying.

He groaned as he saw Owen and waved a hand. Slaves rushed to escort Owen across the room.

"My dear fellow," said the recumbent man. "*Mon très, très cher ami!*"

"I am sorry to see you so afflicted, Pasha," said Owen.

"I was fortunate to escape with my life. They would have killed me."

"Outrageous!"

"*Savages! Jacobins!*"

Like most of the Egyptian upper class, the Pasha habitually spoke French. He looked on the French culture as his own, identifying, however, more with Louis-Philippe than with the present Republic.

"They shall be tracked down."

"And tortured," said Ali Osman with relish. "Flayed alive and nailed out in the sun."

"Severely dealt with."

"I would wish to be present myself," said the Pasha. "In person. Please make arrangements."

"Certainly. Of course, it may all take a little time . . .Legal processes, you know . . ."

Ali Osman raised himself on one arm.

"Justice," he admonished Owen, "should be swift and certain. Then people know what to expect."

"Absolutely! But, Pasha, surely you would not wish it to be too soon? Might not your injuries prevent—?"

"Grievous though they are," said Osman, "for this I would make a special effort."

He collapsed on his face again and a eunuch hastily began to massage him.

"May I inquire into the nature of your wounds?" asked Owen.

"Severe."

"No doubt. But—" eyeing the pummeling Ali Osman was receiving from the eunuch—"confined to the surface?"

"The bruising goes deep."

"Of course. But—bruising only? No stab wounds?"

"Some of them had knives. It was merely a matter of time."

"Yes. It was fortunate that your driver—"

Ali Osman interrupted him. "They let him off lightly. Why did they pick on me? Why didn't they beat him? He's used to it, after all; he wouldn't have felt it as much."

He seemed to be expecting an answer.

"The great," said Owen diplomatically, "are the target for the world's envy."

"Ah," said Ali Osman Pasha, "there you have it."

He lay silent for a while.

"Of course," he said suddenly, "they didn't think of this themselves. They were put up to it."

"You think so?"

"I am sure of it. And I know who is behind it."

"Really?"

"Abdul Maher."

"Abdul Maher?"

"Yes."

"But, Pasha—"

Abdul Maher was a veteran politician, an intimate of the Khedive, a noted public figure. He had occupied some post or other in the last dozen Governments.

The Pasha was looking at him solemnly.

"I know," he said.

"You must have some reason—"

"Motive," said Ali Osman.

"Motive?"

"He wished to take my place. Supplant me in the Khedive's favor."

"I see," said Owen, as light began to dawn. "And that would be particularly important just at the moment."

"Yes." Ali Osman motioned to him to come closer. "This is for your ear alone, my friend," he breathed. "His Highness is close to making a decision. Very close. It has been difficult. He has had to choose between those he knows are loyal to him, those who have served him well in the past. And those others who claim—" Ali Osman snorted—"*claim* they speak for the new."

"But surely Abdul Maher—"

"Belongs with the old, you think? Because he has been part of every Government for the last twenty years? You would be wrong, my friend. Because there is the cunning of the man. He claims he speaks for the new!"

"I cannot believe that the Khedive—"

"Of course not. The Khedive knows him far too well. But he is plausible, you see, not just to the Khedive but to others. He speaks well and some may believe him. So the Khedive—well, over the past week or so the Khedive seems to have been inclining to him. But yesterday he—His Highness, that is—told me personally that Abdul Maher is absolutely *out*."

The Pasha looked at Owen triumphantly.

"So, my friend, if Abdul Maher is *out*, someone else must be *in*."

"You don't mean—"

Ali Osman smiled importantly.

"I think, my friend, that I have reason to hope."

Owen pulled himself together.

"Well, Pasha, I can only hope you're right."

"It is for the sake of the country, of course."

"Of course. And—and you think that Abdul Maher may have got wind of this—change of fortunes and tried to warn you off?"

"Not warn," said Ali Osman reproachfully. "Kill."

"Attack, anyway. That Abdul Maher may have been behind your unfortunate experience yesterday?"

"Exactly," said Ali Osman with satisfaction.

Owen reflected.

"What are you going to do?" asked Ali Osman.

"I shall certainly treat your suggestions very seriously. I shall start investigations at once."

"Excellent." Ali Osman's face clouded slightly, however. "How long do you think it would be before you were in a position to arrest him?" he asked, a trifle anxiously.

"Oh, a week or two. Say two or three. Perhaps four."

"You don't think you could do it more quickly?"

"I would have to complete my investigations."

"Of course. Of course."

Ali Osman still looked unhappy, however.

"You don't think," he said tentatively, "you don't think you could, oh, let it be known, publicly, I mean, that you are investigating Abdul Maher?"

"Why would I want to do that, Pasha?"

"Oh, the public interest. It would be in the public interest. The people ought to know."

"And the Khedive?"

"The Khedive ought to know, too," said Ali Osman, straightfaced.

Owen smiled. He understood Ali Osman's political maneuvers perfectly.

"I am sure," he said, getting up to go, "that this is something you will manage very expertly yourself."

•   •   •

"Ali Osman?" said Nuri Pasha incredulously. "The man's a fool. He stands no chance whatever."

"He seems to think he does."

"The man's a joke!"

"The Khedive has given him a wink. So he says."

"Utter nonsense!"

Nuri looked, however, a little upset.

"Abdul Maher has fallen out of favor."

"Abdul Maher never was in favor. The Khedive detests him."

"Ali Osman considers him his chief rival. He believes he was behind the recent attack on him."

"Ali Osman has a fertile imagination," said Nuri. "Unfortunately, it vanishes entirely the moment he gets in office."

"The attack, at any rate, was genuine."

"Was he much hurt?" asked Nuri, with pleasure rather than concern.

"Bruised a little."

"Oh dear," said Nuri.

"That, actually, was why I've come to see you. There have been a number of such attacks recently. I wanted to be sure that you were all right."

"Thank you. As you see, I am clinging to life with the skin of my teeth. How is Zeinab?"

Zeinab was Nuri's daughter and a more than close friend of Owen.

"She is very well, thank you. She reinforces my concern."

"Have you any particular reason for concern?"

"No. It is just that this could be a time for settling old scores."

A few years before, Nuri Pasha had been the Minister responsible for carrying through the prosecution and subsequent punishment of some villagers who had attacked a party of British Officers, wounding two and killing one. The punishment, on British insistence, had been exemplary; and Nuri had never been forgiven for it.

Nuri shrugged his shoulders.

"It is never not a time for settling old scores," he said. "That is one of the things one just has to get used to."

"Has anything come up?"

"Not out of the ordinary."

"Threats?"

"As always."

Nuri passed him a note. It read: *"To the blood-sucking Nuri: The people have not forgotten. Your time is coming. Prepare, Nuri, prepare."*

Owen passed it back.

"You have been receiving notes like this for years."

"And ignored them," said Nuri, "confident in the assumption that the Egyptian is always more ready to tell what he is going to do than actually to do it."

"A reasonable assumption. In general. However, just at the moment I think I would avoid testing it."

"Have you a suggestion?"

"How about a holiday? The Riviera? Paris?"

Nuri, a total Francophile, shook his head with genuine regret.

"Circumstances, alas, keep me here."

Owen could guess what the circumstances were. Nuri was another of the ever-hopeful veteran politicians. Owen thought, however, that he might be disappointed this time, along with Ali Osman and Abdul Maher. He was too identified with the old regime. There was a need, after Patros, for someone who could satisfy the Nationalists—satisfy, without giving in to them.

"Would you like a bodyguard?"

"The police?" said Nuri skeptically. "Thank you, no. I feel safer without. I have, in fact, taken certain steps already."

Nuri directed Owen's attention to two ruffians lurking in the bougainvillea behind him. They were Berbers from the south and armed from head to foot. They beamed at him cordially.

"I have no fears should there be an attack on me at close quarters. And when I go out I take two Bedawin with me as well. They are excellent shots and used to people attempting to shoot them in the back. No, the only thing that worries me is a bomb."

"Surely there is no question of that?"

"There have been rumors," said Nuri.

There were indeed rumors. Cairo was full of them. Owen's agents brought fresh ones in every day. They came from the Court, from the famous clubs—the Khedivial, frequented by Egyptians and foreigners, the Turf and the Sporting Club, frequented by the British—from the colleges and university, from the cafés and bazaars.

The ones from the Moslem University of El Azhar and the colleges were the most alarming but it was there that the gap between rhetoric and reality was at its greatest. Or so Owen hoped.

The ones from the Court were alarming in a different way, for they were almost exclusively concerned with the current maneuvering about the Khedive, with who had his favor, who didn't, who might be in, who was definitely out. There seemed to be no sense of anything beyond the narrow confines of the Court, no awareness of the impact the delay was having on the country at large.

The rumors from the Club were testimony to the general jitteriness. Owen tended to discount them, not because they were insignificant—in certain circumstances they might be very significant indeed—but because he felt he knew them already and understood them.

It was the rumors from the cafés and bazaars that he gave most attention to, for they were a gauge of the temperature of the city. It was from them that he would learn if things were getting out of hand, if there was a danger of things boiling over.

At the moment he did not get that feeling. The city was tense, certainly, and, given its normal volatility, there was plenty of potential for an explosion. In a city with over twenty different nationalities, at least five major religions apart from Islam, three principal languages and over a score of minor ones, four competing legal systems and, in effect, two Governments, the smallest spark could set off a major conflagration. Owen always had the feeling that he was sitting on a vast, unstable powder keg.

But he didn't have that feeling more than usual. There was trouble in the city, yes, there were incidents, dozens of them, but he felt they would all fade away—in so far as they ever could fade away—if only the Khedive would stop his bloody dithering and form a new Government.

Until that happened he just had to hold on and damp things down. On the whole he thought he would be able to manage that. The Pashas were no great problem. After the attack on Ali Osman they would all be prudently keeping out of sight. The demonstrations, the stone-throwing, the attacks on property, they could all be handled in the normal way.

Even that following business was all right, so long as it stayed at following. It was only if it went beyond that that he would worry.

As in the case of Fairclough.

•   •   •

The attack on Fairclough, simply as crime, did not concern Owen. Investigating it was not his business. Nor was it, curiously, that of the police. In Egypt investigation of crimes was the responsibility of the Department of Prosecutions of the Ministry of Justice, the Parquet, as it was known.

What concerned Owen as Mamur Zapt were the political aspects of the affair. The Mamur Zapt was roughly the equivalent of the Head of the Political Branch of the CID in England. Only roughly, because the post was unique to Cairo and included such things as responsibility for the Secret Police, a body of considerable importance to some previous Khedives when they were establishing their power but now significant only as an intelligence-gathering network.

Fairclough as the near-victim of some private quarrel or dispute did not interest him; Fairclough as the near-victim of a terrorist attack was a very different matter.

Up till now there had been no conclusive evidence that it was one or the other. The Parquet's investigations had so far failed to uncover any private grudge. Nor had they been able to unearth any further information about his attackers.

They had, however, recovered two of the spent bullets and sent them to Government Laboratories for examination. First analysis had failed to match them with any gun used in previous terrorist attempts.

This was quite significant, as in Egypt terrorists tended to cling on to their firearms, using them repeatedly and making no effort to cover their tracks by employing new ones. It was a pattern of behavior inherited from the country's rural areas, where a gun was a treasured possession, jealously guarded and preserved, bound together with bits of wire, until it was long past an age of decent retirement.

If a private quarrel was ruled out, this suggested that a new terrorist group was beginning to operate, a hypothesis Nikos favored on other grounds.

"They're inexperienced," he said. "They fired from too far away."

Beginners often did that, either because they were nervous or because they did not know the characteristics of their weapons. Small arms were effective only at very close range. The most successful assassination attempts occurred when the assailant ran right up to the victim and shot him at point-blank range, a fact which it was very useful to know when arranging protection for the Consul-General or Khedive.

Of course, such evidence was very speculative and Nikos, who took a detached view of such things, was really waiting for other evidence to come along; such as another attack.

Meanwhile, he was attempting an analysis of the reports of following that had come in. There were dozens of them.

"Nearly all of them imaginary," he complained.

"Mine wasn't bloody imaginary," said Owen.

"Wasn't it?"

"Of course it bloody wasn't, I saw two men."

"Yes, but were they anything to do with it?"

"Of course they were something to do with it!"

"How do you know? They were just standing there. They might have been buying a camel or something."

Owen, who found Nikos's pedantic logic very tiresome on occasions, resisted a temptation to kick his ass.

"Anyway," said Nikos, "you haven't described them properly."

"What do you mean, I haven't described them properly?"

"No detail."

"There wasn't time to notice detail."

"They didn't just disappear. They must have walked away. That would take time."

"A couple of steps?"

"Long enough to see something."

"Not from where I was. My view was interrupted."

"It was a chance," said Nikos accusingly.

"Look," said Owen, "there was a reason why I didn't stand out in the middle of the street and examine them carefully. It was that I didn't want to get a bullet in my head."

Nikos bent prudently over the papers on his desk.

Owen stalked indignantly over to the earthenware pot standing in the window where it would keep cool and poured himself a glass of water. He picked up a copy of the Parquet's first report and settled down to read it.

A few moments went by. Then Nikos coughed slightly.

Owen looked up.

"Young or old?" said Nikos.

"What?"

"Young or old? Those two men. Were they young or old?"

"Young, I think."

"Galabeahs?"

"Shirt and trousers, I think."

"Short, fat, tall, thin?"

"About medium, I'd say. Slightly built, perhaps."

"Young," said Nikos.

"Probably. It would go with them being inexperienced."

"They needn't be the same two. The group as a whole might be young. In fact, it probably would be."

"What about the other cases?"

"The other reports? Nine-tenths imaginary or so vague as to be useless. About six worth looking at."

"Including mine?"

"You're on the margin."

"Fairclough's?"

"No detail on the following. Useful detail from the shooting, though not much of it."

"What did you get from the others?"

"Two people, nearly always. Men, young, Western-style clothes."

Owen thought for a moment.

"That could be good," he said.

"Why?"

"It could mean there's only one group operating. If it's the same pattern in each case."

"It's the same pattern, I think."

"I hope it is. That would make things a lot easier."

"Did you think it wasn't?"

"No, no, not particularly. You always worry in a situation like this, with general unrest, that they might all start coming at you, from all sides. It's much easier if there's only one group to handle."

"You've still got the general restiveness to cope with."

"Yes, but you handle the two in different ways. The general stuff is all right provided you keep a sense of proportion. You've got to not let it get out of hand but at the same time you've got to not overreact. If you start thinking they're all bloody terrorist groups you tend to overreact. But that only makes it worse because it provokes people, and then what starts as a demonstration becomes a bloody riot."

"You don't think demonstrations might grow into terrorism if they're not put down?"

"No," said Owen.

"I hope you're right," said Nikos. "We'll soon see, won't we?"

• • •

Keeping a sense of proportion was all very well but it wasn't only Owen who had to guard against overreacting. The next morning he had a meeting at the Residency and when he came out he found that the Army was building roadblocks in all the neighboring streets.

"What the bloody hell is this?" he asked the sergeant who seemed to be in charge.

"Defenses, sir," said the sergeant.

"Defenses? What the hell against?"

"Search me, sir, I don't know. All them Arabs, I expect."

An Egyptian who had been at the meeting with Owen and had followed him out emerged onto the street and turned right, where he walked straight into a roadblock.

"'Ere, where do you think you're going?" asked the corporal manning it.

"Along to the Ministry."

"Not this way, you're not."

"Why not?"

"Because I bloody say so, that's why not. And because I've got this—" the corporal patted the butt of his rifle—"to back me up."

"But I'm only going to the Ministry!"

"'Ard luck."

"I work there."

"You'll just have to work somewhere else."

"But—"

The Egyptian looked around in bewilderment. Owen stepped forward.

"I must get there at once," said the Egyptian. "I've got an important meeting!"

"Why don't you just go away?" suggested the corporal.

"Hallo, Mr. Fahmy," said Owen. "Can I help?"

The Egyptian made a bemused gesture.

"This is the Minister of the Interior," said Owen.

The corporal flinched.

"Sorry, sir," he said, as much to Owen as to the Minister. Although Owen was not in uniform—he was, in fact, on secondment from the Indian Army—the corporal knew at once that he was an Army officer.

"He needs to get to the Ministry," said Owen. "Obviously."

The corporal looked troubled.

"I—I know, sir," he said. "The trouble is, I've been instructed not to let anyone pass along this street. Orders, sir." The sergeant, who had followed Owen along when he saw how things were going, intervened.

"You go and fetch Captain Fenniman," he told the corporal. "I'll look after things here."

Relieved, the corporal took himself off.

"Sorry, sir," said the sergeant, including Fahmy in his "sir." "Would you mind waiting a minute?"

"I'm as much in the dark as you," Owen said to Fahmy.

Fahmy shrugged.

The corporal came hurrying back with a young officer in tow.

"Yes?" he said sharply.

"This is Mr. Fahmy, Minister of the Interior," said Owen. The Captain nodded politely. "He wants to be allowed to get to the Ministry."

The captain hesitated.

"I think he should," said Owen.

Fenniman made up his mind.

"Very well," he said. "Hawley, will you escort this gentleman through our blocks? Bennett, you stay here. Sorry to inconvenience you," he said to Fahmy. "But you'll understand that we have to take precautions."

The Egyptian shrugged again. As he went off with the sergeant he gave Owen a wry smile.

"I don't understand why you've got to take precautions," said Owen.

"Haven't you heard? There's been an attack on a senior member of the Administration. More are on the way, apparently."

"Senior member of the Administration?"

"Apparently."

"Fairclough?"

"I think that's his name."

"Fairclough isn't a senior member of anything. Except possibly the bridge club."

"Oh? Well, that's what I heard."

"There's been an attack, certainly. But why the hell all this?" Owen indicated the barricades.

"Guarding the Residency. The CG could be the next target."

"This isn't your bright idea, is it?"

"It seems a good idea to me," said Fenniman defensively.

"It's a stupid idea," said Owen.

"Oh? And what exactly do you know about it, Mr.——?"

"Owen. The Mamur Zapt. Responsible for law and order in this bloody city. Which you are messing up."

Owen steamed back into the Residency. His friend Paul, the Consul-General's personal aide, who had been secretarying the meeting, was still packing up. Owen told him about the barricades.

"Jesus!" said Paul. "All we asked for was an extra couple of guards."

Owen told him about the Minister.

"The bloody fools! I'll get on to him at once and apologize."

"Can't you do something about the barricades?"

"You think they're a bit *de trop?*"

"I bloody do."

They went back to Paul's office. Paul rang up the Commander-in-Chief's office and asked to speak to one of his aides.

"John? Is that you? What's going on? Have you declared war or something?"

"Not as far as I know. We can't anyway, because I'm playing tennis this afternoon."

"Who's responsible for putting these barricades all over the place?"

"Barricades?"

Paul told him.

"Sounds like Hardwicke to me. Want me to have a word with him?"

"Yes. I have a friend of yours here, an old foe from the tennis courts, who thinks they merely add to the already overwhelming difficulties of his life."

"If he'd only leave Zeinab alone, he'd have a lot less difficulty in his life."

"I'll tell him that. Oh, I think he's heard. Oh, and, John, one more thing: it would lessen the difficulties in *my* life if the Army stopped arresting Ministers of His Royal Highness's Government."

"That the barricades too? OK, I'll see what I can do. Ring you back."

Within a few moments he rang back.

"It was Hardwicke. And I'm sorry to say he's being difficult. He says the CG requested it."

"All we requested was an extra guard. I sent the memo myself."

"He's digging his heels in. If the CG is changing his mind he's got to be told formally."

"I'll send him a chitty."

"That won't be enough. He wants a meeting."

"A meeting! I've got too many of those already."

"With the CG."

"He'll be lucky! The Old Man's off to the coast this afternoon."

"He won't move without a meeting."

"Oh, very well. We'd better have one, then. I'll fix it up. And as for you, boyo," Paul said to Owen, "you're going to have to repay me for this. Richly."

The Army had erected barricades not just round the Residency but at other "strategic points" in the city. As Owen discovered when he returned to his office. These included the railway station.

"Sheer bloody lunacy," Owen complained at the meeting the next day. "There's a Hadji due back from Mecca and they'll all be meeting him off the train and then processing back to his house."

"They'll just have to do without the processing this time," said the Brigadier grimly.

"If you try and stop it, there'll be a riot."

"We know how to handle that."

"We've got enough on our plate without that," said Paul, chairing the meeting in the unavoidable absence of the Consul-General.

Brigadier Hardwicke, at the personal request of the Consul-General, relayed through Paul, had reluctantly agreed to remove the barricades around the Residency. He was digging his heels in, however, over the other barricades.

"This is a particularly tense time in the city," Owen said. "We don't want to do anything provocative."

"If they're shooting our people," said the Brigadier, "we need to teach them a lesson they won't forget."

"We need to teach the people who are doing the shooting, not the others. If we come down heavily on the others, all we'll do is drive them into supporting the extremists."

"You're soft, Owen," said the Brigadier.

"I've seen it in India," said Owen, who knew that the Brigadier's own service had been confined hitherto to the Home Counties. "It didn't work there either."

The argument continued for some time. Eventually Paul, who had been following it with delight, pronounced the verdict on behalf of the Consul-General: the barricades were to come down.

"You might as well confine the Army to barracks," said the Brigadier.

"As a matter of fact," said Owen, who was in an unforgiving mood, "that might be an excellent idea."

"If that's what you want," said the Brigadier, rising from the table in a fury, "then you can have it."

"Do we need to go that far?" asked Paul.

"Yes," said Owen.

The Brigadier walked out. As he reached the door he paused and looked back over his shoulder.

"You'd better be right, Owen," he said. "Because if things go wrong now . . ."

Paul saw him out and then returned for his papers.

"I would not ordinarily agree with the Brigadier," he said. "However, on this particular point . . ."

•   •   •

Nikos brought the note in at once. It had been scribbled in haste and read: *"Am being followed. Have gone into Andalaft's. Will stay there until you come. George Jullians."*

Owen knew Jullians. He was a judge in the Mixed Courts, a calm, experienced man, unlikely to take alarm without cause.

"Tell Abdul Kerim to come," he said, "and send me two trackers."

Andalaft's was in the Khan el Khalil, among the bazaars. It was a shop for connoisseurs. It had only a small stock of tourists'brass and embroideries. Andalaft's real interest was in old enamels, in Persian jewelry and lusterware and in old illuminated Korans.

When Owen went in he was talking quietly to Jullians at the back of the shop. They were fingering lovingly a fine old Persian box, set with large turquoises and used for containing a verse of the Koran.

Andalaft put it down and came to greet Owen.

"The Mamur Zapt," he said. "I'm so glad you've come. I didn't know if my messenger would find you."

Jullians glanced at his watch. "It didn't take you long," he said. "They may still be there."

"You're definite, are you?" asked Owen.

Jullians nodded. "Pretty sure," he said. "I think they've done it before. Yesterday I had a strong sense of being followed and saw these two men. I saw them again today. I tried to shake them off but couldn't. So I dodged into Andalaft's."

"Mr. Jullians often comes here," said Andalaft softly.

"They may even know that," said Jullians. "It depends on how long they've been following me."

Andalaft looked at Owen.

"We have another exit," he said. "Mr. Jullians could have left in safety."

Jullians shrugged. "They'd only catch me some other time," he said, "perhaps when I was less prepared. I thought if I could get a message to you, you might be able to catch them. That's really the only way, isn't it?"

"There may be others," said Owen. "I'd like to catch them too."

"OK," said Jullians. "Well, I'm ready."

"I'd like you to point them out to us. Perhaps we can use your back door?" he said to Andalaft. Andalaft nodded. "And then—do you feel up to walking on?" he asked Jullians.

"So that you can make sure?" Jullians swallowed. "Very well. You're quite right. You can't arrest a man just on my word. Only . . ."

"Don't worry. I've got two trackers outside. They'll stay close."

"OK," said Jullians.

Abdul Kerim had come into the shop with Owen. He was good at this sort of thing, though not as good as the trackers. It took considerable expertise to follow someone in the city, especially in the crowded bazaar area. Owen sent him out to fetch the trackers to the back of the shop. They were waiting when Owen emerged with Jullians.

Jullians pointed out the two men. They were standing some way up the street, apparently deep in conversation. Owen, mindful of Nikos's comments, took a good look at them. There was little to distinguish them from hundreds of others. They were Egyptians—Arab not Copt—in their early twenties and wearing shirt and trousers. He tried to fix their faces in this memory but knew that the trackers would do it better.

"OK now?"

Jullians nodded and stepped back into the shop. He was pale but seemed determined. He probably had a strong sense of duty. You needed one to be a judge in Egypt.

A little later he must have emerged from the front entrance, for the two men looked up and began to move unobtrusively down the street. Even more unobtrusively the trackers fell in behind them.

Owen, waiting in a side street, looked for the guns as the two men went past. They would have to be in their shirts but the shirts were loose and he could not really tell.

He had been wondering how to use Abdul Kerim. He would like him to be pretty close, in case of accidents, but not so close as to constrict the trackers. The Khan el Khalil was crowded and they would have a difficult enough job as it was.

He himself kept well back. Provided they didn't know him, and there was no reason why they should (unless they had been the two who had followed him? Were they? He couldn't be sure), there was nothing to make Owen stand out. He was wearing a *tarboosh*, the potlike hat with a tassel of the educated Egyptian, and with his dark Welsh coloring could easily be taken for a Levantine.

There was the doubt, though, about whether the two men knew his identity, so he kept well back. In any case this kind of thing was best left to the trackers.

He didn't find it very easy to leave it to them, however. He was taking a risk, a risk with Jullians's life. It was always open to him to pick the two men up. The fair-minded Jullians might object that it would be improper to charge merely on his say-so, but other judges might well think differently.

Besides, if the two men were out of the way, only temporarily, until the political crisis was over, that might be enough.

Well, it wouldn't really be enough. If they were terrorists, real or potential killers, they had to be got. Arresting on suspicion and then releasing wouldn't do.

Besides, there might be more of them.

Going through the crowded bazaars, Owen found it difficult to keep them in sight. Occasionally he lost them for a few moments. When he did, and when he saw them again, he was relieved to see that the trackers were always with them, back a little and always with people in between, but near enough.

Owen doubted whether an attack would be made in the bazaars. It would be easy to escape but interference was always likely. They would probably wait until Jullians reached the more open streets. Still, if they started moving up, the trackers would know what to do. They would intervene at once. Risk with Jullians's life was acceptable but only up to a point.

Jullians was leaving the bazaars now. The two men were still making no attempt to approach.

An arabeah came up alongside Jullians. Owen cursed and began to run forward. He hadn't allowed for this!

Somebody got out of the arabeah and embraced Jullians effusively. They began talking animatedly. They obviously knew each other.

Owen hastily stopped running and hoped he had not been noticed.

The two men had been taken by surprise too, for they stopped for a moment as if at a loss and then turned quickly into a nearby shop.

He didn't see the trackers at all.

He caught Abdul Kerim's eye, however. Abdul Kerim was standing in a doorway. He nodded slowly.

Jullians was trying to walk on but his friend, a portly Egyptian, was stopping him. He was clearly trying to persuade Jullians to get into the arabeah with him. He insisted. Jullians declined. Jullians made as if to go, the Egyptian seized his arm. He began almost dragging him towards the arabeah.

In any other country it would have looked almost sinister. In Egypt it was quite normal. Egyptians carried hospitality almost to the point of it being a vice. If you had something and your friend refused to share it, you were really quite hurt. It might be a meal, a pot of coffee or an arabeah. If you had it and you met a friend, he had to share it.

Jullians looked despairingly over his shoulder.

The friend could not be denied. Jullians made a little apologetic gesture with his hand and climbed into the arabeah.

Everyone was undecided: the two men, the trackers, Abdul Kerim, Owen.

The arabeah-driver cracked his whip and the arabeah began to roll off down the street.

The two men turned away.

Owen made up his mind. He signaled urgently to the trackers to keep with him. Abdul Kerim he sent after the arabeah.

The friend seemed harmless but it was as well to be sure. The arabeah was proceeding at a steady walk. Abdul Kerim would have no difficulty in keeping up with it. Even if it increased its pace he would probably be able to stay with it, which was certainly not true of Owen himself.

He waited until they had all departed and then went back to his office.

•　　•　　•

Abdul Kerim was the first to return. He reported that the friend had delivered Jullians to his own doorstep. He had seen Jullians get out and go in.

Jullians rang next. He was very apologetic.

"It couldn't be helped," said Owen.

"Did you get them?"

"That remains to be seen."

One of the trackers was the next to contact him. They had followed the two men into the Law Schools but there, in the crowded buildings with their many corridors, they had lost them. One of them was staying there in the hope of seeing them again, but for the moment they had lost them.

Owen told the other tracker to go back there too and stay there for a few days.

"If they're students," he said to Nikos, "they'll see them sooner or later. If they're not students and just using it as a cover, that makes it more difficult."

There for the moment they had to leave it; but Nikos rejoiced in the accession of hard data: properly observed, as he pointed out to Owen.

"There is, of course, another thing that is becoming clear," he said. "The more examples you get, the more evidence you have, not just about the followers or attackers but also about the sort of people who are followed or attacked."

"Well?"

"Every single one so far has been in Government service—a civil servant."

CHAPTER THREE

I don't think I like that," said Paul.

"Of course, there's not much to go on yet."

"Not many people dead, you mean?"

"There isn't anybody dead yet. All we've got to go on is one attempted shooting and several cases of suspected following. It's early days."

"Look," said Paul, "you may take a detached view but there are a lot of people who won't. All civil servants for a start."

"Do they have to know?"

"Don't you think they ought to be warned?"

"I'm wondering. You see, it's like this. At the moment we've got, I think, only one terrorist group operating. They're different from the usual terrorist group in that the usual group concentrates on one particular target, the Consul-General, say, whereas this group aims at a whole class. I suppose they think that way they'll undermine morale over a much wider area."

"They're dead right," said Paul.

"But the point is there's only one small group. And while it stays like that we've got a hope of localizing it. Now if we warn everybody, it's not just the civil servants who are going to hear. What I'm worried about is if the idea gets around—have a civil servant for breakfast—other groups are going to say, what a good idea, we'll join in."

"You don't think they've got the idea already?"

"No. As I say, I think there's only one group operating. Maybe some people are beginning to put two and two together and are saying, hello, they're having a go at the British, but it's at a very general level. They're not saying, Christ, I'm a civil servant and they're after *me*."

"How long do you think it will be before they get that far?"

"Maybe long enough for us to get the group."

They were having a drink at the Sporting Club after playing tennis. They had, in fact, been standing in for John and his partner, another officer, both now confined to barracks. John was not happy.

"It's a pity you let those two go," said Paul. "You should have picked them up while you could."

"I wasn't sure. Jullians might have been imagining things. Think what a fuss the Press would have made if we'd picked the wrong people up "

"You control the Press, don't you?"

Press censorship was another of the Mamur Zapt's functions.

"I don't control it. I just cut bits out."

"That would do."

"No, it wouldn't. Those are the bits that get around quickest."

"It would have been worth the risk."

"I wanted to get the rest of the group."

Paul ruminated.

"I suppose you're right. You've got to balance risks. However, Gareth, I'm beginning to worry about you. You're taking an increasingly cold-blooded view of things. It's not like you. I shall ask Zeinab to straighten you out."

"It's not something I like."

"No. Well, going back to this question of warning people. I'm still not happy about letting them go as unsuspecting lambs to the slaughter. You know about it and I know about it. Oughtn't others too, so that they could take precautions?"

"What precautions could they take?"

"See they're not being followed. Stay at home. I know it's not much, but oughtn't they to have the chance? The ones most at risk, at any rate?"

"The judges?"

"For instance."

Owen sipped his drink thoughtfully.

"The trouble is," he said, "where do you draw the line? Would you have said Fairclough was most at risk? Don't we leave ourselves open to the charge of looking after the people at the top and letting the poor devils at the bottom, the Fair-cloughs, fend for themselves?"

Paul was silent. After a while he shrugged.

"OK," he said, "so what are we going to do? Leave well alone?"

"I'm not too happy about that either," Owen admitted.

Paul went on thinking.

"What we *could* do," he said, "is issue a confidential warning to Government employees to lie low generally for the duration of the present political emergency. We could tie it to that, not to any terrorist activity. You know, say that choice of a government is a matter for the Egyptians only, that it's best if the British are seen to be having nothing to do with it, that in the circumstances, just for the time being, while the crisis remains unresolved, it might be better if everyone kept out of sight."

"Like the Army?"

"Like the Army." Paul brightened. "That's it! It will look as if we have got a policy. I'll get the Old Man on to it first thing in the morning."

"It'll make the Army happier too."

"Yes." Paul looked at him reflectively. "Although, you know . . . Are you sure you wouldn't like to change your mind? In the circumstances."

"About keeping the Army out of it? Quite sure," said Owen.

•　　•　　•

Fairclough sat uncomfortably on his chair, a worried expression on his face. Dark smudges of moisture were spreading out almost visibly beneath the armpits of his suit. It was very hot in the room. A fan was going but with three people in the small space the temperature had risen uncomfortably.

The Parquet official, Mohammed Bishari, had almost completed his questioning. Owen wondered why he was there. It was not usual for the Parquet to invite him to sit in on its cases. However, he had wanted to find out from Mohammed Bishari how the case was going anyway, so had come readily enough.

Mohammed Bishari was a wiry, intense little man in his early forties. They would have put one of their most experienced men on the case since it involved a Britisher.

He had been taking Fairclough through the events on the day of the shooting, concentrating on the homeward ride. He was very thorough. He had even asked Fairclough where the donkey was tethered during office hours.

He was coming to the end of that part. He must have asked Fairclough those questions before, since they were written up in his preliminary report, a copy of which had been sent to Owen. Fairclough hardly needed to think to answer them. What Bishari was doing, presumably, was confirming things for the record.

The report drawn up by the Parquet official was very important in the Egyptian judicial system. The Egyptian system was based on the Code Napoléon and, as in France, the Parquet had the responsibility not just of investigating but also of preparing the case and carrying through any prosecution. The court often decided issues on the basis of the Parquet's report, or *procès-verbal*, rather than on the basis of testimony in court, which in Egypt was probably wise.

Something in Mohammed Bishari's voice warned Owen to pay attention. He was asking now about Fairclough's private life, whether there was anyone in it who might bear him a grudge.

Fairclough didn't think so.

"Servants?" asked Mohammed Bishari casually. "Servants in the past?"

Again Fairclough didn't think so.

"Someone you've dismissed?"

Fairclough thought hard.

"I've only had three servants all the time I've been here," he said. "There's Ali—he's my cook, and I've had him ever since I came. He was Hetherington's cook and he passed him on to me when he went to Juba, because Ali didn't want to go down there. I've had one or two house-boys. Abdul, that's the one I've got now, I've had for a couple of years."

"Eighteen months," said Mohammed Bishari.

"Well, *he's* all right. No grudge there."

"Before him?"

"Ibrahim? Well, I did sack him. Beggar was at the drink. I marked the bottle and caught him red-handed. But that kind of thing happens all the time. You don't bear grudges. Not to the extent of killing, anyway."

"You didn't beat him?"

"Kicked his ass occasionally. Have you talked to him? He doesn't say I did, does he?" Fairclough looked at Mohammed Bishari indignantly.

"He does say you did, as a matter of fact," said Mohammed Bishari. "But they all say that and I didn't necessarily believe him."

"Well, I bloody didn't," said Fairclough. "I don't believe in that sort of thing. Ask Ali."

"We have. On the whole he confirms what you say."

Fairclough snorted.

"However," said Mohammed Bishari, "Ibrahim also told us something else, which, admittedly after a considerable time, Ali also confirmed. While Ibrahim was with you, he undertook various errands for you. He used to fetch women, for example."

Fairclough flushed and looked at his shoes. "Needs of the flesh," he muttered.

"Quite so. We don't need to go into that. Nor where he got the women. However, on one occasion there was some difficulty. A woman had come to you while her husband was away. When he got back, neighbors told him. He came round to see you."

"He was about off his rocker," said Fairclough. "Foaming at the mouth, that sort of thing. He had a bloody great knife. It took three of us to hold him—Ali, Ibrahim and me."

"You gave him some money. Quite a lot."

"Poor beggar!" said Fairclough.

"In fact, you gave him too much. Because when he had cooled down he realized that you were worth more than his wife was. He divorced her and kept coming back to you."

"Only once or twice. His wife came back too. Separately, I mean, after he'd got rid of her."

"You paid her too?"

"Nothing much. Either of them."

"Enough for it to matter. Enough, after a while, to make you say you were going to stop it."

"Couldn't go on forever," said Fairclough.

"You refused to pay any more?"

"That's right," Fairclough looked at him incredulously. "You're not saying that old Abdul—!"

"He might be considered to have a grudge."

"Yes, but old Abdul—!"

"He came for you with a knife."

"Yes, but that's different. Anyway, it had all blown over."

"You had just stopped giving him money," Mohammed Bishari pointed out.

"Yes, but—" Fairclough looked at Mohammed Bishari and shook his head. "I just don't believe it," he said.

Neither did Owen. Nor, he suspected, did Bishari. The Parquet man, however, went on with his questions, continuing on the same line. Were there other men who might have a similar grievance? Fairclough thought not. In fact, he was pretty sure. But Ibrahim had been on other errands for him, surely? Well, yes, that was true. But he didn't think husbands were involved.

As the probing continued, Fairclough became more and more uncomfortable.

"Doesn't look too good, does it?" he said suddenly. "All these women. Fact is, I'm not very good with ordinary women. Can't manage the talk. Need sex, of course, every man does. But can't manage the patter."

"Ordinary women?" said Mohammed Bishari.

"That's right."

"Ordinary English women," said Bishari.

"I don't think we need to go into this, do we?" Owen interposed. "Mr. Fairclough has been very frank about a particular form of social inadequacy he suffers from. Surely there is no point in pressing that further?"

"Would you allow me to be the judge of that, please, Captain Owen?" said Bishari, looking at him coldly.

He continued with his questions. It was obvious that Ibrahim had provided him with a whole list of women he had procured. He went through them one by one.

Fairclough had turned a permanent brick red.

Owen could not see what Bishari was playing at. Was he just trying to humiliate Fairclough? Was this some kind of personal Nationalist revenge?

He felt obliged to intercede again.

"I fail to see the point of these questions, Mr. Bishari," he said.

The Parquet man looked up, almost, strangely, with relief.

"Are you questioning my conduct of the case, Captain Owen?"

"I am questioning the purpose of these questions."

"Mr. Fairclough has been attacked. They bear on the issue of possible motive."

"Surely the motive is clear? This is a terrorist attack."

"So you say, Captain Owen. But how can we be so sure? It seems to me that the reasons for the attack could well lie in Mr. Fairclough's private life."

So that was it! The Parquet had decided that this was potentially a political hot potato and didn't want to have anything to do with it. They couldn't refuse to handle it but by handling it in this way, treating it as a purely domestic matter and denying that there was any terrorist connection at all, they hoped to force the British into taking it out of their hands altogether.

And incurring any possible odium.

Mohammed Bishari was watching him.

"Of course, if you object to my conduct of the case it is always open to the Administration to terminate my connection with it."

And that, from the point of view of the Parquet, would be even better. If the British could be persuaded, or provoked, into rejecting them publicly then they would not only escape odium, they might even gain credit in the eyes of the Nationalists.

Owen smiled sweetly.

"Far from objecting to your conduct of the case, I am looking forward to an extended opportunity to study the obvious talent of the Parquet in action. Just for the moment, however, I am sure you will agree that Mr. Fairclough has been under very considerable strain recently and would benefit from a recess: quite a long one, I think, will be necessary."

•   •   •

Paul rang.

"There's a perfectly loathsome fellow I would like you to meet."

"No, thanks," said Owen. "I've got a lot on my mind."

"I know you are saving Cairo. And ordinarily I would not dream of interrupting you. But this abominable creature has been left on my hands and he *will* insist on seeing the night life of Cairo."

"Look—"

"I am all for letting him go on his own in the hope that he won't come back. However, the Consul-General and the

Khedive take a different view. He's a member of that delegation that's visiting us and they think he ought to have an escort. Given the present situation. And the fact that they think they can get some money out of him."

"Can't you escort him?"

"No. I'm already escorting somebody else. The one I'm escorting is a Temperance Performer and I don't think she and Roper would mix."

"What about young Bowden?"

"Young Bowden's too young. I like to think he doesn't know the sort of places Roper is bent on going to. And he wouldn't be up to it anyway. Roper's a hard case—he's spent some years in the diamond fields down south. Things could get out of hand. We need someone more mature and used to roughhouses."

"McPhee?"

McPhee was the Assistant Commandant of the Cairo Police.

"Used to knocking people around, certainly. But is he mature? He always strikes me as rather prim. Puritanical, too. I don't think he and Roper would get on."

"I don't think I'd get on with him either from what you say."

"Ah, but you have the brains to subdue personal feeling in the call of duty."

"I don't think—"

"The Old Man does. Owen's just the chap, he said."

"I'll bet."

"True. He thinks it requires a political touch, you see. And he has a high regard for your political touch."

"Why the hell does it require a political touch?"

"Because Roper has powerful friends. He's been sent out here by some Syndicate or other who are interested in the Streeter Concession."

"Emeralds? I wouldn't have thought there was enough of them to interest anyone big."

"I wouldn't have thought so either. However, the Khedive does. The prospect of money, any money, is enough to send him into a tizzy. And the Old Man is just playing along. If the Syndicate finds there are more emeralds than Streeter thinks, then that's good. Good for the Syndicate, certainly, good for Egypt, possibly. If it doesn't, then at least the subject will have occupied the Khedive's mind for a time and kept him out of the Old Man's hair. So that would be good too. I don't know about the emeralds, but Roper's certainly valuable property. And has to be guarded."

"Oh Christ," said Owen resignedly.

"Please please please please. And if that's not enough, the Old Man says it's an order."

Owen made one last attempt.

"How about the Army? Surely some young officer—?"

"Confined to barracks," said Paul. "You suggested it. Remember?"

•　　•　　•

So that evening Owen found himself escorting the impossible Roper round Cairo's night spots. They started with the dancing girls since that was where Roper wanted to start: "The best, mind, the best." Owen took him at his word and led him to a place below the Citadel, since that was the quarter where the Ghawazi gypsies lived, who provided the best dancing girls in the country.

Roper was not, however, interested in the finer points so they moved on to the Sharia Wagh el Birket. The Sharia was picturesque in its way. One side of it was taken up by arcades with dubious cafés beneath them. The other side was given over to the Ladies of the Night. All the upper rooms had balconies; and every balcony had a Lady.

They drooped alluringly over the woodwork and because the street was so ill-lit, indistinct suggestion prevailed over close analysis. The men sitting at the tables of the cafés opposite gathered only a heady impression of light draperies trailing exotically from lofty balconies under the deep night blue of Egypt, while from the rooms behind lamps with rose-colored shades extended diffuse invitation.

"I like a bit of class," said Roper, impressed.

They went into a club beneath the balconies and watched a plump girl doing a belly dance.

"God, man, look at that!" breathed Roper.

Aware of his interest, the plump girl wobbled closer. Although inexpert, she had mastered sufficient of the traditional art to give the impression of being able to move the four quarters of her abdomen independently. Roper, considerably the worse for wear by this time, made a grab at her.

The girl, used to such advances, evaded him with ease. Her tummy settled down to a steady, rhythmic rotation.

Roper made another lunge. This time he caught her by the wrist.

"Not here, sweetie!" said the girl. "Upstairs."

She led Roper away.

Owen beckoned the barman over.

"It would be a mistake if too much happened to him. OK?"

The barman nodded and disappeared into an inner room.

A moment or two later he reemerged and took up his position impassively. However, a glass suddenly materialized beneath Owen's arm.

"For the Mamur Zapt," the waiter whispered confidingly.

Owen was not altogether pleased at being so famous. But Cairo, at that time a small city, was like a village.

A dancer came over and sat in the chair opposite him.

"Hello, dear," she said.

"No thanks."

"Oh, don't be like that."

"I'm the one who's got to stay sober."

"Yes," said the girl, "you'll need to. Your friend won't."

Roper had been drinking three or possibly four to Owen's one. Owen was counting on him lapsing into insensibility before long. That was the only prospect he could see of the evening ending.

"Where are you from, love?" inquired the girl.

"Caerphilly."

"Oh." The girl was plainly disappointed. "I thought for a moment you came from near me."

"Tyneside?"

"Durham."

"The accents can be a bit similar."

The plump girl brought Roper back.

"That was all right," he said to Owen.

"A last drink."

"Hell, no, man. Haven't started."

The dancing began again. This time the second girl was on stage. She was less expert than the plump girl but by this time, no doubt, distinctions were escaping Roper. The café as a whole, mostly Arab, favored plumpness and the applause was muted. Disappointed, the girl came towards Roper. The two went off together.

Owen was fed up. He was one of those people who wake very early in the morning and had been up since five. Conversely, he always fell asleep early in the evening. Or would if he could.

He felt a light touch on his arm. It was a gypsy girl.

"I saw you at the Citadel," she said.

"What are you doing over here?"

"Business is better."

Owen felt his pockets. The girl laughed.

"You're safe," she said. However, as she kept her hand on his arm he took the precaution of transferring his wallet to the button-down pocket of his shirt.

The girl laughed again.

"That wouldn't stop me," she said. "Why don't you just give me some?"

"Would you content yourself with that?"

"Yes."

Owen gave her some money.

"Thank you." She looked around. "They're all busy," she said. "I'll stay here and talk to you for a moment."

The gypsies worked in gangs. Unusually in this Muslim country they used both men and women. The women distracted attention while the men slipped around. Of course, the women were quite capable of picking a pocket themselves.

"What's your name?"

"Soraya. Would you like to come with me?"

Owen shook his head regretfully.

"It would be nice," he said. The Ghawazi girls were noted for their accomplishments. They were without exception strikingly pretty, with thin aquiline faces, long black hair and dark lustrous eyes. They did not wear veils. And what aroused Arab men almost beyond endurance was a general sauciness, a boldness which was almost totally at odds with the self-subjection normally required of Muslim women.

"I'm with someone," he explained.

"Yes," said the girl. "I saw him. He did not like the dancing at the Citadel."

"He is a stranger here. He does not know."

"You are not like him."

"I hope not."

He tried out a few words of Egyptian Romany on her. She looked at him in surprise.

"You speak our tongue?"

"A little."

The language spoken by the Egyptian gypsy was not pure Romany. Much of it consisted of Arabic so distorted as to be unintelligible to the native Egyptian. Some of the words, however, were of Persian or Hindustani origin, and this interested Owen, who had served in India before coming to Egypt.

He told her this.

"I am a Halabi," she said, meaning that she was one of the gypsies who claimed Aleppo in Syria as their place of origin.

"Have you been there?"

"No."

Roper returned, weaving his way unsteadily through the tables.

"Hello!" he said. "Who have you got here?"

"Her name is Soraya."

"How about coming upstairs with me?" he said.

Soraya considered.

"I would prefer to go with you," she said to Owen.

"You can bloody come with me," said Roper.

He fumbled in his pocket and pulled out a wad of bank notes.

"Here!" he said. "Do you want some of these?"

Soraya's eyes glistened.

"No knives!" warned Owen.

"Just keep out of it," said Roper. He grabbed the girl by the arm.

She pulled a knife out of her sleeve and slashed him across the hand. Roper swore and let go of her arm. She snatched the bank notes, ducked under his arm and was gone.

"What the hell!" said Roper, dazed.

He sat down heavily in his chair and looked at his hand. A film of blood spread slowly back to his wrist.

"Well, damn me!" he said.

"Want a handkerchief?" said Owen.

"What do you think I am?" said Roper. "Some kind of pansy?"

"To tie it up," said Owen, "so that the blood doesn't get on your suit."

Roper swore again.

"She a friend of yours?" he said to Owen.

"Not until now."

Roper went on looking in dazed fashion at his hand. Suddenly he thumped on the table.

"Drink!" he said. "Drink!"

The waiter brought him a whisky, which he downed in one.

"That's better!" he said. "Bring me another."

The waiter caught Owen's eye.

"Bring him another," said Owen. "Make it a special one."

Roper drank that too. Owen waited for him to fall. Instead, he clutched at the table and steadied himself. He seemed to be trying to think.

"She bloody knifed me!" he muttered. He looked at Owen. "Friend of yours, wasn't she? Well, she's no friend of mine!"

He lunged across the table at Owen. Owen caught his arm and held him there.

"Shut up!" he said. "You're going home!"

"Am I hell!"

Roper tried to throw himself at Owen, missed, and fell on the floor. Owen put a foot on his throat.

"Get an arabeah," he said to the waiter.

He held Roper there until the arabeah came. Then he stooped down, hauled Roper upright and pushed him towards the door.

A waiter plucked at his arm.

"The drinks, effendi."

Owen put his hand in his pocket, thought better and put it in Roper's pocket.

Roper suddenly tore himself away. He caught hold of a table and hurled it across the room, then swung out at an Egyptian who had been sitting at it. As the man fell, the waiters closed in.

The knot of struggling men edged towards the door. Just as they got there Roper went limp. He stood motionless for a moment, then bent forward and was violently sick.

The waiters sprang back, cursing.

Roper slowly collapsed until he was kneeling on the ground in the doorway, both hands pressed to his middle.

"Christ, I feel awful!" he said.

The second girl, the Durham one, came forward and put a hand under his elbow.

"Come on, love," she said.

Roper got to his feet and looked around dazedly.

"Christ, I feel awful," he said again.

With the plump girl helping on the other side, the Durham girl maneuvered him out of the door. An arabeah was drawn up, waiting. As they tried to get him inside he collapsed again and fell under the wheels, groaning.

Owen bent down, caught him by the collar and tried to lift him up. The girls, used to such scenes, pulled Roper's arms over their shoulders and took his weight. At the last moment, however, he lurched and they fell into a heap. Owen was pulled down too and found his nose pressed deep into the plump girl's warm, soft flesh.

"Owen!" It was McPhee's surprised voice. "Owen! What on earth—"

"Give us a hand, for Christ's sake!"

They eventually succeeded in bundling Roper into the arabeah. Owen took the money out of Roper's pocket, paid the waiters and gave some to the girls. They would probably have picked Roper's pockets anyway.

He was about to get into the arabeah himself when he suddenly had a strong sense that somebody was behind him. He looked up quickly. There was no one there. For a moment, though, he had the impression that somebody was standing in the shadow. But then in Cairo there was always somebody standing in the shadow, waiting.

CHAPTER FOUR

Owen was sitting at his desk in the Bab el Khalk when he heard a cru-ump. He knew at once what it was.

He stayed sitting. Within minutes bare feet came scurrying along the corridor. A man burst into the room.

"Effendi! Oh, effendi!" he gasped. "Come quick! It is terrible."

"Take me," said Owen.

They hurried along the Sharia Mohammed Ali and then branched off left into a maze of small streets, heading in the direction of the Ecole Khediviale de Droit, the Law School. There was confused shouting and a whistle blowing perpetually. There was a great cloud of dust which made Owen gasp and choke, and men running about in the cloud.

The explosion had demolished the entire corner of a building. A wall swayed drunkenly. Even as Owen watched, it crumbled down to join the pile of rubble which lay in a slanting heap against what was left of the building.

A fresh cloud of dust rose up. When it cleared, Owen saw that men were already picking at the rubble. A sharp-eyed, intelligent workman was directing operations, getting the men to pile the rubble to one side.

"Is anyone under there?" asked Owen.

"God knows," said the man. "But it was a café."

A woman started ululating. Through the ululation and the shouting and the screaming the whistle was still blowing. Owen looked up. A police constable was standing in a corner of the square, his eyes bulging with shock. He had a whistle in his mouth which he kept blowing and blowing.

"Enough of that!" said Owen. "Go to the Bab el Khalk and see the Bimbashi and tell him to bring some men."

The constable stayed where he was. Owen gave him a push. The man collected himself and ran off.

There were more galabeahed figures pulling at the rubble now. The subsidiary pile of debris was growing. A few broken parts of furniture had joined the stones.

Owen suddenly became aware that there were other people in the square besides the workers. A peanut-seller lay on his back in the dust with a little crowd around him. He was moaning slightly.

Not far from him an injured water-carrier had been dragged into the shade. His bags of water had left watery trails behind them as they had been dragged with him. Presumably the sellers had been passing when the explosion had occurred.

There were youngsters in European-style clothes, students from the Law School probably. Some were supporting fellow students, others pulling at the rubble.

A large man in a blue galabeah, his face white with dust, went past holding his head in his hands. Two men went up to him but he shook them off and continued wandering around the square in a daze.

A young man in a suit knelt beside a man bleeding from the leg. He was tearing strips from the man's undershirt and binding them round the wound: fairly expertly.

"Are you a doctor?" Owen asked.

"Student," the man said briefly over his shoulder.

"What happened?"

"An explosion. There, in the café."

"Did you see it?"

"Heard it. We were on our way there."

"It's a student café, is it?"

"Yes."

"Christ!" Owen had a sudden vision of a crowded café and bodies buried under the rubble.

"It shouldn't have been too bad. The café's empty at this time of day. A lecture was just finishing."

"What's your name?" asked Owen.

"Deesa."

Owen took note of the name and then went over to help the rubble-workers. They were pulling at a huge beam. He got men to hold the beam while he organized others to pull away the stones which were trapping it. It came clear and they lifted it away.

A large fair-haired man came into the square with a small troop of constables.

"Good heavens!" the man said.

"Hello," said Owen. "It was a café with students. There may be some under here."

"Right," said the man, and began organizing his constables. They formed a chain and began passing debris along it. The constables were simple peasants from the villages and used to this sort of work. One of them, incongruously, began to sing.

After a while Owen left the rubble work. McPhee, a Boy-Scoutish sort of man, was better at this kind of thing than he was. The work of clearing the debris was now proceeding systematically. The sharp-faced, intelligent workman who had got started in the first place was now burrowing deep into the rubble.

The square was filling up with people, eager to help but getting in the way. Owen pulled a constable out and sent him for more help. He tried to get the crowd to keep back. Then, seeing that was useless, he borrowed McPhee's idea and formed them into chains, getting them to clear away the subsidiary pile, which was threatening to topple back onto the rubble.

So far he had seen very few injured people.

The student he had been talking to had finished his bandaging and came over to stand beside Owen.

"Are you sure it was empty?" Owen asked.

"Not empty," said the student. "Emptyish."

He interrupted the large man with the white, dusty face as he went past for the umpteenth time.

"Ali," he said. "Come here."

Ali stopped obediently. The student took hold of his head and stared into his eyes. Then he released him.

"Concussed," he said.

"You're not a law student," said Owen.

"No, medical. I was visiting friends."

"Why," said Ali, in a tone of surprise, "it's Deesa."

"Yes," said the student, "it's Deesa. What happened, Ali?"

"I don't know," said the man. "I came to the door to take some air and then suddenly it was as if a giant put his hand to my back and pushed me. I fell into the street and lay there and when I looked up the building had gone. Where did it go to, Deesa?"

"It fell down, Ali," said Deesa. "That is all that is left." He pointed to the rubble.

The big man shook his head disbelievingly.

"When I looked up, it had gone," he repeated. "Where did it go to, Deesa?"

"Ali," said Deesa. "Try to remember. How many people were there inside?"

Ali shook his head blankly.

"Try to remember, Ali. How many people were there inside? Was Karim inside?"

"No. He is at the mosque."

"God be praised. And Mustafa?"

"Mustafa is at the souk."

"It looks as if Ali was on his own," the student said to Owen. "And if he was standing at the door he couldn't have been too busy."

There came a shout from the rubble. The sharp-faced man had reemerged and was beckoning urgently. McPhee began to organize a special group.

"It looks as if they've found someone," said Deesa. "I'd better see if I can help." As he went across, he looked back over his shoulder at Owen. "I'm only in my third year, though."

"You're doing fine."

Ali sat down and put his head on his knees. Suddenly he looked up at Owen.

"Two," he said. "There were two."

"Sure?"

"At the back. The table at the back."

Owen called across to McPhee. "There are two of them. At least."

"We've found one."

More constables came into the square. They formed into a loose ring holding back the crowd. The crowd had grown so large that it was spilling back down the side streets. Unusually for a Cairo crowd, it was silent.

There was a ripple among the men working on the rubble. A white-dusted form was lifted out. Deesa bent over it.

McPhee came across, inspected the pile of rubbish and shook his head.

"An angrib," he said, "has anyone got an angrib?"

Someone shouted acknowledgment from the back of the crowd and a moment or two later some men appeared carrying a low, rope-matting bed. The form was lifted onto it. Then it was hoisted up and borne off to the hospital.

Deesa started to walk beside it, then turned and came back. "It's no use," he said to Owen.

He stationed himself at the top of the hole down which the sharp-faced workman was already burrowing. The man began to pull at the stones again.

•   •   •

"It was a bomb," said Owen. "I heard it."

The three of them were sitting in Garvin's office—Garvin himself, McPhee, the Assistant Commander, and Owen.

"It had been planted at the back of the café. Probably left under a table or chair. It would have been easy. There weren't many people there that early in the morning."

"How many?"

"Two definitely. That's all Ali, the owner of the café, remembers. There could have been more. Others had been in and out."

"It could have been worse, then."

"Yes. A lot worse. If it had gone off half an hour later the café would have been full."

"Why would anyone want to do it?" asked McPhee. "It's monstrous. All those youngsters!"

"No idea. You wonder if you're dealing with a lunatic."

Garvin turned to Owen.

"Presumably you've got people on it?"

"Yes. I've got them all on it. I hope to Christ nothing else turns up for a day or two."

"What about Fairclough?" asked McPhee.

Owen shrugged.

"The Parquet are supposed to be handling it. Not very well, though. They'd prefer to steer clear."

"It's the possible Faircloughs I'm worried about," said Garvin.

"A note's come round from the CG asking people to lie low," said McPhee. "That might help a bit."

"Do you think the two are connected? The Fairclough business and this bombing?" asked Garvin.

"No. I'd reckoned that the Fairclough business was the work of a specialist group. Specializing in civil servants. The students don't fit into that."

"Maybe they're not so specialized."

"Bombing is a specialist thing too. I reckon we've got two groups," said Owen.

Garvin sighed. "We'll have the whole bloody lot taking a hand if we don't look out," he said.

"Or if the Khedive doesn't make up his bloody mind soon," said Owen.

He felt aggrieved. He had warned Garvin at the Reception and Garvin had more or less turned his back. Now this had happened. If the Khedive had made up his mind earlier it probably wouldn't.

"I don't think that's much to do with it," said Garvin.

"Two groups operating simultaneously would stretch us," said McPhee. "There's all the general policing as well."

"You'll have to look after that," said Garvin. "And you'll have to look after the bombers," he said to Owen. "And the Fairclough business, of course."

"It's a lot," said McPhee, looking at Owen. "I've got some men moving the rubble. Would you like me to carry on with that? We won't find anybody alive now but we'll know how many dead there were."

"Thanks," said Owen. "That would be a help. I'll be going through the witnesses."

"Have you cleared it with the Parquet?" asked Garvin.

"The Parquet can go hang," said Owen. "This is plainly political."

"I suppose it must be," said McPhee. "But why students?"

"Any bombing is political," said Owen, "because you're almost bound to hit other people, people who've got nothing to do with it."

"It's terrorist, all right," said Garvin. "Part of the general picture. The trouble is, it means we've got on to a new stage. Your people haven't picked up anything, have they?"

"In the bazaars? No, no talk of bombs. I saw Nuri Pasha the other day, though, and he said there had been rumors."

"There'll be more rumors now. That won't make things any easier." He frowned. "I don't like bombing," he said. "It's hard to handle. And this will have an effect on people. Worse than that following business, even. They're going to need reassuring."

He looked at Owen.

"Are you sure you don't want to think again? About bringing in the Army, I mean?"

"Quite sure," said Owen.

•   •   •

The lemonade-seller was only too willing to tell all he knew; which wasn't much.

"I had stopped to relieve myself," he explained, "when I heard a mighty roar. I ran around the corner and the square was full of dust. A great cloud enveloped me and all was dark and I couldn't breathe. I gave myself up for lost," said the lemonade-seller with relish.

He eased the tray around his middle to allow himself to squat more comfortably.

"But then the cloud went from me and I saw Hussein lying. Like this!" The lemonade-seller clasped his hands dramatically and quite implausibly. "And I said to myself: 'Surely Hussein is dead.' But then one said to me: 'Not so. He moves.' And I looked again and it was so. And the other said: 'Let us carry him to the side, for if he lies where he is, further harm may befall him.' And one carried him aside and I said—"

Here Owen stopped him.

"Let us go back to the beginning," he said. "You were around the corner?"

"Yes. I was relieving myself. God works in mysterious ways. Had I not stopped I would have been in the square and the house might have fallen upon me."

"The hand of God is in everything," said Owen.

"That is exactly what I said to my wife."

"And what did she say?"

"Not to count upon it when I came to her bed that evening."

"While you were relieving yourself," said Owen, "did anyone run past you coming out of the square?"

"I do not think so. Afterwards, though," offered the lemonade-seller, "many people were running hither and thither."

"But beforehand?"

What Owen was trying to find out was whether anyone had seen a thrower. Terrorist bombs were typically primitive affairs. They tended to be the sort that exploded on concussion and were therefore usually thrown, not left.

"No one came past me."

It was one of the few hard pieces of information that Owen was able to extract. What all the witnesses wanted to do was tell him about their part in the drama, the narrowness of their own escape, their thoughts and reflections, what they had said to Abdul, etc. What they did not want to do was confine themselves to anything as mundane as the bare facts of the affair.

Facts, if they emerged at all, were thrown out rather at random. In order to catch them, therefore, one had to sit patiently by while the story was unfolded in all its glory. Which, with a number of witnesses, took rather a long time.

After a while Owen handed it over to his men and walked round the square to where a group of interested onlookers was watching McPhee's men at work clearing the rubble.

"I am looking for Ali," he said.

The group exchanged glances and then one of them got up, touched Owen on the arm, and led him off to one side of the square.

Ali was sitting in the dust with his back against a wall, his eyes staring unseeingly before him. By his knee there was a bowl of food, untouched.

"He is not well," said the man who had brought Owen over. "He may not hear you."

Owen dropped into a squat.

"Ali," he said softly. "Ali, do you remember me?"

Ali gave no sign of having heard.

"I was with Deesa, if you remember. That day."

Ali stirred. "I remember," he said.

"You helped me that day," Owen said. "You told me there were two inside."

"Yes," said Ali. "There were two."

"Can you help me some more? Just before it happened, did anyone throw anything?"

"I cannot remember."

"Into the café? And run away, perhaps?"

Ali frowned. "I cannot remember," he said. "There was a mighty wind. It threw me to the ground. My head aches."

"Just before the mighty wind. Did anyone throw anything?"

Ali looked puzzled. "I do not understand," he said. "Why should anyone throw anything?" He put his head in his hands and rocked to and fro. "I do not understand," he said. "I do not understand anything."

"He is sick," whispered the man who had brought Owen.

"It is the shock," said Owen. "Get him to the English hakim at the hospital. Tell him the Mamur Zapt sends him."

"I will take him," said the man.

Ali had stopped rocking.

"Ali," said Owen. "I shall ask you only one more thing. Then you are to go to the English hakim and he will make you better. That morning, when it happened, there were two inside. But had there been others? Had others come and gone that morning?"

"My head aches."

"Try," said Owen. "Try to remember, Ali."

Ali put his head on his hands again and frowned with concentration. Some inner pain made him wince and close his eyes.

"I am trying," he said. "I am trying to remember."

"Good. That morning. Before. Were there others?"

Ali bowed his head in concentration.

"Yes," he said suddenly. "There were others."

"Many? Do you remember them?"

"Not many."

Ali's head came up. "I do not remember them," he whispered. "I was working."

"But you saw them?"

"I cannot remember."

"Can you remember one of them? One I could ask about the others?"

Ali frowned with concentration. Suddenly he burst into tears.

•   •   •

Owen managed to find a small boy who knew the way. The boy took him down a dark alleyway which opened out into a small courtyard completely enclosed by crumbling blocks of flats. There was a pump in the middle of the courtyard round which small children were playing. A strong smell of fried onions came from one of the houses.

A man in a galabeah and skullcap came out of the house. It was the sharp-faced workman who had organized things at the scene of the bombing. He greeted Owen politely and led him inside. In an inner room a woman was busy cooking.

There were no chairs but the man produced a worn leather cushion for Owen to sit on. He himself sat on the bare floor.

The floor was clean, which was not always the case in the houses of the poor. But then, as poor went, perhaps this man was not so very poor. The flat seemed to have at least two rooms and the furnishings, though sparse, were of good quality and well looked after.

A woman came in from the other room and placed little dishes of olives beside them. She wore her veil over her face but only over half her face. Intelligent, interested eyes regarded Owen curiously. She observed the proper forms but there was an independence about her which went with that of her husband.

The husband's name was Ibrahim and he was a mechanic; one of a new breed of workman which was growing up in the city. He worked at the transport depot repairing trams. It was a skilled job and he received good wages.

"I know you, of course," he said to Owen. "I saw you the other day. You are the Mamur Zapt."

Owen bowed his head in acknowledgment.

"And I know you," he said. "It was easy to find your house. Everyone knows Ibrahim and speaks well of him."

Deliberately he spoke loudly enough for the wife to hear in the other room.

Ibrahim now inclined his head.

"We have been here a long time," he said.

"I would like to ask you some questions. But first I wish to thank you for all you did that day."

"It was nothing. Who would not have wished to help? I was there first, that was all."

"Not all. Not all, by any means. But tell me, how was it you came to be there first?"

"I was passing when it happened. I had just come into the square when I was struck by a puff of wind. It was like a blow in the face. I stopped in surprise and then there was a great roar and the house began to crumble. Ali was standing in the doorway and he was thrown forward. He was on hands and knees in the street and great stones were bounding all over the square. I saw a man struck, a water-carrier, I think, but then there was dust everywhere, it was like a haboob, and I couldn't see anything. When the dust cleared there was just the great pile of rubble where the café had been and I ran forward in case people lay buried."

"That was brave of you and quick. For the rubble would have been unstable and when such things happen one is stunned for a time."

"Well," said Ibrahim modestly. "I don't know about quick. But the rubble was certainly unstable. As I reached it, it was still moving. Then it seemed to collapse and steady."

"Were there any cries?"

"From inside? No. I think it happened too suddenly. The boys were killed at once. But sometimes people are trapped in spaces where they can breathe and if you get to them quickly they can be pulled out alive. I have helped before when a house has fallen. It is not uncommon in Cairo—it is the way the houses are built. I sometimes fear about this one. That is why, when we have saved enough, we shall move to another. Also we shall want a bigger house for our children."

Owen looked around.

"You have good children," he said. "They are very quiet. Or are they playing outside by the pump?"

"If they are still playing," said Ibrahim, "it is inside. For as yet they are still in my wife's stomach."

There was a stifled laugh from the other room.

"God grant you a fine boy."

"A boy first. But then I would like a girl to help her mother."

This too was unusual. In most families girls were unsought for, if accepted when they arrived.

"One first, then the other. Not both together," said Owen. Again there was a laugh from the other room.

Something Ibrahim had said came back to him.

"You said that Ali was standing in the doorway of the café when you came into the square?"

"That is so."

"Are you sure?"

Ibrahim thought for a moment.

"Yes," he said.

"And then, almost at the same moment, there was the explosion?"

"Yes."

"Was there anyone else by the door?"

Again Ibrahim thought.

"No," he said.

"Did you see anyone running away?"

"No." Ibrahim looked at Owen. "I do not think anyone would have thrown anything," he said, "if that's what you're asking. They would have had to have thrown it in through the doorway and I do not think Ali would have been standing there so calmly if they had."

"In that case it must have been left there beforehand. I have spoken with Ali. He says that there had been people in the café earlier that morning."

"There is always somebody in there."

"The trouble is Ali can't remember who it was."

"The students will know."

"It might not have been students."

"It usually is. It's mostly students who use that café."

There was a wail from outside in the courtyard. Ibrahim's wife stuck her head into the room and said something to him. Ibrahim half started to get up, then stopped.

"It is the pump," he said. "It has got stuck again. Someone must have jammed it."

"Let me not hinder a man who is called on for help," said Owen politely, and stood up.

"The fact is, they're always calling on me," said Ibrahim.

They went out into the courtyard. It took Ibrahim only a moment to strip the pump down.

"I tried to do that, Ibrahim," said one of the boys tearfully, "but when I put it back together again it wouldn't work."

"That is because you put this bit back the wrong way round. Otherwise it would have."

He showed the boy and they put it back together.

"You can be the first to try it," said Ibrahim.

There was a gush of water from the spout and a cry of triumph went up from the assembled children. Within a moment they were all playing happily again.

"The young are God's gift," said Ibrahim, watching them.

"Who, then, would wish to harm them?" asked Owen.

"You are thinking of the students?"

"Yes."

Ibrahim hesitated.

"I have asked myself that," he said. "I said to myself: who could do such a terrible thing."

"And did you find an answer?"

"Yes. Other students."

"Other students?" said Owen, taken by surprise.

"Yes. For they were too young to have other enemies."

Owen did not reply at once. He and Ibrahim began walking slowly across the courtyard towards the exit.

"If it was a quarrel," said Owen, "then it was a terrible revenge."

Ibrahim spread his hands. "The young are immoderate in their hates," he said, "as in their loves."

"I still find it hard to understand," said Owen. "Revenge on an individual, yes. But this would have blown up everyone in the café!"

"I wondered," said Ibrahim diffidently, "if it might be one Society lifting its hand against another."

Owen stopped in his tracks.

"Was it a café used by Societies?"

Ibrahim shrugged.

"I do not know," he said. "But where there are students, there are Societies. I don't know what's come over them these days." He looked back at the pump and at the children playing. "We could do with more good workmen," he said, "and fewer Societies."

•   •   •

"I hardly knew them," said Deesa. "Of course, I had seen them, often. They came most days and they always sat in the same place, in the back room. But they didn't join in much. You know, if there was a general argument they didn't say anything. They kept themselves to themselves. We thought they were rather dull. You know, typical engineering students."

Owen picked up Deesa at the Medical School after morning lectures and they had gone on to a café. Deliberately Owen had chosen one some distance from the Schools so that there would be less likelihood of interruption; and it was not a student café.

He did not think Deesa would mind being seen talking to the Mamur Zapt, but in the tricky world of student politics, especially just at that time, such conversations were liable to be misinterpreted.

Deesa had impressed him at the scene of the bombing and he had made a mental note to talk to him again. When he had approached him, Deesa had agreed readily enough. "Though there won't be much I'll be able to tell you," he had warned. "I wasn't even in the café that morning. I was just passing. "

In fact, Deesa had been the first person Owen had talked to who had been in the habit of using the café, and, as a student, the perspective he afforded was doubly useful.

"Why did they come to Ali's cafe anyway?" asked Owen. "It's quite a distance from the Engineering School."

"There's a lot of crossing over," Deesa said. "Take me. What was I doing at Ali's? I'm a medical student. Well, I've got friends at the Law School and they often go to Ali's—it's very handy for them—and if I want to see them, I know I've a good chance of finding them there."

"Yes, but you said these two didn't mix in much. Did they have any friends? Who came in the café, I mean?"

"I can't say I ever noticed," Deesa admitted. "If they did have any friends, they were as quiet as themselves. Anyway, that might not have been the reason for their coming to Ali's. They might have come for the opposite reason—to get away from other Engineering students. I sometimes feel like that," said Deesa, laughing.

"What did they do in the café?"

"Do? Drink coffee, talk, read. They used to read a lot. They brought their books with them. They used to go through·them together."

"What sort of books?"

"I don't really know. Engineering books, I suppose. Now I come to think of it," said Deesa, "I did once see one of their books. We were at the next table. It had a lot of drawings in it, diagrams, that sort of thing."

"It seems very sad," said Owen. "Ordinary students, getting on with their work. And then to die like this!"

"I know," said Deesa. "We're all very upset."

What Deesa had told him tallied with what he had already heard. The two students had been in their second year. They had completed their first year successfully, though without being outstanding in any way. Their teachers remembered them as being very quiet. Both had come up from the country, though from different parts, and had been overawed at first by life in the city. Perhaps that was what had drawn them together, for the staff remembered them as inseparable from the first.

Owen had not yet had time to look into their families. If they were from the country it was unlikely that they were the children of the professional families whose offspring filled most of the Higher Schools. Very few professionals were prepared to work for long in country districts.

More probably they were here by virtue of the patronage of some local Pasha, exercised as the consequence of some operation of the intricate network of favor and obligation that bound Egyptian society together.

Someone would miss them, though. Some uncomprehending family in Upper Egypt would have learned by now and would be grieving.

"What sort of café was Ali's?" asked Owen.

"It was all right. Nothing special. It was handy for the law students, that was all."

"What about Ali himself?"

"He was all right too. He didn't mind students. Some people don't like them, you know. You go into a café sometimes and you know at once that they don't want you there."

"But Ali wasn't like that?"

"No. He wasn't bothered. He would leave you alone. You had to pay your bill, of course, he made sure of that. But nobody minds that."

"How did he handle quarrels?"

"Quarrels? I don't think there were any, not while I was there, anyway. Arguments, of course, there were always lots of those, and they sometimes became heated. But coming to blows, is that what you mean? It didn't usually come to that. Ali would have stopped it, I suppose."

"You ask yourself about that sort of thing," said Owen. "I just wondered if those two boys could have quarreled with anybody?"

"Them? They're not the sort. Much too quiet. Anyway, if they had, that doesn't mean anyone would want to throw a bomb at them!"

"Of course it might not have been them. I mean, not them particularly. The bomb was left so it could have been anybody."

Deesa shook his head. "That is what I cannot understand. How anyone could do a thing like that!"

"I suppose," said Owen tentatively, "it couldn't have been anything to do with the Societies, could it?"

Deesa stared at him. "Societies?" he said. "Why should it be anything to do with the Societies?"

"A bomb is aimed at a group," said Owen, "or at any rate anyone who throws or plants a bomb knows it's likely to hit more than one or two. I just wondered if one Society could be trying to hit another."

"I don't know," said Deesa. "I wouldn't know anything like that."

"Was the café used by Societies?"

"Not as far as I am aware. I dare say some of the people in it belong to Societies, but that's not something that anyone's going to tell you."

"They didn't talk about it?"

"About Societies? No."

"Indirectly?"

"There was a lot of talk about politics. There always is. But about Societies, no."

"There were no obvious groups in the café?"

"There were groups of friends. You could say I was in a group. But none of us in a Society."

"Well, if you didn't get the feel that it was a Society café, it probably wasn't one."

"There aren't many Societies," said Deesa, half accusingly. "Not as many as you might think."

Owen laughed. "I know," he said. "It's just that the ones there are do things like this."

He steered the conversation onto safer ground, asking Deesa about his medical studies and telling him about his recent encounter with Ali. Deesa said that he would make sure Ali had actually gone to the hospital.

"It sounds as if he ought to see a proper doctor," he said, "not one like me."

"You're all right," said Owen, "or you will be when you're qualified. Still, I'm not sure that Ali's troubles are purely medical. He's still suffering from shock. But other things are hitting him as well. He's still trying to make sense of the whole business."

"Can anyone make sense of it?" asked Deesa. "Who could do an awful thing like that?"

CHAPTER FIVE

It was the British," said a tall student fiercely. He had tribal scars and came from the south.

Owen at first thought that no one was going to demur but then a fat Greek said mildly: "The British are to blame for most things. But not this, surely?"

"They are, by God!" said the student, banging his hand on the table.

"How so?"

"If the British hadn't been here this wouldn't have happened," another student said.

"We'd still have had to have got rid of the Khedive," a third student objected.

"Yes, but that would have been easy," the second student declared. "He's only there now because he's kept there by British bayonets."

"We'd still have had to have got rid of him. He wouldn't have gone easily. Those old men around him would have seen to that. We'd have had to force him out."

"With bombs?" asked the Greek. He seemed on good terms with the students even though he plainly wasn't one himself. He had come with them and they were already discussing the incident when they entered the café.

"If necessary," the third student said.

"We'd have used arguments first." This was the second student, who was clearly more moderate than the others.

"They never work," said the third student contemptuously.

"You've got to do it by argument," said the fat Greek. "Otherwise you can't object if they throw bombs at you when you're in power."

"If we were in power they wouldn't *want* to throw bombs at us."

The Greek smiled gently.

"That wasn't what I meant," said the tall student who had spoken first, the one with the tribal scars.

"What did you mean?" inquired the Greek.

"The British did it. No, really did it. They planted the bomb."

"In a student café?"

"Yes, yes," the earnest faces chorused.

"Why would they want to do that?"

"Because we're the people they fear."

"We are in the front rank of the revolutionary struggle."

"We are the point of the knife," said the student with tribal scars.

"Yes, but even so—"

"Don't you see? If they break us, they break the revolution."

"And so they planted the bomb?"

"Yes."

"It seems a drastic solution."

"We've got them worried."

"I'm sure you have. Even so! A bomb!"

"The British are bastards."

"They certainly are," agreed the Greek. "Even so, a bomb!"

"We'll pay them back."

The Greek, though, was still doubtful.

"Why did they pick that café? he asked. "Was it a head-quarters or something?"

"I don't think so. It was just where we went between lectures."

"I wasn't thinking of you. I was wondering if someone else used the café. You know, someone they might want to get rid of."

"Such as?"

"Well, a Society, say."

"Lots of Societies use it."

"Yes, but was there a particularly active one?"

"What do you mean—active?"

"Well, there have been a lot of incidents lately. Was there anyone at the café who was particularly involved?"

"Why do you ask?"

"Because that would explain it," said the Greek. "I mean, if the British thought there was somebody dangerous there, that might explain why they left the bomb."

Sympathetic brown eyes gazed trustingly at the students. He was obviously a bit naïve but didn't seem to intend any harm.

"It would explain it," said the more moderate student. "I don't think there was anyone there like that, though."

"We wouldn't tell you if there was," said the scarred student.

"Oh? No, of course not. Quite right, too."

The Greek backed off hurriedly. He wasn't really nosey, he was just a bit childlike.

"Well," he said, "one thing's certain anyway. You won't be using that café again."

"No," said the scarred student, "we've got to use places like this." He waved a dismissive hand.

"What's wrong with this?" demanded one of the other customers, lowering his newspaper.

"Nothing's wrong with it," said one of the other students hurriedly. "It's just not our kind of place."

The customer disappeared again behind his newspaper. There were several other newspaper-readers in the café, among them Owen. In his light, Cairo-made suit, dark glasses and *tarboosh*, there was little to distinguish him from the Levantines at the other tables. There were a lot of them. The café, though near the Law School, was on a boulevard-like main street and its cosmopolitan clientele included businessmen, civil servants, journalists and teachers, as well, of course, as plenty of people who it seemed had absolutely nothing to do.

Quite a few people spent most of the day in the café. They came first thing in the morning, picked up a newspaper and ensconced themselves in their favorite seat. At some point in the morning coffee and perhaps a roll would appear before them and just before lunch the coffee would be supplemented by aniseed.

The café would empty at lunchtime and begin to fill up again once siesta was over. In the evening it was so crowded that its tables spilled out into the road. It had a vigorous life of its own and the students were invaders.

"I kept thinking about those boys," said the fat Greek, "the poor boys who were killed. How their parents must have felt! They had families, presumably?"

The students weren't sure.

"They kept themselves very much to themselves."

"They must have had families, though," said one of them.

"They came from the country, didn't they?"

"I don't know. I never really spoke to them."

"They weren't law students, you see," one of the students explained.

"They weren't?"

"No. They were at the School of Engineering."

"What were they doing over here?"

"We get around a lot. They had a friend, I expect."

"If they had, he hasn't come forward."

"Perhaps he's under the rubble. They're still looking, aren't they?"

"I thought they'd finished," said the Greek.

"You'd have expected them to have finished."

"They're not really trying. Shocking, isn't it? They don't really care."

"When are they being buried?"

"It's not known yet. The British haven't released the bodies."

"When they do we ought to see that it doesn't go unnoticed."

"We ought to have a procession."

"Yes!"

The students blazed up.

"That's what we'll do! We will go to the British and show them the bodies and say: 'These are the corpses of the men you have murdered.'"

"Yes!"

"Yes!"

Newspapers rustled.

"What is it now?" asked someone wearily.

"We are going to have a procession."

"Another one? Don't you ever do any work?"

"What is work?" said one of the students. "This is our work."

"Don't you ever have any exams?"

"They're not for a bit yet."

"They ought to have them more often," said another newspaper-reader.

The scarred student sprang to his feet.

"This is what we're fighting against!" he declared, with a dramatic sweep of his arm. "You are what holds us back!"

"I'm not holding you back," a newspaper-reader objected. "I'm all for study."

"We all are," someone else said. "It's just that we'd like you to do it a bit more."

"You don't care about Egypt, do you?" said the scarred student in a fury.

Someone lowered a newspaper.

"Egypt? What do you know about Egypt? You're a Sudani by the look of you."

"I come from Halfa," said the student with dignity.

"There you are! That's the Sudan. It's a bit hot down there. Perhaps it's affected your head."

Friends pulled the student down. Other friends sprang up in his place.

"Halfa belongs to Egypt," they shouted.

"He's as good an Egyptian as you are!"

"Better! At least he tries to do something about what is wrong!"

"You just accept it! Slave!"

"You are all slaves! Slaves to the British!"

Not a newspaper was batted.

"One day we'll sweep you all away!"

"One day the examiner will sweep *you* all away," retorted a newspaper-reader. "And that day's likely to come first."

"Slaves!"

"Tyrants!"

Despite the turmoil around the students' table, the rest of the café was surprisingly calm.

Suddenly, through the uproar, there came the sound of a bell. The students looked at each other in consternation.

"It's the next lecture!"

They rushed out.

"*Ah, ces révolutionnaires!*" muttered someone.

• • •

"Why students?" said the fat Greek. "The British, I can understand. Pashas, I can understand. But students?"

He and Owen were walking back to the office together. His name was Georgiades and he was one of Owen's most useful agents. People would pour out their soul to Georgiades. He had a most remarkable capacity for eliciting confidences. One glance of those soulful, sympathetic brown eyes and people were ready to confide their innermost secrets.

Particularly their problems. Everybody had problems and Georgiades somehow was the sort of person you wanted to talk to about them. He seldom came up with solutions, as

Nikos pointed out, but for pure sympathetic listening Georgiades had few equals.

He had spent the last two or three days listening in the Law School and already seemed to have been part of the place forever. No one was quite sure what he was doing there. He didn't quite seem to be a student—he was a bit old for that. He certainly wasn't a lecturer.

People rather gathered the impression that he was a student from a previous year. Perhaps, if the truth be known, several previous years, one of those unfortunates who regularly came unstuck when it got to exam time.

No one quite liked to ask him because that would have been unkind. The truth, actually, was obvious, though no one wished to press it. The poor chap was none too bright.

You had to explain a lot of pretty obvious things to him. He didn't seem to have even heard of them. Not just legal things, the sort of points that came up in lectures, but ordinary things you took for granted, like the fact that Cairo was clearly in a revolutionary situation, or the tensions between evolutionary determinism and the autonomous "I," or the roots of crime in neo-Imperialist substructures.

Mind you, he was quite able to pick them up when you explained them to him, which only went to show how unjust and partial the examination system was. The poor chap was a victim. That's what he was: a victim.

So Georgiades was not only tolerated, he was actually the object of considerable sympathy in the Law School. People talked about taking another look at his case and seeing whether something couldn't be done for him. But that, of course, would have to wait on the whole system being put right, which, fortunately, was just around the corner.

"You're making the assumption they're connected," said Owen. "They might not be."

"Two groups?"

"Yes. One shooting and following, the other bombing."

"Perhaps." Georgiades was unconvinced.

"There's only one thing they've got in common," said Owen, "apart from timing and the fact they're all acts of terrorism. And even that's pretty tenuous. Make the assumption that the two men who followed Jullians are in some way connected with, or the same as, the two men who followed and shot at Fairclough. Where our trackers lost sight of those two men was the Law School. And the Law School is right by Ali's café."

"The Law School is what they've got in common?"

"It might be."

"Pretty tenuous," said Georgiades, "as you said."

"It's not so nutty. We know, or at any rate we're pretty sure, that we're dealing with at least one Society. Societies are strong among students. The sightings we've had always report the men as being in European dress. That rules out El-Azhar, and makes it more likely they're from one of the Higher Schools. If they're from one of the Schools, it's more likely to be the Law School, not just because that's the one we've got the most pointers to, but because that's the one that always causes the most trouble."

"One of the things that always puzzles me," said Georgiades, "is how it is that all the lawyers I know are loving, conventional, rather dull people, whereas law students are rebellious, troublesome and a general pain in the ass. What happens to them?"

"The bright ones are too busy making money to make trouble. The next brightest go into the Parquet. The dimmest become Public Prosecutors in country districts. Oh, and the troublesome ones become politicians."

"There ought to be more politicians," said Georgiades.

"What about that lot in the café?"

"Parquet, I think."

"There was a lot of big talk."

"That's right—big talk."

"They said they were members of Societies."

"There are Societies and Societies. The ones we're bothered about are not the ones that do the talking."

"You don't reckon there's anything in it?"

"I don't reckon there's anything in it. Nor, incidentally, do I reckon there's much in your notion of Ali's café being a Society headquarters. I thought they ruled that out."

"It was only an idea. And it provided a reason for somebody to bomb it. Without that we don't have any reason at all."

"As I said," said Georgiades. "Why students?"

•   •   •

"You think so?" said Ali Osman doubtfully.

"I'm sure of it, Pasha," Owen said heartily. If he could get Ali Osman out of his hair it was worth any amount of deceit.

For the last few days his messengers had been coming every day. One day it was a sinister-looking man lurking at his gates; the next it was a complaint about trouble-makers being allowed to gather across the street from him and shout abusive words and threats.

Owen replied soothingly to all the messages and otherwise did nothing about them. This morning, however, he had secured a message which made him pause.

Ali Osman reported that he had been followed.

"He's just heard that other people have been," said Nikos scathingly. "Take no notice."

Owen, these days, was reluctant to take a chance on it, not just because of the Khedive's solicitousness on behalf of Ali Osman. He took the message and went down into the yard, where, as he had hoped, the messenger was still waiting.

The messenger was a cheerful Sudani from the south, middle-aged and sensible looking.

"Hello," said Owen. "You're far from home, aren't you? Where is it you come from?"

"Dongola, effendi."

"Then you *are* a long way from home. I've been there once but it was a long time ago now."

"It's even longer since I was there," said the messenger. "The Pasha brought me as a boy to his estate at Hamada, where I have been ever since. That is where my wife and children are too. But for the last four years I have been at the Pasha's house in the city."

"Long enough to know your way around," said Owen.

"I know the city pretty well. The Pasha often makes use of me."

"He has sent a lot of messengers to me lately but I have not seen your face before."

"No. But this time is different."

"Why is it different?"

"He wants to be sure the message reaches you."

"His messages have always reached me."

"So they should. But this message is important and he wanted to be sure."

"You know what the message was?"

The man hesitated. "The Pasha does not tell me these things," he said, "nor can I read them."

"But you know."

"Well . . ." said the man.

"The Pasha believes he has been followed by bad men."

The messenger nodded.

"Were you with the Pasha when he was followed?"

"No. Hamid was."

"He has spoken of it?"

"A little."

"About being followed?"

"He told us about it when he got back. He said the Pasha was disturbed."

"Did he himself see those who followed?"

"Suleiman was with him. The Pasha said: 'Do you see those two men?'They both looked and Suleiman thought he saw the men. Hamid was not sure. The Pasha said: 'I saw them before, in the Midan Nasriyeh. Now I see them again. Let us go home quickly. Tell me if you see them again.'"

"And did they see them again?"

"No. Suleiman thought they might have seen them looking and knew they were on their guard. But the Pasha was mightily disturbed and hurried home."

"Tell him I will come," said Owen.

"You are wasting your time," said Nikos, when Owen went back to the office to fetch his hat. "He's imagining it. It doesn't fit the pattern."

"What do you mean?"

"It is only people like Mr. Jullians who are followed. People who serve the Administration. Not Pashas."

"Pashas sometimes serve the Administration."

"Ali Osman?"

"He was a member of the Government."

"Pashas are not part of the pattern," Nikos repeated stubbornly.

All the same, Owen went.

He found Ali Osman, as before, lying on the dais, plumped up by cushions and surrounded by servants. The Pasha's eyes lit up when he saw Owen.

"Ah! The Khedive has sent you?"

"I am afraid not. Not on this occasion. I came in response to your own message."

"Ah well. It doesn't matter."

Ali Osman seemed, however, downcast.

He waved a plump hand and servants arranged the cushions for Owen to sit on the edge of the dais.

"It is good of you to come, old fellow," said the Pasha. "Things are getting serious."

"Abdul Maher—?"

"*Not* Abdul Maher," the Pasha said soberly. "Not this time."

His own description of what had happened matched the other ones Owen had received, was similar, indeed, to his own experience. It was sufficiently similar to incline Owen to take it seriously, despite what Nikos had said. At the same time it was as sketchy as all the other accounts and there might be nothing in it.

"I need your help, Captain Owen," said Ali Osman Pasha, "badly."

He clapped his hands. Two servants came into the room carrying an object covered with a cloth. They put it on the dais beside Owen and removed the cloth. It was a marvelous old mosque lamp of enameled glass made at the end of the Middle Ages with a workmanship which had not been equaled since.

"For you," said Ali Osman.

Owen took it in both hands.

"It is exquisite," he said. He was not a true collector but even he could see at once what a remarkable piece it was. "Exquisite!"

He put it down regretfully.

"Alas, Pasha, much, very much, as I would like to, I cannot accept it. These tiresome English customs, you know. It is our masters at home. They are so afraid of our falling into the delightful ways of the East that they make it a rule that no one in Government employment can accept or give presents."

"Oh, it's not a present," said Ali Osman, "it's a loan. Think of it as a loan, a long loan. And if it worries you, you can lend it yourself to the Collection in the Museum until such time as you leave Egypt, when you can take it with you as a small memento of your time here."

Owen laughed. "You are very persuasive, Pasha, and I can see how successful a Parliamentarian you must be. But even a loan—well, I'm afraid not. Though I shall retain the memory of your kind gesture and take *that* away with me as a delightful memento of our friendship."

Ali Osman let the lamp remain on the dais as continuing blandishment.

"In any case," said Owen, "it would make no difference to our eagerness to offer you as much protection as we can. I can certainly arrange a bodyguard, if you wish. However—"

It was then that he had made his suggestion, the same one he had made to Nuri. Might not this be a good time for a fatigued public servant to take a vacation, either abroad or on his estates? At any rate, away from Cairo.

Unlike Nuri, Ali Osman did not at once dismiss it.

"You think so?" he asked.

"If the Khedive can spare you."

"Alas," said Ali Osman gloomily, "the Khedive seems able to spare me only too easily."

•   •   •

Owen caught sight of Fairclough across the bar. There was a crowd of people in between them and Owen wasn't sure that

Fairclough had noticed him. However, a little while later Fairclough touched him on the shoulder.

"Owe you one for stepping in the other day. That silly beggar would have gone on forever. What'll you have?"

As Fairclough bore his glass away for a refill, Owen wondered whether a drink constituted a present. A drink was acceptable, wasn't it? Why not Ali Osman's beautiful lamp? Try as he might, he couldn't persuade himself. Ali Osman's lamp was not like that.

He sighed.

"Terribly sorry, old man," said Fairclough, appearing beside him. "It's taken bloody ages. They had to go to the storeroom to fetch some more and that meant getting the key from the Effendi and all that sort of thing."

"That's OK."

He raised his glass.

"Cheers," said Fairclough, drinking deep.

He put the glass down.

"Been thinking," he said. "Wondering why they picked on me. But maybe it wasn't like that. Maybe it was a question not of picking *on* me but of picking *out*. Different thing. You see, if it's not a matter of what a chap's done but just of him being British, anyone British would do. But there's still the question of why pick this one and not that one."

"A matter of luck, I would say."

"Yes, but there must be something that makes them notice you. I mean among all the others. Now, I don't flatter myself I'm a particularly noticeable chap—"

"Oh, I wouldn't say that!"

"—but there must be something. So I've been asking myself what it was."

"And have you found the answer?"

"Yes," said Fairclough triumphantly. "The salt business."

"I beg your pardon?"

"Salt—you know, the stuff you put on your dinner."

"That's what I thought you said. But—?"

"I had a big role, you see. Well, maybe not that big. I had to go down and look at the stuff. Make sure the figures tallied. But I thought that's when they might have seen me. Otherwise I'm just in an office. I mean, no one sees me."

"Let's get this straight," said Owen. "You had to go somewhere—"

"Hamada," said Fairclough, "in Minya Province. That's where it was."

"Hamada. To see some salt. Now why exactly," said Owen cautiously, "was that?"

"Contraband. It's all the stuff they confiscated during the time of the Salt Monopoly. I had to value it."

"I thought the Monopoly had ended?"

"It has. It was abolished in 1904. But there's still all the stuff they confiscated when it was in operation. It's a hell of a place round there, I can tell you. You see, there's all these naturally occurring salt deposits which the Bedawin have been using for hundreds of years. When the Government gave the salt trade away as a monopoly to some foreign company the Bedawin couldn't understand it at all and carried on as they always had done."

"Christ, yes!"

Owen was beginning to remember. Before 1904 salt other than the company's was considered contraband and possession of it was an offense. The prisons of Upper Egypt were full of poor fellahin and Arabs whose only crime was the possession of salt. It was, of course, precisely that which had led Cromer to abolish the Monopoly.

"It's a hell of a place," said Fairclough, "around Hamada. The Thieves' Road passes right by. There's cattle-rustling from the south, camel-rustling from the north, and bloody brigands in the sugar cane."

"Not to mention salt smugglers," said Owen. "All the same, wasn't that all in the past? The salt smuggling, I mean? Now that the Monopoly's gone, they can surely do what they like? Why should they have anything against you, if that's what you're saying? All you're doing is putting a price on it."

"Yes, but they think it's theirs. Which, in a way, it is, of course. They think the Government's taken away what rightfully belongs to them."

"Yes, but they're not going to blame you for that, surely?"

"As far as they're concerned, I'm the Government," said Fairclough dolefully.

"Christ, that's down in bloody Hamada!"

"It's the only time I've been out of the office, you see. They sent me down there specially."

"I don't think that's got anything to do with it. I think the reason why you got picked out was simply that you were the one they saw riding past."

"Dare say you're right." Fairclough examined his glass. "Got an apology to make," he said. "All that stuff. The women, you know. You don't want to hear about that kind of thing. Sorry to inflict it on you."

"You didn't," said Owen. "It was that bastard, Mohammed Bishari."

"All the same," said Fairclough. He looked into his glass. "Needs of the flesh," he mumbled.

"I let it go on too long," said Owen. "I didn't want to butt in because it's really the Parquet's business. They're supposed to be conducting the investigation."

"Thought you were?"

"Formally it's their responsibility. I just—look over their shoulder."

"Glad somebody's looking," said Fairclough. "Don't want the damned thing to happen again."

•   •   •

"Salt?" said Mohammed Bishari incredulously. "No, I don't think so. I don't think that's got anything to do with it. I think the reason why they picked him out was simply that he was riding past."

"Glad you said that," said Owen. "I thought the last time we met that you were on a different tack."

Bishari had the grace to look embarrassed.

"Sometimes you have to take a different line," he muttered.

They were sitting, amicably enough, at a table outside a small café. Reflecting in the bar on the part played by hospi-

tality in easing social communication, his conscience stirred
by the conversation with Fairclough, Owen had come to the
conclusion that it was time to do the equivalent of buying the
Parquet investigator a drink.

Unfortunately, Mohammed Bishari did not drink; and
when Owen had made tentative approaches towards a social
rapprochement they had been rebuffed. That they were there
at all, and sitting amicably, was due to the efforts of the third
person at the table, a friend of Owen's, Mahmoud el Zaki.

Mahmoud, like Bishari, was in the Parquet. He was a
younger man than Bishari but already higher than him,
something which might make for difficulty if he interceded
too openly.

"It doesn't have to be a formal meeting," Owen had said.
"In fact, it would be better if it wasn't. Couldn't you arrange
an accident?"

Mahmoud's fancy had been tickled by this and he had
arranged it with gusto. It had been easy to find a pretext for
inviting Bishari to take coffee with him. And it was only natural that Owen, passing by, should pause to greet his friend.
Equally natural that he should be invited to join them for coffee.

"What tack did you think Mohammed was on?" asked
Mahmoud.

"It's this Fairclough case," said Owen.

"The man on the donkey?"

"Exactly. The victim, as we both now agree, of a terrorist
attack. In his questioning, though, Mr. Bishari was probing
the possibility of private motives."

"One has to explore all avenues," Bishari said defensively,
"especially when, as in this case, there turns out to be a history."

"But I take it that now you are satisfied that the examples
belong to history?"

"History has a way of repeating itself," said Mohammed
Bishari drily.

"And although the examples may belong to history, their
effects may not," said Mahmoud.

"I don't think it was like that here," said Owen.

"You would be inclined to discount such effects, though, wouldn't you, Captain Owen?" said Mohammed Bishari.

Owen guessed this was a reference to his own relationship with Zeinab.

"I just take a look at the facts of the case," he said, "and when I see terrorism I don't try to conceal it."

There was an awkward little silence. Then Mahmoud said, as if à propos de nothing: "I think I have heard of the case."

Owen knew this was a warning. The Parquet's policy in the matter would almost certainly have been discussed at high level within the Department, in which case it was quite possible that Mahmoud had been party to the discussion. He was telling Owen to keep off.

Owen knew he had to take the hint. He looked at Mohammed Bishari and smiled.

"I think in any event that Mr. Bishari and I had reached a compromise," he said. "The strain was obviously telling on Fairclough and Mr. Bishari felt obliged to adjourn his questioning until he was in a better state of health. While Mr. Bishari's inquiries are interrupted I shall naturally proceed with my own."

"That seems a very reasonable compromise," said Mahmoud.

Mohammed Bishari appeared slightly relieved.

"I was hoping that Mr. Bishari might be able to assist me by letting me have a look at his notes."

"You have received copies of my reports," said Mohammed Bishari.

"Ah yes."

Mahmoud grinned. "I am sure we can do better than that," he said, "in the circumstances."

"You can have them," said Bishari, "though I don't know that you'll find them very helpful. Frankly, we weren't getting anywhere."

"It was help with the identification that I was hoping for."

Mohammed Bishari shook his head.

"No such luck," he said. "Truly."

Mahmoud and Bishari left together, but a few moments later as Owen was walking along the road Mahmoud caught up with him.

"Satisfied?" he asked.

"Reasonably. Thanks anyway. You've been a great help." Owen hesitated. "I'm still puzzled, though. Why is the Parquet taking this line? What's special about this case?"

After a moment Mahmoud said: "It's not the case that is special. It's the circumstances."

"I can see the political situation is something special. But why should that affect the case? The Parquet doesn't usually take a purely Nationalist line. Not overtly, that is. Why now?"

"Can't think," said Mahmoud. He looked at Owen deadpan. "Perhaps our Minister has aspirations?"

•   •   •

"That *would* make a difference," said Paul. "He wouldn't want to be identified with the British. Not just now."

"Pity about the case."

"It's only hanging fire. They'll pick it up again once the Khedive's come to a decision."

"Any sign of that?"

"None."

"Does he stand a chance?"

"He'd be good. He's bright."

"Doesn't that rule him out?"

"Now, now," said Paul. "Though it's certainly true the Khedive's scared stiff of him. Not just because he's bright but because the Khedive thinks he's too radical. The Khedive wants Nationalism without the pain. But Sa'ad is actually in quite a strong position. He's got a strong following in the Assembly and he's popular in the country as well."

"And just at the moment he doesn't want to risk that popularity?"

"A bit more than that. He wants to capture Nationalist support. Then he can go to the Khedive and say, look, I've got the Nationalists in my pocket. Appoint me and you don't have to worry about them. It's a strong card."

"A winning one?"

"The Khedive's resisting. He's frightened of Sa'ad and hopes that if he hangs on a bit, Sa'ad's support will crumble. Sa'ad on the other hand reckons that if he's seen to be riding the wave then he'll come in with it."

"So we just have to sit and wait?"

"That's it."

"Oh, good," said Owen. "That's just what I need."

CHAPTER SIX

Outside in the yard Owen could hear scuffling.

"God protect us!" someone cried in an agitated voice.

There were other cries of alarm. A door banged and feet came running. An orderly burst into the room.

"Effendi! Come quickly! Come quickly indeed!"

"What is the matter?" said Owen, rising from his desk.

The orderly pulled at him.

"Quickly, effendi! Come quickly!"

As he hurried along the corridor there were further shouts and everyone seemed to be running.

"What is it?"

"A bad man, effendi, oh, a very bad man."

Owen came out into the sunlight of the yard. A large, fierce individual was struggling with a knot of orderlies.

The knot suddenly fell apart.

"Guard thyself, effendi!" cried someone in an agonized voice.

The fierce man shook off the remaining restraining hands. An orderly dropped to the ground and remained there praying.

"Effendi!" cried the interloper, a great beam of delight spreading over his face.

He was a tribesman from the south, a giant of a man and bristling with arms from head to foot. There seemed something familiar about him.

He was holding a short piece of iron piping carefully in front of him.

"Effendi!" he cried. "I have found you!"

"Effendi! Effendi! It is a bomb! Do not let him come near you!"

The man stepped forward.

"They tried to keep me from you. The dogs!"

He put his foot firmly on the praying orderly's head and stood on him.

"They said you were not here. The lying sons of Shaitan!"

"We tried to keep him from you, effendi," said someone faintly.

Owen pulled himself together.

"What is your business, man?" he said sternly, wishing he had brought his gun with him. It was tucked away in a filing cabinet in his room, buried beneath a pile of estimates.

"You know me, effendi," said the tribesman confidently.

"I do?"

The tribesman looked anxious.

"Surely you remember, effendi? The other day, at Nuri Pasha's."

Light began to dawn.

"You are one of Nuri's men. I saw you in the bougainvillea."

"I knew you would remember. I told them so." He gave one of the orderlies an enormous push.

"What is your name?"

"Omar."

"Well, Omar, what brings you to see me?"

Omar held out the piping.

"Nuri told me to bring this to you."

"What is it?"

"It is a bomb, I think."

"Jesus!"

"We told you, effendi," murmured one of the orderlies faintly.

Omar held the piping up to his ear and shook it.

"For Christ's sake, don't do that! Here! Give it to me!"

Owen took it gingerly.

"Hassan! Go and get a fire bucket and put it by the wall!"

"At once, effendi!"

Hassan scuttled off with alacrity and reemerged with a pail full of sand.

"Over there! By the wall."

"At once, effendi."

Owen walked across and set the piping firmly in the pail, taking care to keep it upright.

"Nikos!"

Nikos appeared from a side door. On occasions like this he considered his role to be a backroom one.

"Ring Explosives and tell them to send someone over here immediately!"

"Harrison Effendi is away at the moment."

"Get them to send someone else."

"Ja'affer?"

"No, not that stupid bastard. Someone else."

"There isn't anyone else."

"Ring Mines, then. Surely they've got someone."

Nikos disappeared inside. Owen cleared the yard and posted orderlies to keep people away. Then he led Omar up to his office.

"Sit down, Omar."

Omar sat on the floor.

"Now, Omar, let us get this straight. Nuri Pasha told you to bring this to me?"

"Yes, effendi."

"How did you come by it?"

"It was thrown at the car."

"The car? Nuri Pasha's car?"

"Yes, effendi."

"I don't understand. Did it hit the car?"

"No, effendi. I caught it."

"Caught it?" said Owen incredulously.

"Yes, effendi. I was watching the crowd and I saw a man's arm move and then this came through the air and I caught it."

"Jesus!" Owen was impressed.

"I showed it to Nuri Pasha and he went pale and then he told his driver to drive very fast and then he stopped and told me to get down—"

"Get down? said Owen. "Where were you?"

"On the running board. I stand on one, Ahmed on the other. So I got down and Nuri bade me take it to you and then he drove off again very fast."

"Did you see the man who threw it?"

"I saw the arm but not the man."

The movement. That had been enough for Omar.

"Well, Omar, you have saved your master."

"That is my job," said Omar modestly.

"You have performed it well. And Nuri will no doubt reward you."

"Nuri Pasha will," said Omar. "When I go home I shall be able to double my herd of camels. And buy another wife as well."

"And tell your friends this story."

"It was nothing. There was no real fighting in it."

•   •   •

The man from the Mines Department arrived shortly after. His name was Plumley and he was a shy little man with a nervous manner which disappeared completely when he was examining the bomb.

"Oh yes," he said, "I can see how this works."

He had taken off one of the screw-top ends and was poking about inside. Now he unscrewed the bottom end and extracted a long metal cylinder containing a liquid.

"Picric acid," he said.

He showed Owen the other end of the piping. Inside the lip there was hung a small glass bottle closed with a loose plug of cotton-wool.

"Nitric acid in this one," said Plumley. "It's all right as long as the thing is kept upright. Once it gets out of the vertical, though, the nitric acid oozes into the picric and detonates it."

"Then how the hell—?"

"Don't know. Perhaps it stayed vertical."

Owen thought of Omar holding it up to his ear and shaking it.

"There are a lot of lucky people around," he said.

"Well, yes. It's quite effective even though it's very simple. The only thing is, you'd have to be very careful with it. I mean, it could so easily go off."

Georgiades took up the piping gingerly.

"It's safe now," said Plumley.

"I was hoping that."

He examined the bomb carefully.

"There's nothing special about the piping," said Plumley. "Any piping would do."

"What about the picric? And the nitric?"

"Easily obtainable. Any decent lab. The only difficult bit is fitting the screw-caps and hanging the bottle. And that's something anyone can do. A workshop would be a help but you could manage without."

He inspected the ends of the piping.

"A bit amateur, if you ask me," he said.

•　　•　　•

"Another one that doesn't quite fit the pattern?" asked Owen.

"It fits in some respects," said Nikos defensively.

"Not a public servant."

"Isn't a Minister a public servant?"

"Nuri's an ex-Minister. And I thought you were ruling out Pashas."

"Clearly some Pashas should be included," said Nikos coolly. "As more data comes in we can be more precise about our categorization."

"Maybe your original categorization only applies to one of the groups," said Georgiades. "That is, if there *are* two groups. Suppose there are two groups," he said, amplifying. "One is a following/shooting group and one is a bombing group. The following/shooting group confines itself to public servants—Fairclough, Jullians, that sort of people. The other group, the bombing one—"

He stopped.

"Pashas," said Owen.

"Students," said Georgiades. "That's the hard one to explain."

"Anyway," said Nikos, "it doesn't work. Ali Osman is in the Pasha category and also in the 'following' category. That is," he added with a sniff, "if he genuinely is in the 'following' category."

"I would have thought the 'following' might cut across categories," said Owen. "It's part of the homework you'd do before making an attack of any kind."

"What about the attack on Nuri?"

"They'd have had to have known that the car was going to be going past. Presumably it's a regular journey."

"If it is," said Georgiades, "you can bet that Nuri's changing that!"

"We ought to check. We ought to check in the street where the bomb was thrown, too. Someone may have seen something."

"It would all have happened too fast. The car didn't stop."

"Better check, anyway."

"OK," said Georgiades. "I'll do that. There's something else I want to do, too." He picked up the piping. "Mind if I take this away?"

•   •   •

One of the perquisites of the Mamur Zapt's office was a box at the opera. How this had come about Owen did not care to ask. The office of Mamur Zapt in Cairo had been tradition- ally one of considerable prestige and among Owen's Ot- toman predecessors had been those who had known how to turn that to advantage.

Owen was fond of music and, coming from a Welsh back- ground, had an ear for singing. Until he had arrived in Egypt he had not, however, ever been to the opera. Now, though, he went almost every week. And he saw no reason why, just because of the present crisis, that custom should be broken.

He had, moreover, an extra reason to be there. Plumley had mentioned that that evening he would be taking a guest to the opera and in the course of conversation it emerged that that guest would be Roper.

Owen had rung Paul immediately.

"What the hell are you doing?"

"It's nothing to with me," said Paul defensively. "It's Mines. That's where he's based now."

"Yes, but—Plumley!"

"I'll have a word with them."

A little later he rang back.

"It's OK. They know each other. Plumley's the bloke he's working with."

"It's not OK. It took about five men to get him into an arabeah last night."

"Drunk?"

"He's always drunk. But sometimes he's fighting drunk."

"Oh." There was a pause. Then Paul said: "Are you going to the opera yourself tonight by any chance?"

"Yes, I am and I'm taking Zeinab and I'm bloody going in order to enjoy the opera."

"I shall be there myself, too," said Paul, "with similar hopes. Still, it is encouraging to know you will be there. It is always helpful to have around a man who can knock other people on the head if the need arises."

"Yes, but that's not what I had in mind for this evening. Whose bloody crazy idea was it to take Roper to the opera anyway?"

"Plumley's. He's fond of opera himself and thought it would be a nice thing to take a visitor to."

"He's insane. Or possibly a bit simple. All those people who muck around with explosives are. Can't you talk to him?"

"No. He and Roper are out at Gebel Zabarrah. They'll be out all day. They'll just have time to get back and change."

"Look, the only thing Roper will be interested in after a day in the desert is drinking himself into insensibility as speedily as he bloody well can. Not in going to the opera."

"Don't you think he might point that out himself?"

"There's a chance, I suppose. All the same . . .!"

All the same, when Owen entered the foyer with Zeinab on his arm, there were Plumley and Roper, dressed in cool white suits, their hair still wet from the shower, dutifully scanning the program.

Roper greeted Owen warmly. His eyes automatically undressed Zeinab.

"You've got a nice piece there," he said. "How much was she?"

"*Qui est ce cochon?*" Zeinab asked Owen.

"You won't say that when you get to know me, sweetheart," said Roper.

"She isn't going to get to know you," said Owen.

Plumley went pink.

"I've seen you here before, haven't I?" he said hastily to Zeinab. "Have you a passion for opera?"

"You bet she has," said Roper. "And other things as well."

"Da Souza won't be singing tonight, I hear," Plumley continued heroically. "She's unwell."

"I feel unwell too," said Zeinab. "Perhaps I will not stay."

"Oh no. Do, please do, I'm sure—"

"I do not like the people here."

"She doesn't have a knife, does she?" Roper asked anxiously. "I mean, that other girl of yours—"

"What girl was this?" demanded Zeinab ominously.

"Someone we met," said Owen. "She didn't like him either."

Paul suddenly materialized beside them.

"Hello!" he said. "Hello, Zeinab. You're looking marvelous this evening. That gown! The Princess noticed it at once. I think she'd like to ask you where it was from. Paris, of course, but which of the houses? Is someone doing something new? I was out of my depth, I'm afraid, so I said I'd ask you if you could bear to join us at the interval. I have a table . . ."

Etcetera. Zeinab, pleased, simmered down. The warning bell rang and they started to make their way to the boxes.

"Where is this table?" asked Roper.

Paul looked over his shoulder.

"Not you, you shit," he said.

•   •   •

The Princess Lamlun was a Cairo institution. She owed her position in society formally to the fact that she was the Khedive's aunt, but without the addition of her formidable personality the simple status would have been nothing. It was rumored that the Khedive was terrified of her. Certainly his spirits lifted noticeably when she returned to Deauville at the end of the Cairo season.

During the season, however, she held sway over Cairo Society. Her salon was the major center of intrigue and gossip and although her sphere of influence was theoretically limited to the social, as was proper for a woman in an Islamic society, there were many who felt that it extended covertly to other areas as well, including the political.

The party which gathered, then, at the Consul-General's table during the interval was an imposing one and Zeinab, despite herself, was impressed. Owen didn't believe for one moment that the Princess had said anything at all about Zeinab's dress, but when they joined the party Paul so managed it that within seconds she and the Princess were chatting away happily together.

Owen took the opportunity to slip away. He had qualms about leaving Roper with Plumley. Christ knows what might be happening.

In fact they were talking quietly by the bar. There was already a row of empty glasses in front of Roper and Plumley was looking rather green. He had switched to orange juice; too late.

He looked up with relief as Owen came across.

"Got to go!" he whispered. "Just for one moment."

He rushed off in the direction of the toilets.

"Funny little bugger," said Roper, looking after him. "Knows his job, though."

"I gather you've just got back from Gebel Zabarrah."

"Yeah. Dry place, the desert."

The bartender added a fresh whisky soda to the row.

Obviously Roper and he had come to some arrangement, for as Roper was finishing one glass another appeared. There was no gap between them.

"How are the emeralds?"

"All right. Don't know that we're going to be interested, though. It's a bit small for us."

"That's the trouble with Egypt," said Owen. "There's lots of stuff here—emeralds, gold, copper, iron, lead, coal—but it's all in small amounts."

"It wasn't small originally," said Roper, "but it's all been worked."

"Yes," said Owen. "The Pharaohs, the Greeks, the Romans, the Arabs, they've all had a go. There's not much left now."

"Of course," said Roper, "we can go deeper than they could."

"You think there might be more lower down?"

"Not in emeralds."

Plumley reappeared, washed out.

"You go easy, son," Roper advised him. "We've got to be out early tomorrow morning."

Plumley eyed the row of glasses but said nothing.

"Don't worry about me," said Roper. "It's just replacing what I've lost in sweat."

"Where are you going?" asked Owen.

"Tomorrow? Down into Minya Province."

"I thought there was nothing there but salt?"

"Oh no," said Plumley. "There's more than that. There's a lot more than that."

"Really?"

Roper looked at his watch. "Wasn't that the bell?" he said. "Time we were back in our seats, old son."

He moved purposefully away. Owen knew he had been cut short. He shrugged his shoulders. It wasn't any of his business.

There was a crowd in the doorway and he caught up with Roper and Plumley as they went out. Something came into his mind.

"If you're going down to Minya," he said, "watch out for the camels. The Thieves' Road runs through there and camels have a way of disappearing."

"I'll do that," said Roper. "But I wouldn't worry, if I were you. I've met this kind of thing before. It's the other people who'll have to look out—if they don't want a hole in their head."

•   •   •

Zeinab didn't say anything until they got back to their seats. Then she said: "Did you find her?"

"Who?"

"That girl."

"What girl?"

"The one that man said you were with."

"I wasn't looking for her. Anyway, I'd hardly find her in a place like this."

"Why not?"

"She's a gypsy girl."

"Ah, you like the gypsy girls?"

"Not particularly. Look, what is this? I met this girl once, when I was taking Roper to that bloody night club. She came up to our table."

"What was she doing there, dancing?"

"Picking pockets."

"Picking pockets?" said Zeinab as if she could hardly believe her ears.

"Yes, and—"

"I know what she was doing there," said Zeinab, "and it certainly wasn't picking pockets."

•   •   •

When Owen received Georgiades's message it was almost noon and as he walked through the streets the stalls were already closing down. He had chosen to go through the narrow side streets where he could twist and turn. Since his experience on the Masr el Atika he had not been too keen to offer much of a target to potential followers.

Of course in the crowded bazaars or side streets it would be easy for anyone to walk right up to him and shoot him in the back. Somehow, though, he felt less exposed than in the broader streets of the more well-to-do areas.

In the streets like the Masr el Atika you could be shot at a distance. All they had to do was step out of a doorway. Here, where it was more crowded, they would have to come right up to you and he thought he would stand a better chance of seeing them.

It was, however, unpleasant to have to think about such things. It spoiled the walk. Usually there was nothing he liked better than a pretext to wander through the streets of the Old City, smelling its smells, seeing its oddities, catching its conversations. Now it was different.

And if it was different for him, how would it be for other people? How long would it be possible to pretend that things were normal?

There would come a point when the pretense could no longer be maintained. That point, of course, was when he would have to swallow his pride and call in the Army.

He didn't want to do that; not just because he didn't like swallowing his own words, but because, or so he told himself, it was the wrong way. Call in the Army, put soldiers everywhere, and everyone would be affected. No one would be able to avoid being reminded that the British were an occupying power. They would be having their noses rubbed in it.

Bringing in the Army was the surest way to stir up massive resistance. You'd have problems right across the board rather than limited, as they still fortunately were at present.

And would you be any nearer catching the ones you really did want to catch? Would the Army be any better at it than he was? Owen didn't think so. The attacks would surely continue, even increase. The Army would swipe out blindly in all directions, antagonizing even those at present moderately disposed to it. People would resist, the Army wouldn't be able to tell their resistance from genuine terrorist attacks, would react heavily and everything would get worse.

No, the only thing was to be selective. You had to hit the ones you wanted to hit and take care not to antagonize the population as a whole. Keep things normal, was Owen's instinct. Normality was his greatest ally, because, despite what politicians said, most people just wanted to get on with their daily lives. Genuine terrorists were few and far between.

Which was all very well, but at the moment so far from things being normal he was scared of his own shadow, and far from hitting those responsible, he had not yet succeeded in hitting anybody.

•　　•　　•

He found Georgiades sitting down, which he had expected, but on the pile of rubble from the bombed café, which he had not expected. With Georgiades on the rubble were several workmen, who looked as if they might have been working. Part of the rubble was in the shade, however, and offered an opportunity too tempting to be resisted.

"Ah!" said Georgiades, as if he had only been waiting for Owen to arrive before he burst into action. He scrambled down off the heap and pulled something out from under a piece of sacking.

Even Owen could see at once what it was: a length of piping, battered and mangled by some enormous force.

"When you know what you're looking for," said Georgiades, "it's not too difficult."

Owen turned it over in his mind.

"It's the same," he said.

Georgiades nodded.

"Yes," he said. "When I saw the other one I just wondered."

"How long did it take you to find it?"

"Two days."

"Anything else alongside it?"

"If there was, it's been moved. Since the blast, I mean. The whole pile's been shifted." He hesitated. "If you wanted," he said, "we could go through it again. We haven't really done it properly."

"Is there any point? All we'd find is glass."

"There's some of that inside." Georgiades showed him. "There's some in one of the bodies, too."

Georgiades sat down on the rubble again. Owen put the pipe back in the sacking and then sat down beside him.

"Send it to the Lab," he said. "That's where the other one is. They'll be able to do tests on it and establish whether the acids are the same."

"It's the same principle, anyway," said Georgiades.

"Yes," said Owen. "And that surprises me a little. I had expected it to be one of those that work with fuses."

"Because it was left?"

"Seemed to have been. Not thrown, anyway. Or so I would have said until I saw this."

"It can't have been thrown. The man was in the doorway."

"Unless the person who threw it was inside."

"Can't have been. They wouldn't have had time to get away. They'd have killed themselves at the same time."

"Are we sure no one else was in there?"

"We haven't found any other bodies."

"How about this for an idea: one of them threw it at the other."

"The same arguments still apply. It would have been suicidal."

"Maybe that's what he wanted."

Georgiades was silent for a little while. Then he said: "I prefer the other possibility. That it was left and set up to explode."

"So do I. But how did they do that? Setting it up would have taken a lot of skill, a bit of time anyway. There were people coming and going all morning."

"Of course," said Georgiades, "if they were really ingenious they might have set it up the night before."

"They'd have had to be really ingenious. Otherwise they wouldn't have been able to count on it exploding at the right time—the right time to get those poor devils."

"If they wanted to get those two. Maybe they just wanted an explosion and weren't particular about which poor devils it got."

"If that was the way it was," said Owen, "then they weren't very nice."

"Whichever way it was," said Georgiades, "they were going to get students."

"Yes," said Owen. "That's what it all comes back to."

•　　•　　•

It was among the students that, for the moment, they were pursuing their inquiries. It was about the only avenue open to them.

The Fairclough case was at a standstill. Mohammed Bishari had sent his notes around as promised, but, as he had warned, they contained little hard information. Owen did not blame him for that. His own men had failed to unearth anything either.

Similarly with the Jullians case. The trackers had remained in the Law School for over a week but had failed to spot anyone resembling the two men they had followed. It was expensive using good trackers in this way and Owen didn't dare do it for too long. He pulled one of them out altogether. The other he kept there but only for half of each day, varying the time.

Georgiades, too, continued to hang around the Law School in his spare moments, maintaining the impression that he was somehow part of the proceedings.

Owen took care not to use him for ordinary inquiry work on the case. This was a pity, for Georgiades was far and away the best man that he had. But the Greek had achieved a position on the inside of student life which he didn't want him to compromise. It might pay dividends later. As in the case of the tracker, Owen was making an investment.

He had not really expected the routine inquiries his men were making to produce anything, but surprisingly they did.

Checking the backgrounds of the two students who had been killed in the bomb blast, Owen's agents came across someone who knew them a little better than the previous informants. They brought him to the Bab el Khalk.

Owen went down and took him for a walk under the trees of the square rather than seeing him in his office, which was often inhibiting for Arabs and might be especially so for a student.

He was a tall boy, a student, in his third year at the School of Engineering. His face was pocked with smallpox scars, and although he had been for some time in the city he was still suffering from bilharzia, which was endemic in the country districts.

"Yes," he said, "I knew Abu. He came from near us, from a village at the other end of the estate. The Pasha sent him to the School, as he did me."

"How was it that the Pasha's choice fell upon you two?" asked Owen.

The boy shrugged. "We were cleverer than the others at the school, I suppose. Our teacher spoke for us. And then the Pasha owed my father something. It was like that for Abu, I expect."

"Abu came to the great city the year after you, is that not so?"

"It is so. He looked me out when he arrived, for my father had spoken to his father. For the first weeks he slept on the floor of my room. But then he found his own room and I did not see so much of him."

Owen asked if it was about this time that Abu had taken up with Musa, the other boy killed in the bombing.

"It was soon after. I know, because the first time I went to see Abu in his room he was alone and finding it expensive. He said he would have to leave it or else find someone to share with him. When I went again, he was sharing with Musa."

Owen inquired about Musa.

"Musa? He was a boy like Abu. Like him, he came from the country, but it was north of us. His Pasha had sent him too, I think. But he did not like his Pasha and seldom spoke of him. He and Abu were like brothers. They went to lectures together, they studied together, they ate together, they worked and played—"

"What did they do in the evenings?"

The boy stopped short. "What did they do in the evenings? I do not know. Worked, I expect. They did not go out much. They had no money, of course."

"Had they friends?"

"Few."

"What were they doing over in Ali's café? It is a long way from the School of Engineering."

"I do not know. Perhaps they wished to work quietly, without interruption from other Engineering students."

"They did not go to meet friends."

"They *had* a friend in the Law School. Perhaps they went to meet him."

"Do you know him?"

"Alas, no. But I remember Abu speaking of him. He was the friend of a friend. The friend must have spoken to Abu of him, for as soon as he reached the city, Abu went over to see him. Perhaps someone in the village had given Abu his name, the way someone gave him mine. It is right for country boys to stick together."

"Was he a good friend? Did Abu see him often?"

"He spoke of him warmly. But I do not know how often he saw him."

"You think Abu knew of him before he came to the city?"

"Yes."

"He did not come from Abu's village?"

"I don't think so."

"Are there others from Abu's village here?"

"No. There was once but that was some time ago. I think the last one lost the Pasha's pleasure and so for a time he did not send anyone."

"Why did he lose the Pasha's pleasure?"

The boy shrugged. "Who knows? It is easy to lose a great one's pleasure."

Owen asked what the Pasha was like.

Again the boy shrugged. "Pashas are Pashas," he said. "They are the great and they hold us in their hand."

"What happens after you have finished your studies? Do you go back to the Pasha?"

"I would prefer to work for the Khedive. But I do not think I am clever enough. I shall probably go back. Hamada is not such a bad place, after all."

*   *   *

"Hamada?" said Nikos, when Owen told him. He went back into his office and began to burrow through his files.

*   *   *

Ali had had two men working for him in the café. Their names were Karim and Mustafa. When the café was bombed, they had both been out, Karim at the mosque, Mustafa at the souk, where he had been buying things for the café. That was definite; Owen's men had checked.

They had also discovered that the two men slept every night on the floor of the café. It counted towards their wages. They had slept there the night before the bombing. The door was kept locked and they were sure no one could have forced their way in without waking them.

"That takes care of the setting-it-up-during-the-night theory," said Georgiades. "I never did think much of it."

*   *   *

Attention now focused on the time between the café's opening in the morning and the point about halfway through the morning when the bomb exploded. Gradually Owen's men traced all the people who had been in the café during that period. All except one were students.

Owen himself questioned them very carefully. They were eager to help. The killings had shocked students generally. At the end, though, Owen was none the wiser. Nobody had seen anything suspicious: no strange package lying around, no one fiddling with anything that might resemble a bomb, no one carrying anything or doing anything untoward.

The evidence was even a little more negative. About fifteen minutes before the bomb exploded, and ten minutes before Ali took up his position at the door, the last two students—apart from Abu and Musa who had been in the back room—had left the café. Before doing so they had made a "sweep" of the café looking for some books one of them had lost. That was, in fact, the reason why they were the last of their group to leave. They had seen nothing out of the ordinary.

Nikos came into Owen's room.

"Hamada," he said. "Remember it?"

"It's where the student came from. Abu. And I've heard of it lately in some other connection. I've got it. Fairclough. That's where he'd been to check the salt contraband. He thought someone might have seen him there and remembered it later."

"I don't know about that," said Nikos, "but Hamada was the scene of an interesting event about two years ago. There was an explosion. A boy blew himself up. Or that's what they think happened. It was out in the desert and not a lot was found. He was a local boy and they couldn't understand it. The Prosecutor down there investigated it but didn't get anywhere. So they reported it and forgot about it."

"Hamada?"

"Yes, Hamada."

"Well," said Owen, "we're not getting anywhere here, either. So why not go down to Hamada?"

CHAPTER SEVEN

There were two ways of getting to Hamada. One was by the river, the other by the desert. Approached by the river, Hamada was a clearing surrounded by fields of sugar cane. But in Upper Egypt cultivation was restricted to the Nile banks, and two or three miles from the water the vegetation ceased and became sand. Approached from the desert, Hamada was a brief thread of green in a thousand miles of brown.

Owen went by river, his felucca skimming gracefully across the blue water, three Bedawin trackers sitting uneasily beside him. He had left Georgiades behind. The Greek was a city man and outside the city his expertise dwindled to incapacity. Besides, in the city there were things to do.

There was no landing stage, just a bare stretch of bank which Owen would have taken for a chance interruption of the cultivation had it not been for the little group of figures waiting above the water.

As the felucca nosed in, two of the figures splashed out and took the rope. One of the crew joined them and the captain guided the boat to the side with a paddle.

One of the figures on the bank was dressed in a suit. This was the local Mamur, or Police Inspector. He shook Owen's hand warmly but looked anxious. It was not every day—in fact, it was never—that he received a visit from one of the Cairo élite and who knew what errors of commission or omission might be discovered?

Owen gathered the impression as they talked, though, that he was not more than ordinarily stupid—that is, for a country Mamur—and there was an easy camaraderie between him and the villagers that Owen found reassuring. In remote areas the Mamur could not but be the Pasha's man and Owen had feared, after talking to the student, that the Pasha's hand might lie heavily on the village. Although the use of the *curbash*, or whip, had been abolished by Cromer some years before, it was often still used in the country; and too often it was the Mamur who used it.

The Mamur led him up to the village. It consisted of a single irregular street with mud-brick houses loosely grouped about it. The houses were single-story and flat-topped. Poking over the tops Owen could see the piles of brushwood for the household fires and occasional heaps of onions or melons or other garden produce.

This meant that the village was not one of the most desperately poor ones. There was food here, perhaps not much, but enough. Several of the houses had rabbit hutches on top. Rabbits were bred for food and that again was a sign of a slight margin between living and subsistence.

The Mamur led Owen to a house at the end. They did not go inside. Instead, the Mamur produced his cane chairs and they sat outside in the shade where it was cooler.

The three trackers slumped down in the shadow of the wall and looked at the villagers disdainfully.

Within moments of sitting down Owen found himself covered with flies. The warm, stagnant heat of the cane fields produced them in profusion. In the desert it would be better. But Owen had no intention of spending longer than he could help in either the cane fields or the desert; or the village, for that matter.

"Tell me about the boy," he said.

"He was a good boy," said the Mamur. He looked across the street to a man sitting patiently on the ground in an outer ring of observers. "That is his father," he said. Behind them in the shadow of a doorway stood a group of women. "And there is his mother."

"If he was a good boy," said Owen, "how was it that he came to blow himself up?"

The Mamur scratched his head.

The wife called something across to her husband. Reluctantly he stood up.

"It was not his fault, effendi."

"Why was it not his fault?"

The man seemed confused. He started to say something, then stopped and looked at the ground.

The woman called out something. The man lifted his head.

"It was the other boy's fault," he said.

"What other boy was this?" asked Owen, surprised.

"There was another boy with him," said the Mamur.

"Why was this not in the Report?"

"Wasn't it in the Report?" The Mamur looked alarmed.

"No, it wasn't. There was no mention of any other boy."

"There must have been," said the Mamur, looking worried.

"I have it here." Owen tapped the paper on his knee. "It says nothing of any other boy."

The Mamur looked completely flummoxed. He shrugged his shoulders in bewilderment and turned the palms of his hands outwards as if appealing to the heavens.

Owen sighed. The Reports that came from the provinces were often next to useless. Compiled by people who wrote only with difficulty, they often consisted of a few illiterate scrawls, formulaic clichés scrambled together. They did, however, usually contain the basic facts.

He glanced down at the piece of paper, smudged almost to the point of unreadability by the Mamur's original sweaty labors, crumpled by the journey down in Owen's pocket.

"It says here that one afternoon when the village was still sleeping there was a mighty clap as of thunder."

The semicircle of observers nodded vigorously.

"That is true, effendi."

"It woke me from my slumbers," said one.

"And me. I went outside and, lo, in the sky a hundred birds were circling."

"They were beyond the fields. I remember them."

"We wondered what it might be. So we woke the Mamur."

"I had heard it," said the Mamur defensively, "but I thought it was some miracle of nature."

"You thought it was brigands in the sugar cane," said one of the villagers tartly.

"And so you did nothing?"

"Not at first, effendi. But then we made him come with us. We went to the edge of the fields where the birds were circling. And there we found Hamid lying."

"Hamid?"

"My son," said the man.

"We went to Hamid at once but he was already dead."

"So was the other boy."

"The other boy's body was the more broken," said an older villager, "so I think it was he who had been carrying it."

Owen considered for a moment.

"What was it that he was carrying?" he asked.

The villagers were silent.

"We do not know," one of them said.

"What did you see?"

"A piece of iron."

"Other pieces, too."

"What happened to them?"

"We left them lying."

"You didn't bring them back?" said Owen, looking at the Mamur, who was supposed to collect the pieces of evidence.

"They were still too hot."

"You did not go back later for them?"

The Mamur shrugged.

"Well," said Owen, "perhaps they are still there. If they are, we shall find them. Let us continue. You saw the bodies and you saw the iron. What then did you do?"

"We bore Hamid back to the village."

"And the other boy?"

"We left him there. The body was much broken."

"The boy had a family, too," said Owen reprovingly.

"He did not come from our village."

"From a nearby one?"

"No. He came from the city. When Hamid came home— that was in the summer when all the Great Schools close— this boy was with him."

"Was he, too, at the Great School?"

The villagers were silent.

"I do not think so," said the woman across the street.

"I do not think so," her husband echoed obediently.

"Did Hamid speak to you of him?"

Owen addressed the question to the man but it was aimed at the woman. It was the woman who answered.

"He said only that he was his friend. That was enough for us."

"And so you took him in?"

"We took him in," said the man.

Owen considered.

"He did not speak of his family?"

The man looked at his wife.

"No," said the woman.

The man shook his head.

"No," he said.

"Nor where he came from?"

"No. In the house he said little."

"But outside?"

"He and Hamid were always talking. They talked together, though, not with others."

"The young are like that," said Owen.

"I wish the boy had never come." The woman lifted her voice. "It was a black day for us when he came to Hamada. Had he not come my son would have been still alive."

"You said it was his fault?"

"And so it was. My son was a quiet boy, a good boy. The whole village knows that. What happened to him when he went to the great city? When he came back to us he was changed."

"In what way—changed?"

The woman hesitated. "He was different. He was—bitter."

"Against the Pasha?"

The woman drew her burka over her face.

"Yes," she said, "to our shame."

"And this other boy?"

"Like him."

"They talked together of this?"

"I think so. I did not hear them. Only once, when they were by the house. I upbraided them and after that they went into the fields. They always went into the fields."

The woman's voice broke. The other women in the doorway muttered among themselves. One of them began to ululate softly. Owen knew he would have to stop.

"In the fields," he said, "the men saw iron. Did the boys have iron with them in the house?"

"No," said the woman. "If they had I would have seen it and I would not have allowed it."

"Then how—"

"It was the brigands," said the Mamur. "It must have been the brigands."

The women began to ululate together.

•   •   •

The sugar cane ended abruptly and gave way first, briefly, to thorn scrub and then to sand. Close to the fields the sand was red and gravelly but almost at once, within twenty yards, it became thin and silvery. It washed over the feet and into Owen's shoes. It was too hot for the villagers to walk barefoot.

The Mamur led them to the edge of the sand and then stopped.

"Wasn't it somewhere around here?" he said to the villagers.

"Surely not!" objected one of the villagers. "We came the other way."

"Did we? It was a long time ago."

"Show me," said Owen.

The little procession turned right and walked back along the edge of the sugar cane. After some time another track emerged onto the desert.

"We came up this one."

"So it was somewhere around here?"

"I think so." The villager suddenly sounded less confident.

Owen looked out across the sand. The desert stretched out to the horizon, empty and featureless except for the occasional stunted thorn tree.

The trackers had already begun patrolling the sand. They walked in line abreast, a few yards apart, their eyes fixed on the ground ahead of them. They had already marked off in their minds a stretch of desert extending from one track to the other and a little beyond.

The villagers watched from the sugar cane.

Twilight came early in this part of Egypt. The trackers worked until then and then came to Owen.

"OK," he said resignedly. They would have to carry on the next day. He cursed the Mamur under his breath. This was taking more time than he wanted.

The trackers came for him even before the sun had risen and they went up together through the sugar-cane fields. The sun was just beginning to tinge the desert red as the trackers set to work.

This early in the morning it was not only pleasant, it was beautiful. Owen felt a twinge of nostalgia for his first few months in Egypt when he had been posted up to Alexandria to learn the ropes under Garvin and had ridden on desert patrols.

It was only a twinge, for Owen was not really a desert man. There were men in the Government's service who liked

to spend all their time in the desert. Funny little Plumley
might even be one of these. They were in the tradition of the
great English Arabists, who were typically more at home
among the simple Bedawin of the desert than among the
more sophisticated people of the town.

Owen, however, was a town man through and through. He
was a sociable Welshman who liked talking to people and
enjoyed the bustle and variety and complexity of the big city.
For him the life of the boulevard café, not that of the campfire.

All the same he loved the early morning in Egypt, the
cool, the quiet, the staggeringly beautiful colors. And this
morning, as he walked alongside the sugar cane, and
watched the sparrows dodging in and out, he felt he might almost settle for a comfortable provincial office.

This indulgent feeling wore off as the sun rose. By mid-
morning it was baking hot. Even through his shoes he could
feel the heat of the sand. He moved in closer to the shade of
the sugar cane but even here the warmth trapped in the dense
vegetation seeped out at him making the sweat run down his
face and turning his shirt into a sodden mass. The birds
stopped singing.

The trackers walked up and down, impervious, apparently,
to the heat, oblivious of the birds. But when the sun had risen
until it was directly overhead even they retreated into the
shade.

The shade was where the Mamur and some old men from
the village were already to be found. The active men were at
work in the fields. Owen went round the old men individu-
ally, talking to them, checking the account of the explosion
that had emerged the previous day.

He asked them about the boy, Hamid. After the almost rit-
ual "he was a good boy," Owen sensed qualifications. The
qualifications referred to the somewhat changed Hamid who
had returned from the city after his first year at the School of
Engineering to spend the summer back at home.

Nothing very explicit was said but Hamid had obviously
picked up some of the radical notions current among the students and said enough about them to disturb the conservative

villagers. Perhaps realizing that, after a while he had stopped saying anything and with his friend, the other boy, Salah, had taken to going for long walks up beside the sugar cane and out on to the desert.

About the other boy the villagers said even less. Again Owen sensed reservation. "He did not come from our village," was about the most the men would say, but in that expression of difference Owen detected condemnation and rejection. "It was the other boy's fault," Hamid's mother had said. Whether that was true or not, the blame generally was placed on him.

After the afternoon break the trackers went back to their patrolling. Owen walked down to the village and found someone who would take him by boat to a village a couple of miles upstream. The village was also on the estate and counted as Hamada; and it was where the most recent boy to leave the estate for education in the great city had come from: Abu, one of the boys killed in the café.

The parents were still numb from the shock. This boy had grown up with them for all these years and then had gone to the great city. And there he had died. It was remote, unbelievable.

The remoteness, the unbelievableness, was about all that they could express. They had not seen their son since he had left for the city. He had not written—he could write but they could not read. Others would have read the letter to them, but the boy had not written. It would have been expensive, anyway, to send a letter. They had heard nothing of him. And then this.

The other villagers confirmed what there was to confirm. Abu had been a hard-working boy, not interested in politics, not interested in very much, plucked out by the Pasha and sent up to the city with the same bewilderment as his parents now shared in their loss.

Owen asked the question he had come to ask. Had Abu known Hamid? The villagers could not recollect that he had. He might have met him but the difference in age between them—Abu would have been three years younger than

Hamid—mattered at that point in their lives and they would not have been close.

Besides, in walking terms, in the heat, the distance between the villages was significant. To people on horseback, on camels, to the Pasha and his men, the villages were close together, hardly distinguishable as separate parts of the estate. To fellahin in the fields, working all their lives near their own village, the other village was in a different country.

Abu would, however, have heard of the explosion; might, indeed, have heard the explosion.

Owen stayed on in the village until the young men came back from the fields. He wanted to talk to boys who had known Abu, were part of the young men's grapevine. He asked them the same question.

They thought it possible that the two had at least spoken. Again, though, there was the gap in age. What would they have spoken about? Hamid at that time, over two years ago, would have been an exalted creature, singled out by the Pasha to go up to the great city. Abu would have been a small boy, not knowing yet that he would take the same path, not even quite understanding in what the distinction might lie, knowing only that Hamid was a remarkable man and remarkably fortunate.

The other boy, Salah? They did not remember him. Perhaps the two, Hamid and Salah, had come to the village on one of their long walks. Who knew?

Who might they have spoken to? Owen asked. Were there other boys of Hamid's age? Or might they have spoken to the teacher? They might have spoken to the teacher but he could not recollect it. As for the other boys, well, they thought they could remember Hamid but certainly nothing of what he said. It was not anything special.

Political? They looked at the ground and shuffled their feet.

Political, then. But it could have been only brief. And at this distance in time they could remember no names.

Owen had to take his boat back. No boatmen like traveling by dark. He had, anyway, he felt, got all that he was likely to get.

It wasn't much. It was not much at all that he had gained from his visit to Hamada. Down there in the vast, monotonous sugar-cane fields and the intense, dripping heat, with the great desert stretching out on the sides into a void, definiteness had a habit of seeping away. A boy killed in an explosion had become two boys. The place of the explosion, so obvious in Cairo, had slipped way into uncertainty here. The evidence it might contain might now be buried under the sand.

How long could he afford to spend down here? He himself would soon have to go back. Who knew what might be happening?

The trackers, too, how long could he leave them? They were expensive and there was work for them to do elsewhere. How long could he afford to have them combing the desert fruitlessly?

He had expected to come down, find the spot and make his inquiries at the most in the space of a couple of days. It was already certain that it would take longer.

And what did he hope to gain? From a few fragments of metal he hoped to be able to tell whether the bomb was of a type similar to the one thrown at Nuri Pasha and the one left in the café. What would that tell him?

From a few whitened bones he hoped to find out—what?

Was it worth it?

And yet, and yet, the parallels had become sharper, if anything. In each case a student—two students, in fact—and a bomb. If the bomb was of the same type it could not be coincidence. And Hamada was the common ingredient. He would not leave it yet.

When he stepped out of the boat he found the Mamur waiting for him.

"You must come quickly," the Mamur said agitatedly. "The Pasha is expecting you."

High up on the bank a man was waiting with two horses. He led one of the horses over to Owen.

"The Pasha bids you welcome. His house and all he has is yours. He is waiting to receive you."

The house was about three miles away through the sugar cane and it was quite dark by the time they reached it. They rode through a gate in a high mud-brick wall and dismounted in an enclosed courtyard.

Servants with lamps escorted Owen into a long inner room with divans, on one of which a man was lying.

"Why, Captain Owen, it is you!" a familiar voice said in surprised tones. "What brings you to these uncomfortable, oh, so uncomfortable, parts?"

It was Ali Osman Pasha.

•　•　•

"I followed your advice," said Ali Osman, "and retired to my estate."

"This is your estate?"

Ali Osman looked around with an expression of distaste.

"Yes," he said, "unfortunately."

The room was if anything slightly larger than the corresponding one in the Pasha's Cairo house. Because of the heat there were fewer carpets on the walls, but the floor was as elaborately tiled, and over in the darkness a fountain was playing. Among the silk and leather cushions occasional little silver boxes caught the light from the lamps the servants were holding.

"It is so awful here," Ali Osman complained. "The people are barbarous, there is nothing to do, no one to talk to." He looked at Owen hopefully. "And what are you doing here, my friend? Surely you have not come here for your health too?"

Owen decided to tell him only half the truth.

"I am working on a case," he said.

"A case? Down here? Alas, my friend, you must have fallen out of favor. Like me," said the Pasha gloomily.

"The case concerns someone on your estate. A boy."

"A boy?" said Ali Osman, reviving. "How interesting!"

"A student, Hamid, who killed himself with a bomb two years ago."

"That is much less interesting," said Ali Osman. "In fact that is not interesting at all."

"You remember the boy?"

"Barely. Is he worth remembering?"

"You paid for his education."

"A big mistake," said Ali Osman. "Obviously."

"What led you to select him?"

"Did I select him?"

"Someone selected him."

"It was probably one of my servants."

"You had nothing to do with it yourself?"

"I probably saw him," Ali Osman granted. He frowned in concentration. "Did he have large ears?"

"You sent him to the School of Engineering."

"Where apparently the only thing he learned was how to make a bomb."

"Why did you send him to the School of Engineering?"

"I send them all there. In the hope that they might learn something useful. Useful to me, of course, not to them."

"Do you send someone every year?"

"After that unfortunate incident," said Ali Osman drily, "a gap seemed advisable."

"A strange incident," said Owen, "especially strange in that it happened at Hamada. In Cairo, yes, it would be nothing out of the ordinary. But in Hamada!"

"It just goes to show," said Ali Osman, "that even on your estate you can't be safe. I should have remembered that when you suggested coming here."

"It was surely not intended for you."

"Wasn't it? Who else in Hamada is worth bombing?"

"Were you here at the time?"

"No."

"Well, then—"

"They were preparing," said Ali Osman, "getting ready for the next time I came."

"They knew you would be coming."

"Some time I would come," said Ali Osman. "It might be years—I visit Hamada as infrequently as possible—but they would be ready. You don't know these people. They are terrible people, backward. They store things in their hearts. For years. And then one day—poof!" He spread his hands.

"They would surely not be making a bomb just on the off chance—"

"Education," said Ali Osman, "that's at the root of it. It's a big mistake trying to educate these people. It just fills their heads with idle nonsense. Or worse. And then they come back to places like Hamada and there's nothing for them to do, so they have time to think about the terrible things they have heard. And then if they are particularly inclined they turn to making bombs."

"Invariably?"

"In my experience. Yes," said Ali Osman. "Education's at the root of it. It must be stopped."

"Surely—"

"That's why I've given it up. Educating these boys from the estate. It's wasted on them. It only spoils them."

"Actually," said Owen, "you haven't given it up. You only stopped it for a year or two."

"Really? Don't tell me I've sent another boy up to the School?"

"Yes. He—"

"He must be brought back. I'll have him sent home at once."

"It's too late. He's dead."

"Really?"

"A student café was bombed. He was one of the victims."

"Another one! This is frightful!"

"It's slightly different. In this case the boy was merely a victim."

"All the same," said Ali Osman, "we can't have this sort of thing. I don't want my people mixed up in anything to do with bombs. It gives them the wrong ideas."

Owen went on to explain the circumstances. Ali Osman was already slightly bored, however. He clapped his hands and servants started bringing in supper: soup, curried fowl, quail, fish stuffed with crab, mutton and salad, beef with eggplants, asparagus, macaroni, grapes, figs, pears, Camembert and coffee.

• • •

The desert was less featureless than it appeared. From time to time the trackers pointed out objects to him: the carcass of a bird or dog, the ribcage sticking up through the sand; a broken jar, the remains of a cane basket, an ant-eaten saddle belt. They did not find any human bones, however, nor any metal.

He stayed with the trackers for two more days and then returned to Cairo. He couldn't, he really couldn't, allow himself to be absent from the city for longer at such a time.

He almost pulled the trackers out, too, but decided to reprieve them for another week. After that he would offer the small boys of the village a reward if they found the remains and reported them to him. Owen was a great believer in small boys.

He was not, however, entirely guileless in the matter and knew that if a reward was offered then it would be claimed. Plausible bones would suddenly appear in just the right spot. He would have to find some realist to vet the claims locally.

That would not be the Mamur, for he was probably corrupt and certainly incompetent. Nor would it be one of the villagers, for they would have a vested interest and would pronounce the claims valid in return for a share in the reward.

When the time came he would have to go to Ali Osman's household. The villagers, and certainly the boys, would be wary about going there, however, so another solution would be preferable.

For the moment the decision could wait. The trackers would continue. Perhaps they would make the decision unnecessary.

He returned to Cairo and was relieved to find that nothing had happened in his absence. He had feared some further outrage. There had been no progress either, but this, as Nikos pointed out with asperity, did not mean that people had not been working hard.

The fact was that in terrorist cases all one usually had to go on were the circumstances. It was no good researching, for instance, the background of the victims since motivation was not located in the personal context.

The circumstances, however, typically yielded little data. While Owen had been away the forensic lab had done a complete analysis on the spent bullets and confirmed that they had come from two guns and that the guns had not been used in previous terrorist offenses. They had found nothing distinctive about the picric or nitric acid used in the two bombs, nor really in the bombs themselves.

No further eyewitnesses had been found and no further details had emerged from questioning of the eyewitnesses they already had.

"We'll just have to wait until more data is available," said Nikos.

"You mean until there is another killing?"

"That's right," said Nikos.

Owen found it difficult to take such a calm view of things and instructed Nikos to analyze reports of current followings in the hope that, having sifted out possibles from totally unlikely ones, they might be able to second-guess the terrorists and anticipate where the next attack might come. This was not very fruitful because of the highly subjective nature of the reports. However, it made Owen feel better.

He also got Georgiades to check the background of the boys killed in the explosion at Hamada. It was easy to find out about Hamid, but about the other boy, Salah, at this distance in time little could be established.

He had definitely not been a student of the School of Engineering, nor had he shared a room with Hamid. One or two people thought they might remember seeing him; but that was all.

On Hamid himself the details gleaned were rather similar to those obtained about Abu, the boy from Hamada killed in the café bombing. He had been a quiet boy who had not stood out in any way, certainly not for academic merit. Like Abu, he appeared to have been lost at first in the great city, overawed and bewildered by it. But this was no different from the countless other country boys sent up by their Pashas to be educated in the High Schools.

There was, however, one difference between Hamid and Abu. Hamid had definitely been interested in politics. There was a report of his having participated in a student demonstration outside the Abdin Palace. Nikos checked and there had indeed been a demonstration at about the time reported.

Armed with that information, Georgiades began to make covert inquiries among the older students, but so far without result.

At the end of a week Owen pulled the trackers out. The bones of the second boy and the fragments of the bomb appeared to have been lost forever beneath the shifting sands of the desert.

Hamada continued to niggle at him, however. He felt obscurely dissatisfied. Something told him that there was something important to be found out at Hamada. Whatever it was, he had not found it out. Somehow or other he would have to go back.

The opportunity came about ten days after he had left.

An urgent message came from Ali Osman Pasha: *"They have followed me down here. Come at once."*

CHAPTER EIGHT

They were waiting for me," said Ali Osman. "I saw them."

"Where was this?"

"At Nag Balyana. It is across the river," Ali Osman explained.

"In the sugar cane?"

"No, no. Beyond the cane fields. In the hills. I rode around some rocks and there they were."

"How many were there?"

"Two." Ali Osman looked at him soberly. "As usual."

"You have been followed before?"

"In Cairo," said Ali Osman. "Not here. Until now."

"But were they following? Pardon me, but you said you came upon them."

"The following time was past," said Ali Osman. "Now they were waiting."

"They were armed, I take it?"

"I saw their rifles."

"And they were waiting?"

"Yes," said Ali Osman. "They were waiting for me."

Owen hesitated.

"Forgive me, Pasha," he said, "but I need to ask these things. How do you know they were waiting for you? Might they not have been a group of ordinary villagers—?"

"Fellahin," said Ali Osman, "do not carry rifles. Nor would they have been in the desert."

"Camel-herders?"

"Camel-herders do not wear city clothes. Nor, before you ask me, do brigands. Not in Hamada they don't."

"City clothes," said Owen. "That makes a difference."

"It made a difference to *me*," said Ali Osman. "I turned my horse and bolted."

"You were on a horse?" Owen could not keep the surprise out of his voice.

"How else would I get to Nag Balyana?" asked Ali Osman rather tartly.

"Forgive me, Pasha. I had not thought of you as a desert man."

"One has one's roots," said Ali Osman with dignity.

"Of course. It was just that, well, I wasn't sure that you had recovered so completely from the bruising you received."

"Battering," said Ali Osman, "battering. At the hands of the mob."

"I am glad to see you so recovered. May I ask what was taking you out to Nag Balyana?"

"Sport. Yes, sport. I was hunting hare." Sensing that this sounded unlikely, Ali Osman modified his claim. "And duty. I was combining pleasure with duty. It is a part of the estate I seldom visit. Justifiably. There is nothing there, *mon cher*, absolutely nothing there. All the same, they should have an opportunity of seeing their Pasha. Occasionally, that is. *Very* occasionally," said Ali Osman with emphasis.

"It was a kind of regal progress?"

"Exactly." Ali Osman was pleased by the thought. "I am, after all, their king," he said modestly.

"And while you were—showing yourself, so to speak, you came upon these men?"

"Afterwards. I couldn't take too much of it, you know. The heat!" Ali Osman fanned himself at the mere thought. "In the fields it was terrific. After a while I had had enough. So I went hunting here."

"Not unaccompanied, I trust?"

"Naturally I had a few servants with me. My retinue," said Ali Osman, still enjoying the regal image.

"And they were with you when you came upon the men?"

"Of course. Though not for long. They departed from the spot even more quickly than I did."

"Could you show me the spot?"

"They could. I see no reason to return personally to that detested place." He clapped his hands and spoke to a servant. "They will be waiting for you outside. It will do them good to have to return to a spot they quit in so cowardly a fashion."

The servants, however, when Owen questioned them on the way to Nag Balyana, were unabashed.

"They were bad men," they said, shaking their heads vigorously, "oh, very bad men."

"How do you know?"

"We could see at once."

"They were not from these parts."

"They were dressed like foreigners," put in an older man.

"So they could not have been brigands?"

"Oh no." The men were definite. "We know the brigands. They are friends of ours."

"I see."

"Besides, the brigands stay in the sugar cane."

Ahead of them Owen suddenly caught sight of the river. It was about half a mile wide at this point, blue and glinting in the sun.

They walked the horses down to the water's edge and stood waiting for a boat. One or two of the men dismounted and splashed water over their heads. The rest stayed on their horses enjoying the cool river breeze.

The boat when it came was a small one and could take only two horses at a time. Owen crossed first with the oldest servant and had a long wait on the other side. They let their horses nibble at the sparse grass on the river bank and squatted down on the baked earth.

"It always takes a long time," said the servant, watching the boat tacking back through the sandbanks, "especially when there are a lot of you. When we are with the Pasha, it takes forever."

"It is fortunate that you don't have to do it often," said Owen, commiserating.

"Often enough lately," said the servant. "Since the Pasha came down we have been going almost every day."

"Every day?" said Owen, surprised. "Not with the Pasha, surely?"

"Oh yes. It surprised us. He wasn't so fond of riding when he was here before."

"There can't be that many villages on this side."

"There aren't any. Well, there's one further up the river. You see, the cultivation on this side of the river is fairly recent. In the old Pasha's time there wasn't any. It's only in the last twenty years that they're starting growing over here. The villages are all on the other side, where the house is. People come over here to work."

"What's the Pasha doing over here, then?"

"There's a holy shrine on the slopes of the jebel. He goes to that."

"Every day?"

The servant shrugged. "He's become very holy all of a sudden."

"It's a bit out of the way, isn't it?"

"That makes the shrine more powerful, of course. Perhaps the Pasha needs a powerful saint to intercede for him."

"He doesn't come over here to hunt for hare?"

"Hare?" The servant looked at him as if he had gone off his head.

·   ·   ·

When at last the party was all across they mounted their horses again and rode on through the sugar cane. On this side the cane grew more thickly. Even on horseback they were not high enough to see over it. It was like riding through a tunnel.

Owen was glad when he saw the desert ahead of him. The horses were glad too and perked up. When they emerged into the open they burst of their own accord into a little gallop.

Ahead of him, some way off across the sand, Owen could see the rocky outline of the jebel, rising like a tooth out of the flatness of the desert.

The jebel was further off than it looked and the horses soon slowed to a walk. There was a slight but firm desert wind which blew all the time. At first, after the enclosed heat of the sugar cane, they found it very pleasant. Soon, however, the servants and the trackers wrapped a fold of their galabeahs across their faces.

Owen wished he could do the same. When he had ridden patrol in the north he had worn the same headdress as the other men and he wished he could do that now. Although the wind was slight, there was the perpetual small sting of particles on his skin, and he had virtually to close his eyes against both the sand and the sun.

He was carried back to his early days in Egypt, when he had just transferred from India and was exhilarated by the space and emptiness of the desert after the dense, close-packed humanity of the Indian coastal towns.

Very soon, however, he was being reminded uncomfortably that it was some time since he had last done much riding. He wondered how Ali Osman had found it.

Why all the story about showing himself to the villagers and hunting hare? The Pasha was obviously a fantasist. Perhaps he had invented it all to compensate for the comparative austerity of provincial life. Or perhaps beneath the hedonism was buried a remnant of the traditional harshness and sparseness of the desert.

Perhaps the Pasha was going out into the desert like some modern Elijah or Elisha to commune alone in the hope of spiritual renewal.

Or perhaps that was how he saw himself. That was more likely. Another expression of his fantasy. Extruded from the great city which was his natural element, perhaps the only way in which he could come to terms with a place like Hamada was by adopting a role which translated the exile into a great personal drama.

Somehow Owen could not quite see Ali Osman as a spiritual explorer. What he could see him as was someone playing at being a spiritual explorer.

Provided that this did not involve too great an affront to the flesh. The journey to Nag Balyana was just about right: sufficiently far and sufficiently uncomfortable for Ali Osman to be able to persuade himself that he was donning a spiritual hair shirt, not so far that he could not return at night to the comforts of his cushions and his people and the coolness of his house.

For a long time the jebel did not seem to come any nearer at all and Owen slumped into the daze which seemed an inherent part of any lengthy desert expedition. But then he emerged from the daze to find the rock looming up in front of him.

The ground had become stonier and they were riding now over just buried rock. The hooves of the horses tapped sharply on the hard ground.

The rocks began to break through the surface and the horses had to wind their way through them. Ahead the jebel rose steep and sheer.

It was a ridge of low, rocky hills which ran across in front of them for not much more than a mile. At first the line of the rock seemed unbroken but as they drew closer they could see gaps and recesses, outcrops which they had to skirt and which could easily conceal someone.

Owen began to understand how it was that Ali Osman had come so suddenly on his pursuers.

If, indeed, they had been pursuing him. Owen would have dismissed the whole thing long ago as another figment of Ali Osman's fantasizing had it not been for one thing: the fact that the men had been dressed in city clothes.

They were riding parallel to the face of the jebel now. The horses instinctively took the easiest way through the rocks. In the sand Owen could see marks that other horses had traveled that way before.

Or perhaps the same horses. The trackers weren't interested.

They came around an outcrop and then the leading servant pointed. Unnecessarily; the trackers had already seen.

They slipped from their horses and walked in towards the main face of the rock. A few yards short of it some large slabs lay in an extended curve around the foot of the cliff, bending back into a rift. The trackers stopped at the sharpest point of the bend and stood looking at the ground.

Owen walked across to join them. The sand was chewed up by the feet of several camels and to Owen it seemed that all individual tracks had been obliterated.

"Six camels," said the leading tracker, "two of them baggage camels being led. I think the foreigners would have been on these camels." He showed Owen some indistinct sets of pad prints. "They stopped here and then they turned and went back."

"How long ago?" asked Owen.

"Three days," said the tracker.

One of the trackers started following the tracks around into the rift.

Was it worth following the trail? Owen could not make up his mind. In three days the men could be a long way away, halfway down the Thieves' Road. There must be at least four of them. The three trackers were all armed. Owen, as usual, wasn't. The Pasha's servants certainly weren't and were keeping well back.

The men were probably simple camel thieves and the threat to the Pasha a product of his own easily alarmable imagination. Owen couldn't afford to spend a long time away from the city. Perhaps he should leave it at that.

He would have but for one thing.

"Can you tell from the tracks whether any of them were city men?" he asked the trackers.

"Oh yes. This one and this one," said the trackers, pointing to the pad prints again.

"How do you know?"

The tracker found it hard to put into words.

"It is the way they ride," he said. "You can see that they have backed up into the rocks here, which is a silly way to ride. And then they are not sitting properly." He thought hard and then spread his hands helplessly. "You can just *see* that they were not brought up with camels."

"Very well," said Owen. "We will go after them. A little," he amended.

They went back for their horses and then rode on round the face of the jebel.

High up in the rocks there was the flash of something white.

"What's that?"

"A shrine," said one of the trackers indifferently.

"It is the shrine of the Haji Abbas," said one of the servants.

"Where the Pasha goes?"

"Yes. There is a path up from the rift."

"Have you been with him?"

"Yes. We waited outside while the Pasha prayed."

The ground now was covered with boulders and the horses picked their way with difficulty. There had been a heavy fall from the cliff above.

"How far are you going, effendi?" asked the servant. "If you don't turn soon you won't be at the river before it gets dark."

Owen was wondering that too.

They came to the edge of a fall of scree. The horses hesitated and then plunged across it, their feet sliding and slipping on the loose stones.

The servants stopped.

"We will go back now, effendi," they said.

"Very well. Only lend me your headdress," Owen said to one of them. "It will be evening soon and you will not need it."

"All I have is yours," the man responded automatically and swept his headdress off. Owen sensed, however, a slight discomfort. No Arab felt at ease if he was bareheaded for long.

"And in exchange, take mine," he said.

The man beamed, took Owen's hat, and rode off rejoicing.

"Bring it to me tomorrow!" Owen called after him.

On the other side of the scree the ground sloped away sharply down into an enormous hollow. It was like riding down the slope of a dune.

One of the trackers muttered something. All three suddenly seemed to have found something ahead which interested them.

On the other side of the hollow was another set of tracks. It came over the sand and joined the trail they were following at right angles. The tracks blended together.

"Friends?" asked Owen.

The leading tracker shook his head.

"It is the same people," he said. "Only the track is fresher."

"What is it that you are saying?"

"It is the same party, but a later day."

"How much later?"

"Earlier today."

"In that case," said Owen, "let us ride on."

They were coming now to the end of the jebel. The trail still kept close to the bottom of the cliff following the line of rock. As the steep line of cliff fell back the tracks bent around with it until they were going first due east around the end of the jebel and then north behind it.

Still they kept close to the rock. Little ridges ran out on this side like the buttresses of a cathedral, requiring them to make continual detours and blocking the view ahead.

It was for this reason that they came upon the men quite suddenly.

They had climbed to the top of a spur and were just about to plunge down the other side when the trackers stopped. At first Owen could see nothing. And then on the far slopes he saw a group of tiny figures: four men and six camels. Two of the men were Bedawins. The other two were Roper and Plumley.

* * *

Owen swore. To have come so far, to have gone to such lengths, and then to find—this!

He cursed Ali Osman for luring him down here with his tales of being followed, he cursed himself for his credulousness in believing them. Most of all he cursed himself. What was he doing riding around the countryside like a lunatic when he ought to be in Cairo where Christ knows what was probably happening?

The trackers looked at him admiringly.

"That was a mighty curse," said one. "It does a man's heart good to hear it."

Resignedly Owen gave the sign to ride over to Roper and Plumley.

They were just about to ride over the brow of the spur when there was the sharp crack of a rifle. It was followed at once by several others.

The figures on the far slope seemed to freeze for a moment and then plunged desperately towards some rocks to one side of them.

The rifles cracked again and there was the distinctive ping of a bullet hitting rock. There was no echo, but here where the air was clear the sound came with peculiar sharpness.

So far as Owen could see, the figures reached the rocks without mishap, leaped from their mounts and took up position behind cover.

A moment later they began to fire in return.

From where he was Owen could see their assailants clearly. A handful of men in galabeahs lay sprawled among the rocks at the bottom of the slope blazing away.

"Brigands," said Owen.

"Gypsies," said one of the trackers contemptuously. He raised his rifle to his shoulder.

Owen stopped him. "Let's get closer," he said.

The two parties were so far apart that there was little chance of them doing much damage to each other, and Owen's party was further off still. The Bedawin—and certainly his own trackers—were good shots, but their besetting sin was to blaze away at absolutely maximum range where a kill would certainly be spectacular but was highly unlikely.

Besides, Owen was supposed to be keeping the peace.

They rode quickly down the spur, keeping out of sight. At the bottom there was a dried wadi which ran roughly in the right direction. At the end of that there were some rocks.

They left their horses in the wadi and ran crouching through the rocks. The trackers, recruited from unruly desert tribes, were in their element.

Owen was not. Once again he had been caught without a gun when he particularly needed it.

From time to time he heard occasional splatters of fire. Neither party had left its cover. The assailants seemed reluctant to press their attack.

That would probably be so if they were indeed gypsies. Like anyone else in the desert, they would take a chance if one came along, and a small party with baggage camels was an opportunity not to be missed. However, it was unlikely that they would have gone out positively looking for trouble.

Owen thought that if he could get close enough he could get them to surrender *en masse*. What he would do with them he wasn't quite sure but it was better if you could do that, for then you could bring home to them that there *was* somebody ostensibly keeping law and order in the land. Otherwise, if you just scared them, they would run away and consider the attack quite a success.

The trackers, entering into the spirit of it, took him through the rocks so quickly he could hardly keep up. The rocks brought them right up to the gypsies and they were upon them before the men could see them coming.

The shooting from the top of the slope had died away. From their higher position Roper and Plumley had probably watched it all.

The trackers slipped into position behind some rocks and trained their rifles across their tops. Owen got them to fire a volley over the heads of the gypsies.

The firing stopped abruptly.

Owen shouted to them to put down their guns. The volley, and then the English voice, would probably be enough to convince them that retribution was at hand.

Nothing seemed to happen.

Owen got one of the trackers—one only, because he did not want to give away the small size of his party—to fire another shot. This time the tracker deliberately put it just to one side of a man who might be the gypsies' leader. There was a little puff of sand about a foot to the left of the man as he was lying.

The man hastily scrambled up and put his hands in the air. One by one the others did the same.

Owen walked out from the rocks with one of the trackers. The others gave him cover.

"Stay where you are!" he said.

The tracker went around collecting the guns.

Owen told the men to sit down. They did so glumly. Now he was close he saw that they were indeed gypsies.

Out of the corner of his eye Owen saw that the party on the hill was beginning to come down towards them.

The tracker stacked all the guns in a pile and sat on them. As an afterthought he pulled three of the guns out, loaded them and leaned them carefully over his knee. Meanwhile the barrel of his own gun did not waver.

"This is a Government party that you've attacked," Owen said to the gypsies sternly.

"I know," said one of them sadly, "and now we are for it. You will take us to prison."

"We did not really mean to kill them," said another gypsy.

"When God had put such bounty in our way it seemed wrong to spurn it," another explained.

"You cannot go around attacking peaceful travelers."

"They were foreigners. We thought that didn't count."

"It counts; as you will shortly find," said Owen severely.

Roper arrived in a shower of sand.

"I take my hat off to you, Owen," he said. "How the hell did you know this was going to happen?"

"What are you doing here?" Owen asked ungraciously.

"Doing a survey," Roper replied. "With our little friend here." He indicated Plumley.

"I thought it was all right here?" said Plumley anxiously. "We said we'd be somewhere around here."

"It's all right. On the whole."

Owen looked at the crestfallen gypsies.

"Are you planning to go on with your survey?" he asked.

"Might as well finish it," said Roper.

"We just don't want these beauties interfering again."

"What are you going to do with them?" asked Roper. "Shoot them or kick them up the ass?"

"I ought to take them in."

"We don't usually bother," said Plumley shyly.

"Usually?"

"Well, of course, this sort of thing happens now and again," said Plumley apologetically. "Usually they shoot at us and we shoot at them and after a bit they go away again."

"It happens all the time when you're surveying, does it?"

"Not all the time. Occasionally."

"Not worth reporting?"

"Well, hardly. Is it?"

It wasn't. By the time a police force had reached the spot the attackers would be hundreds of miles away.

"I may take one of them back with me," said Owen. "Just to show them."

"You won't be able to do that tonight," said Roper, looking at the sun.

In fact, the trackers would have been able to find their way just as easily by night as by day. However, Owen thought he'd better spend the night where he was. That way he could keep an eye on the gypsies. In the morning he would let Roper and Plumley get off first and give them a start. Then he'd start the gypsies off in the opposite direction.

The other thing he'd have to watch out for was theft during the night. The gypsies might not be great gunfighters but as simple thieves they were in a class of their own.

Roper was evidently thinking the same thing. He beckoned to one of the gypsies and made him sit down on the ground. Then he tied his feet together. He then confronted the assembled gypsies.

"If anything goes missing during the night," he said, tapping his gun, "then his head goes missing too. Got it?"

The gypsies understood the mime if not the English.

Owen made his own arrangements. He instructed the gypsies to retire to the bottom of the hollow, where he ordered them to make camp. As soon as they did so, other gypsies, mostly women and children, began to emerge from the rocks.

Owen was standing watching them when he suddenly felt a hand moving over his hip. He caught it and held it as he spun around. It belonged to a woman who had crept up behind him unnoticed.

"You cheeky bitch!" said Owen. "Bloody robbing me while I was standing there!"

"I wasn't robbing you!" the woman protested. She explained where she had intended to put her hand.

"Jesus!" said Roper. "There's that woman again."

It was Soraya, the Ghawazi girl from the night club.

"You get around," said Owen.

"I'm a gypsy."

"What the hell are you doing down here?"

"We always come down here at this time of year. We go up the river to Assiut and then across the desert to Hurghada and then up the coast to Suez. Then sometimes we go straight to Alexandria, other times we go to Aleppo. I am a Halabi."

"Yes, I remember. I also remember what you were doing in the night club."

"You could come to me tonight," said Soraya.

"Bloody take up the offer, man!" urged Roper. "What's wrong with you?"

"I've got other things on my mind. Like seeing they don't cut your throat."

"I'll be all right," said Roper, and wandered away.

"*Would* you like me to cut his throat?" asked Soraya.

"Christ, no."

He found he was still holding her arm and released it. Soraya seemed disappointed.

"You go back there," said Owen firmly, pointing towards the gypsy encampment.

Soraya went off sulkily.

As soon as it began to grow dark Owen went to the gypsy camp and drew a line in the sand with his foot. He then summoned one of the trackers and presented him to the gypsies.

"This is Hosein," he said. "He is a famous tracker. He can see in the dark. If anyone crosses that line between now and dawn he will shoot them."

Hosein agreed with enthusiasm.

The gypsies looked at the other camp, the space and the tracker appraisingly. Owen was under no illusion that their calculations were necessarily the same as his.

He went back to the other camp and joined Plumley and Roper for supper.

Plumley, not one of the Bedawin, was the cook and he prepared a meal with all the expertise of one used to camping and used to the desert.

"I quite like it out here," he said. "Of course, I wouldn't want to do it all the time, there are things in Cairo I'd miss. But it's nice to get away from the office occasionally."

"Do you usually travel on your own?"

"I have a couple of men with me when I'm surveying. You need one to hold the theodolite and it's best to have another holding the camels."

Roper went to sleep soon after the meal.

"He's not used to it now," Plumley apologized. "He gets tired if there's a lot of riding."

Owen and Plumley remained sitting by the fire.

"Presumably you didn't come down to Hamada just to save us?" said Plumley quietly.

"No."

Owen told him about the bomb. Plumley listened attentively.

"That's interesting," he said. "That's very interesting."

"It doesn't seem to be getting us anywhere. I can't even find the place where it happened."

"I might be able to help there," said Plumley.

"Really?"

"Yes. I think I may have seen the place. I was surveying over that side, oh, about a year ago and I came across the bones. They were already bones by then. You know, hawks and ants. And I couldn't work it out. That close to the village they would normally have been properly buried. And then I could see it had been an explosion."

Plumley looked at Owen again almost apologetically.

"I'm used to that sort of thing, you see. Explosions. Anyway, I couldn't make it out. How could there be an explosion like that *there?* The man would have had to have been carrying gelignite or something. And then I looked around and I saw the piping and I reckoned it had to be a bomb, a homemade bomb. But a bomb, there?" Plumley bobbed his head diffidently. "Anyway, it stuck in my mind."

"A year ago. Do you think you could still show me the spot?"

"Oh yes. I noted it down. I was surveying, you see. Anyway, I think I could remember. Would you like us to come back with you tomorrow?"

"Very much. Normally I wouldn't want you to disrupt the surveying, but just now—"

"It won't disrupt it very much. We were going to go over to that side of the river afterwards. We'll just circle around."

As Owen stretched out on the sand a little bit later, his hand on his saddle-bag, he thought he might call back the curses he had heaped on Ali Osman; some of them.

The mighty tracker, Hosein, who could see in the dark, could not see well enough. Owen had not been asleep long when he awoke to find a hand crawling over his body. He grabbed it and twisted over to pinion his attacker. There was a surprised grunt and then a soft voice complained: "You are always hurting me."

"What the hell are you doing here?"

"Well . . ."

• • •

Plumley led them right to the spot. It was not in the strip they had been searching but to one side of it. There was a track leading back to the village.

"Why on earth didn't they tell us about this one?" demanded Owen.

"It goes out of the village at a bit of a tangent," said Plumley. "If they wanted to get to the desert they wouldn't go this way."

"Then why did they go this way when they heard the explosion?"

Plumley, high on his camel, looked back over the sugar cane.

"They were following the sound, presumably."

And the Mamur had just forgotten, thought Owen bitterly. Or perhaps he hadn't.

When they emerged from the sugar cane, Plumley paused for an instant to consult his mapwork and then set out unhesitatingly across the desert.

The trackers saw it first: a white ribcage, rounded like a wicker basket, collapsed back into the sand. As they drew nearer, they saw other bones lying. And then as they drew nearer still there was the black sheen of metal and a short length of piping, twisted and gnarled and now choked up with sand.

"It's exactly the same, you see," said Plumley, dismounting. "Of course, I wasn't to know that at the time. But this kind of bomb has become pretty standard over the last few years. In Cairo, I mean. I've been called out before."

The bones were scattered over quite a wide area.

Plumley took out a sketchpad.

"I'll draw it for you if you like," he offered. "It's always a help to the lab."

The trackers began to work over the ground methodically, uncovering fragments, exposing bones, but leaving them lying.

Roper watched for a time but then, bored, walked his camel off and began a wide circle in the desert studying the lie of the land.

Owen bent over the remains of the bomb. It was exactly the same as the one used in the bombing of the café and the one thrown at Nuri. Standard, no doubt, as Plumley had said; but what was it doing down here?

One of the trackers beckoned him over. There was a shoulder blade lying in the sand. The tracker directed his attention more closely. Half fused to the shoulder blade was a tiny, studlike thing. It took Owen a moment to realize that it was a button. Caught round the button were a few wisps of cloth.

The tracker scraped away more sand and uncovered some smaller bones. One of them looked like a collarbone. As the tracker gently prised it out Owen saw that there was some more cloth sticking to it, preserved in the dry air and the sand.

The tracker turned it over with his finger and thumb. It was about an inch square, yellowing and oddly shiny. There were some faint scratches on it, faded marks.

Suddenly Owen realized what it was: the tailor's label of the suit.

"Would you like to borrow a magnifying glass?" Plumley offered diffidently. "I use it for examining rocks."

The scratches and marks became clearer. They were writing. Owen thought he could make out the letters "Guill—" Then the label was torn across.

He gave the magnifying glass back to Plumley.

"Thank you," he said. "You have been very, very useful."

CHAPTER NINE

Yes," said the tailor, "it's one of ours."

"Would you be able to trace it?"

"We have a list of all the suits we've sold and to whom they've gone. It helps getting the money."

"How far back do you go?"

"Fifteen years," said the tailor with a touch of pride.

"Five would be enough."

The tailor ducked down some steps into an inner cellar in which half a dozen men were busy sewing. He returned with a bound leather book.

"They're all in here. Would you like to copy down the names?"

Owen opened the book. It contained name, address and measurements.

"Can I borrow it for a couple of days?"

The measurements might help Nikos. The lab had been able to give them a rough indication of height and build, not precise enough to tally exactly but sufficient to rule out some combinations.

"I promise it will come back," he said, seeing the man hesitate.

"I should hate to lose it. It's—it's, well I started it the day I started here. Fifteen years ago."

"You've done well," said Owen, looking around.

It was a small shop. Garments hung on racks around the walls leaving barely enough space for two men to stand in the middle. It was a tailor's for men only, the sort of place which made suits for the hundreds of clerks and minor civil servants with which Cairo abounded.

Every man who worked in an office wore a suit. It was a mark of social achievement. The dark suit, the little potlike hat with a tassel, were the badge which distinguished the educated professional, or semi-educated, semi-professional, from the galabeahed figures in the street.

Students wore suits, even schoolboys in the secondary schools did. Though not usually when they went into the country. Owen was a little surprised at that. Of course there was no guarantee that the second boy, Salah, had been a student but somehow Owen had expected it.

Perhaps he had simply not had a change of clothing.

"Do you get many students?" he asked.

"Not many. They are usually too poor. Or, if they are lawyers, too rich. It's clerks, teachers, that sort of person, who use it."

The suit was, in fact, traced to a teacher, a Salah Foukhari, who taught in a Government primary school in one of the poorer parts of the city. Had taught, rather, for some eighteen months previously, at the end of the long summer term, he had walked out of the school and not come back.

"I am afraid that happens occasionally," said the headmaster apologetically. "It is not easy being a teacher, and there is not much money in it."

"Did you make any attempt to trace him?"

"I went to his house. That was at the start of the next term when he didn't appear. I thought he might simply have forgotten the date term started. That happens, too," said the headmaster, "occasionally."

The house, or rather the simple room in the house that Foukhari had occupied, was now occupied by another. Owen asked what had become of Foukhari's belongings.

"There weren't any," said the landlord. Possibly truthfully.

"Friends?"

The headmaster thought.

"He had made no friends while he was here. He kept himself very much to himself. But I think he had friends. Perhaps he made some at the Training College?"

At the Training College they remembered Foukhari well.

"After all, it's only three years since he left."

Could they remember his friends?

No, but they could put Owen in touch with someone who had been a student at the College at the same time as Foukhari, had indeed been a classmate.

"Though not exactly a friend," the former student said when they visited him at the primary school where he was now teaching. "Salah didn't have many friends. Not among us, at any rate."

Among whom, then?

"Well, he was always going off with somebody. To the Law School, I think. He was friendly with some law students. He used to go to meetings with them, that sort of thing."

Meetings?

"Public meetings."

"Political meetings?"

"Yes."

"Nationalist?"

The former student hesitated. "Probably," he said neutrally. "I'm afraid I really can't remember."

"He was politically active?"

"I really couldn't say. You'll have to ask someone who knew him better."

Like whom?

Here the former student actually was able to help. He remembered that in his final year at the College Salah Foukhari had become a member of a radical debating society. The society still existed and met regularly in a café near the Great Schools.

"One for Georgiades, I think," said Owen.

He went along to the café himself, however, and sipped coffee and read a newspaper—a radical Arab weekly—while the innocent-eyed Georgiades engaged in fierce conversation with a group of students at an adjoining table.

The upshot of that and several similar conversations was that Georgiades was invited to a meeting of the society, which took place in an upstairs room.

"The End of Imperial Rule, the Necessity of Nationalism, the Coming Revolution," he reported to Owen afterwards, "all that sort of stuff. Harmless."

"Just talk?"

"It's a debating society, after all."

Foukhari had continued to attend debates at the café for a year after he had left the Training College.

"Then he drifted away, apparently," said Georgiades. "He and a few friends. They said the debates weren't getting anywhere. They wanted action."

"Real action? Or more talk?"

"More talk at first. I got the name of someone who went with them. When it started moving towards action, this one pulled out and went back to the debating society. He wanted talk."

"Did you get any names?"

"One name, Abdul Rashid. A lecturer at the School of Law."

"A lecturer? Then he would still be there."

"He might be." Georgiades hesitated. "If he is, do we want to approach him directly? I mean, if he was involved in something then, he might be involved in something now. Do we want to put him on his guard?"

"No. No direct questioning. Not at this stage. Discreet inquiries, that's all. And they'd better not be by you. We don't want anyone at the Law School finding out your links with us. I'll put someone else on to it."

"What do you want me to do?"

"Go on hanging around the Law School?"

Georgiades went on hanging around the Law School and other agents made the discreet inquiries. Nikos, who saw his role as analytical, especially in hot weather, collated the findings.

"He is a radical and he's almost certainly been involved in extremist attacks. But we've never been able to pin anything on him. The closest we came was four or five years ago—that was before your time, of course."

Nikos liked to remind Owen that he was a junior partner.

"What happened then?"

"A law student threw a bomb at the Sultan Hassan. Someone caught his arm and the bomb missed but it exploded in the street and several people were hurt. The student gave himself up. Said he was trying to kill Hassan and had no wish to injure ordinary decent Egyptians. He repeated it in court. They sentenced him to death of course, though it was later reduced to life imprisonment."

"How does Rashid come into it?"

"There were associates, clearly, but the student refused to say who they were. Obviously we offered to do a deal over the death penalty but he refused to say anything. Said he was proud to die for Egypt. The Sultan reduced it anyway. He didn't want a martyr."

"And Rashid was one of the associates?"

"Almost certainly. There was a small group of them, extremists. The others fled but Rashid stayed on. Admitted the sentiments, denied the action. And while Elbawi kept quiet he was safe."

"Elbawi was the student?"

"That's right."

"Where is he now?"

"Cutting stone in the quarries at Tura, presumably."

"Go on about Rashid."

"Elbawi had been one of Rashid's students. There was a small group of them, as I said, all extremist. The others went abroad. Rashid said he wasn't responsible for the actions of a few hotheads. The rest of the staff supported him. Academic freedom and all that. It was a *cause célebre*."

"And he became a hero, I suppose?"

"That's right. But a modest hero. And he's stayed modest ever since. Puts out pamphlets, that kind of thing. Doesn't do anything too obvious, nothing that we could really catch him on."

Among the things that Rashid could not really be caught on was membership in various radical groups: such as the debating society that Foukhari had belonged to.

"In fact, he was the one who introduced Foukhari in the first place. Foukhari was a friend of one of his students. They'd met, talked in cafés, that kind of thing, and apparently Rashid had suggested they might both like to join the society. They went along to a few debates and then Rashid suggested it was all a bit tame and not really getting anywhere and wouldn't they like to get involved in something more real?"

"Which was?"

"A cell of some kind. My informant—who was the law student friend of Foukhari I spoke about—never found out. He isn't sure whether it actually existed. Rashid kept talking mysteriously about some 'project' they might get involved in but it never came to anything. Not in the informant's case, anyway. He drifted away and lost touch. But Foukhari stayed."

"And later died messing about with bombs."

"While Rashid remained on the fringe, as usual."

"I wonder what he's on the fringe of now? There's nothing to link him with the café bombing, is there?"

"Well," said Nikos, "there might be. Those two students who were killed."

"Yes, but they came from the School of Engineering."

"And had a law student friend. Remember?"

"You think it was Rashid?"

"No. I don't think he works like that. He does it indirectly through students, friends of students, friends of friends. My guess is he's always on the lookout for potential recruits. He

tries them out in something safe like the debating society.
Then if they show promise he switches them to something
more serious."

"Yes, but I don't think that would have been the case with
those students killed in the café. I mean, they were victims,
not—"

"Were they?" asked Nikos. "Are you sure about that?"

• • •

"Look at it this way," said Georgiades. "No one threw the
bomb into the café. So someone must have taken it in. Ali's
two men slept in the café overnight and swear blind it wasn't
taken in then. And we've gone through all the people who
used it the next morning and drawn a blank there too. The
only way a bomb could have got in there was if those two
students took it in themselves."

Georgiades had been invited to join the discussion and
had sided with Nikos.

"With the aim of blowing themselves up, along with
everybody else?" said Owen skeptically. "I don't believe it."

"That might not have been their intention. They might
merely have gone there to hand the bomb over to someone.
Say that law student friend of theirs."

"Yes, but to take a live bomb into a crowded café. For
Christ's sake!"

"It wasn't a crowded café. They picked a time when they
knew it wouldn't be."

"Yes, but a live bomb!"

"Engineers are casual about such things. Think of Plumley."

"They may be casual but they're not bloody daft."

"It fits," Nikos insisted. "You see, it's where they come
in. As engineers, I mean. They made the bombs. They knew
how to do it and had access to the materials and equipment.
That's what they were used for."

"They weren't politically active." said Georgiades, "not in
the ordinary sense. They didn't go to meetings, speak up,

carry banners, march in demonstrations, distribute leaflets. They weren't the type. What they could do was make bombs."

"Not well enough: they blew themselves up."

"It often happens," said Nikos. "Look at the records. Look at that business at Hamada for a start."

"What the hell were they doing with a bomb down there?"

"Trying it out. Trying to make a better one. And, incidentally, that was another engineering student."

"Let's get this straight," said Owen. "What you're suggesting is that the explosion in the café was an accident?"

"That's right. And that the people killed were the people who'd planted the bomb. Only the bomb wasn't really planted. It was taken in probably to be handed over to somebody."

"Somebody from the Law School."

"That's right."

"Well, it's an idea," said Owen reluctantly. "What do we do with it?"

"It doesn't seem to me to alter anything much," said Georgiades. "It's just another thing to tie in with the Law School and possibly Rashid."

"We should be looking at Rashid," said Nikos.

"Go back a minute," said Owen, "to what you were saying earlier. That Elbawi fellow—the one who was sent to prison for throwing a bomb at Sultan Hassan, and who might have been a friend of Rashid: oughtn't we to take a look at him as well?"

"We could take a look, certainly," said Nikos, "but don't expect to get anything out of him. They tried at the time."

"That was four years ago. He's been cutting stones since then. He might have changed his mind."

 •   •   •

Elbawi had indeed changed his mind; interestingly.

Conditions in the Khedive's prisons had improved greatly over the past decade—Cromer's reforming hand was felt even there—but remained harsh. Forced labor had always been part of the Egyptian penal system and, indeed, had its good side. It was better for prisoners to be out in the open air and removed from the unsanitary and unhealthy conditions which usually prevailed in prisons.

But for prisoners like Elbawi, who had made an attempt on the life of one of the royal family, the labor was kept deliberately hard. It did not come much harder than working in the stone quarries at Tura.

Elbawi might have been broken; but he was neither broken nor set permanently in defiance. He was bitter, understandably, but his bitterness was not now directed just or even, it seemed to Owen, primarily at the Khedive and the British; it extended to those who had induced an inexperienced young student to commit what he now regarded as a crazy act.

"They used me," he said to Owen at their third meeting, when he had got to know Owen a little and seemed inclined to trust him. "They got me to do the dirty work and stayed comfortably out of trouble themselves."

"Did they actually suggest a target?"

"I don't know now," Elbawi confessed. "We talked and talked. At the time I thought it was I who had had the great idea but now I am not so sure. I think they may have made me think that."

"They provided the means, presumably?"

"The bomb. Yes."

Elbawi, carried back, stayed sunk in thought for a while.

"Perhaps if they'd not actually given me the bomb I wouldn't have done it," he said suddenly. "I was wavering. I couldn't make up my mind. To do it or not. But then when I actually had the bomb in my hands—I mean, it was hard to go back on it."

"How old were you?"

"Seventeen." Elbawi shrugged. "I'm not blaming them entirely. I did it. I meant to do it. I saw it as a great blow for freedom. Something that would help Egypt. Well, perhaps it would have. But I think now that, well, one doesn't have to be so drastic. There are other ways, after all. Of course, there's a Nationalist Party now, which there wasn't then." He looked at Owen. "Do you think they'll make it?"

"Into the Government? Not this time."

"You're probably right. It's too much to hope for."

"What'll probably happen, though, is that the Khedive will have to appoint someone sympathetic to the Nationalists."

"You think so? You don't mind? You think the British will let it happen?"

"We'd let it happen all right. In fact, if we could only bloody *get* it to happen!" said Owen, forgetting himself at the chance to expatiate on a favorite theme.

He found Elbawi looking at him curiously.

"It makes for stability," he explained lamely.

"Ah yes." Elbawi fell silent.

"It seems strange, though, all the same," he said after a while, as much to himself as to Owen. "It makes you wonder . . ." He shrugged. "Things change. Or the way one sees them change."

His eyes met Owen's.

"Why have you brought me here?"

"To see if the way you see things has changed."

"It has. But I still don't know that I'm going to tell you anything."

"You still feel loyal to them?"

Elbawi hesitated.

"I wouldn't say that. I just don't think I'm going to tell you anything, that's all."

"The reason why I'm asking is that I think they're still doing it—using naïve young students in the way they used you. Only getting them killed."

"Killed?"

Owen told him about the café and about the boys down at Hamada.

Elbawi sat thinking for a long time. And, while he sat, Owen was thinking too.

"What is it you want?" said Elbawi at last.

"Not information. Because I think I already have that."

Elbawi looked puzzled.

"In which case—?"

"I want more. I want you to help me. And in return for that I will see that you are released."

"Tell me more," said Elbawi.

• • •

"Are you sure you wouldn't like some help?" asked Paul.

"Of course I'd like some help. God's, preferably."

"I wasn't thinking of going quite as far as that." Paul hesitated. "I was thinking of the Army, actually."

"Look, I've told you—"

"OK, OK." Paul held up a hand soothingly. "But you've got to be reasonable. This is going to be very big. It's going to stretch you everywhere. Not just at the Palace itself but right along the route. You haven't got enough men."

"I'll get some more in from outside Cairo."

"You've said yourself—often—that policemen from the provinces are next to bloody useless in Cairo."

"Why are you so keen on the Army all of a sudden?"

Paul sighed. "We're getting questions from home. Why have an Army if you're going to lock it up all the time in barracks? If that's what you do with it, do you really need an Army? One of that size? One at all? Savings might be made. The very mention of savings scares the wits out of the War Office. They're on to us all the time, wanting to know what we're doing. Get the Army out on the streets and show how important, nay, indispensable, it is!"

"I've got enough problems policing Cairo without policing the bloody Army as well."

"There's another thing. All those men cooped up in barracks. It's very unhealthy. Suppose an epidemic breaks out? It'll kill the lot. My God, Gareth, you're carrying hostility to the point of vindictiveness. Will nothing satisfy you but the wholesale butchery of the British Army? And what about John's tennis?"

"That is a consideration, I must admit. We could relax the order for recreational purposes only. That ought to make them happy."

"No, it won't. Unless brothels are included under the recreational heading."

"I want to keep them away from the Egyptians just at present."

"We won't be able to keep it up for much longer. I'm giving you advance warning."

"Can't you tell them that the Army is in fact deployed? It's just being held in reserve, that's all."

"Should be in the front line. That's the Army's proper place."

"Well, they are in the front line. Virtually."

"In barracks?"

"That's just a ruse on our part. In actual fact they're all armed to the teeth and ready to rush out at a second's notice."

"Actually," said Paul, "it might not be a bad idea if they were. Just for the next day or two. Coinciding with these demonstrations."

"All right," Owen conceded ungraciously. "If it will make you feel any better."

"Thank you. It will."

•   •   •

The demonstrations were to start, as demonstrations usually did, at El Azhar, the great Islamic university. From there the procession would march through the narrow streets of the Old City down to the Bab Zouweleh Gate, where it would turn right so that it could pass provocatively through the Place Bab el Khalk and in front of the Police Headquarters.

It would then march past the Palace of Ali Basha Cherif on the right and the Law School on the left, where its numbers would be augmented considerably, until it turned left into the square in front of the Khedive's Palace.

There it would be addressed, for many hours, by eminent leaders of the Nationalist movement, including Sa'ad, the Minister of Justice.

"Though how he squares that with being a Minister I fail to see," said Garvin sourly.

"Why don't we pick him up?" suggested McPhee.

"And make a hero of him? That's just what he wants."

"It doesn't seem right," said McPhee obstinately. McPhee, despite his many years in the country, remained irredeemably straightforward, a quality which had handicapped him greatly when for a few months before Owen arrived he had taken over the post of Mamur Zapt in an acting capacity.

"What does?" said Garvin shortly. While McPhee was thinking about that, Garvin turned to Owen.

"At least his presence there means that things are unlikely to get out of hand."

"Does it?"

"Yes. It's one thing impressing the Khedive with the mass of support you've got behind you. It's another thing letting them run amok in front of the Palace. That's no way to convince the Khedive you're just the chap to be his right-hand man."

"What I was doubting was whether Sa'ad had that degree of control over them."

Garvin looked down at his papers.

"Well, if he hasn't," he said, "you'd better bloody have."

Owen and McPhee left together. As they went out, Owen said to McPhee: "All this wouldn't be necessary if the Khedive could only make up his confounded mind."

McPhee grunted noncommittally.

"There's still a chance," he said.

"Is there?"

"So I've heard. A new name has come to the fore."

"Which one's that?"

"Ali Osman," said McPhee.

•   •   •

"It's true," said Nuri Pasha glumly. "He's made a comeback."

"How the hell did he do that? The last I heard he was down in Hamada."

"He returned to Cairo last week."

"When I saw him he didn't reckon he had a chance."

"Things have changed since then."

"They've changed damned quickly! What has changed them?"

"Money. Somehow Ali Osman has suddenly got hold of a lot of money. This always impresses the Khedive."

"Yes, but—Ali Osman!"

"Quite so." Nuri said it, however, without his usual vigor.

"You really think he's got a chance?"

"He's closeted with the Khedive all the time now."

"What about the Nationalists? Ali Osman would be absolutely anathema to them."

"That, of course, is the purpose of the demonstrations: to point that out to the Khedive."

"Don't worry," said Zeinab, coming into the room and hearing the last bit. "The demonstrations will scare the Khedive off Ali Osman. But they'll also scare him off the Nationalists. Then he'll come back to you."

"You think so?" said Nuri Pasha, brightening.

•   •   •

"I don't like asking you," said Owen, "but—"

"I'll do it," said Mahmoud at once.

Now Owen was even less sure. He felt he was taking advantage of Mahmoud; of their friendship, of Mahmoud's sense of duty, of, well, Mahmoud's sheer Arabness. There was an emotional impulsiveness about him, a tendency, in British eyes at least, to overrespond.

Owen wanted to damp him down. This of all things ought to be approached coolly.

Britishly.

Unfortunately Mahmoud wasn't at all British.

"Yes," he said, firing up with enthusiasm. "I'll do it."

"We could catch the lot, you see."

"Yes. Yes."

"It's a lot to ask."

"Nothing!" Mahmoud declared.

"Well, it *is*," Owen insisted. "The risk—"

Mahmoud shrugged it aside. "For you, perhaps. No, certainly. It would be impossible for you. For me, however—"

"There's a real risk," Owen insisted. In his anxiety to get Mahmoud to think about it properly before committing himself, he was now beginning to talk himself cold on the whole idea. "Suppose they know you, for a start?"

"Why should they know me?"

"You're a lawyer, aren't you? You went to the School yourself."

"A long time ago."

"Someone is sure to remember you."

"What if they do?"

"They'll think you're a plant."

"They may find out I'm in the Parquet. That doesn't make me a plant."

Owen, however, with an inconsistency that was hardly Anglo-Saxon—though possibly Welsh—had now convinced himself to exactly the opposite point of view.

"No, no. It's a daft idea. Forget about it. I'll find somebody else."

It had been irresponsible of him. Persuading someone else to risk his life. Someone who he knew was not likely to turn him down.

"No, no. Forget about it. It was a stupid idea in the first place."

But as he had grown cold, Mahmoud had grown hot.

"It's a good idea," he said enthusiastically. "We could get the lot. And it's right, it's proper, to come to me. To the Parquet." Mahmoud had a great pride in his job. "It's right that the Parquet should provide someone. That brings it into the normal processes of law and order."

Mahmoud viewed the operations of the Mamur Zapt with the disapproval of a strict constitutionalist. He liked the man but opposed the post on principle.

"No," he said definitely, "no, I will do it."

There was a moment's silence after this declaration. Owen was trying to think how he could now persuade Mahmoud out of agreeing. Mahmoud, however, had gone on to think of other things.

"There could even be advantages," he said. "Think about it. What if they do check and find I'm a member of the Parquet? What else will they find? That I'm a Nationalist, yes? As you frequently complain. That last year I was taken off a case at British insistence because I was politically biased—"

"That Senussi business?* For Christ's sake, everyone knows—"

"No, they don't. You know and Garvin knows and the people round the Consul-General know. The people in the Parquet know. At least, the ones high up do. But apart from that people don't know. All they know is that I was very publicly taken off the case and might be excused for feeling bitter. Bitter enough to want to hit back."

Owen, despite himself, saw the logic.

"You think it might work?" he said, half-persuaded.

Mahmoud, now that he was faced with the prospect of action, had characteristically calmed down.

"I think it's worth a try," he said. "Would you like me to see Elbawi?"

•   •   •

Owen's time was taken up preparing for the demonstration and Zeinab, who from her experience in her father's household found it hard to take political crises seriously and felt that anyway they should yield precedence to her private life, complained.

Owen offered opera but they had already been to all the opera houses in the past fortnight and Zeinab stuck out for something which would require him giving his attention exclusively to her.

That meant dinner. Dancing would have suited Zeinab better, since she enjoyed it and also enjoyed establishing a position of superiority over Owen who didn't and wasn't very good at it. But the only places where men and women could dance together Western-style were the hotels and the regimental balls.

Owen didn't feel that the latter were a good idea just at the

*The Mamur Zapt and the Donkey - Vous.

moment and Zeinab disdained the hotel dances on the grounds that they were too touristy and contained too many fresh English girls just out of London whom she regarded as potential rivals.

That meant dinner, although they might manage to combine that with a little dancing if Zeinab felt soft and Owen felt softer.

Here again, though, was a problem, for the hotels provided far and away the best food in Cairo. Apart, of course, from that served at the French Chargés, but there too one ran up against tourists and fresh young girls just out from England.

In the end they settled for a nice spot known only to Cairo initiates, the roof garden at the Semiramis, small and intimate and possessing the most wonderful view over the river.

Unfortunately, the Semiramis was known to initiates and was already quite full when they got there. Owen thought he could hear Paul's voice over beyond the potted palms. The waiter brought them, however, to a solitary palm-protected table and Zeinab was quite prepared to be content.

Owen was too. Zeinab was never a person to be overlooked, but she was more striking than conventionally pretty. She had a thin, bony face and a severe Arab nose. Seen in repose she looked rather ordinary.

But then, Zeinab was very seldom seen in repose. Her normal state was fired up. Then the big eyes would flash, the brow would furrow wrathfully, the lips would quiver and her beauty became formidable.

Owen was used to this and adored it. On the other hand it was sometimes a strain to live with. Sitting at the table in the Semiramis roof garden, with Zeinab's face in the shadows and only the big eyes looking over the candles, with the moon already silvery on the river but with a touch of red and gold still lingering on the water in the west, with the big, red-sashed suffragis moving unobtrusively among the tables, Owen's ever-impressionable Welsh heart plunged once again.

Zeinab, perfectly aware of this, was pleased. What she required was not so much Owen's subservience as at least his total attention, which, in her view, she seldom got.

The meal proceeded in agreeable, leisurely fashion. In the center of the floor was a tiny space where couples were dancing. It was so small that however bad one's dancing one could hardly come to grief; and Owen was sufficiently moved by the moonlight to take Zeinab onto the floor.

As they threaded their way through the tables they passed a large group of Europeans sitting solidly in a recess. It was the visiting delegation, escorted by the Consul-General himself, his wife and Paul. The whole delegation was there; including Roper.

He sat on the outskirts of the party, a little row of glasses already on the table in front of him, looking bored.

His eyes lit up when he saw Owen.

"You're the lucky one," he said, "what with her *and* that girl down in the desert."

"Girl in the desert?" said Zeinab.

The rest of the evening was not a success.

•   •   •

From where he sat, high up on his horse, Owen had a good view. So far—and it had been a long distance, the speeches were in their fourth hour now—the demonstrations had been orderly. The square in front of the Palace was a sea of people, but all the faces were turned raptly towards the speaker on the hastily erected makeshift stand in front of the Palace railings and there had been no trouble.

If trouble came it would come from the fringes of the crowd where the zealots shook their banners. But there too, massed in the side streets, were policemen on foot, holding their clubs uneasily, and policemen on horse. The crack mounted police of the Cairo force, itching to display their prowess once again.

And less than half a mile away, in the huge barracks beside the river, waited the Army.

Owen intended them to wait a long time.

So far all was well. The procession had marched good-humoredly through the streets gathering support as it went. By the time it had passed the Law School it was immense. If

Sa'ad Pasha was seeking to impress the Khedive by the scale of his popular support he was probably succeeding.

Not that the support, of course, was genuinely his. The demonstration would have gone ahead in much the same way if he had not been there at all. All that the Nationalist politicians had done was to insert themselves adroitly at the head of it.

Sa'ad, even more adroitly, had inserted himself at the head of *them*. His speech was the climax of the whole affair and he made the most of every bit of it.

He did not attack the Khedive directly but condemned his advisers, hinting that the Khedive himself was only too ready to place himself at the service of a Nationalist crusade but was held back and obstructed by men of the past. The Khedive would have liked that; Ali Osman wouldn't.

His fiercest attacks were naturally reserved for the British. The technique lay in spacing them out so that they could be used to revive slumbering attention and quickly abandoned if they showed signs of creating too much heat.

At the beginning of his speech the incendiary passages had been well apart. Now they were following closely on each other. Sa'ad must be coming to the end. He would certainly finish on a major vituperative note.

And that, of course, would be when the trouble would break out.

Owen glanced along his forces. They were all ready.

As Sa'ad rose into his peroration the crowd began to chant with him. Experienced orator that he was, he was able to incorporate the chants into his own speech, posing a question, waiting for the returning chant, repeating it and making it his own, inviting them once again.

This was Sa'ad, expressing the will of the people.

On the fringes of the crowd little groups began to break away and try to scale the railings.

Owen raised his hand and the police moved in.

The chanting was continuous now. Sa'ad had come to a stop but no one noticed. The crowd surged forward.

But already the police had moved in between them and the railings, a solid, uniformed wall. The clubs were poised.

Someone mounted the stand and tried to urge the demonstrators to go home. His voice was lost in the roar.

The front of the crowd was pressing against the police wall. Owen could see McPhee's tall figure directing proceedings.

The crowd pushed but the wall held. On the wings, though, fighting broke out. Clubs began to rise and fall.

The crowd surged and the wall wavered. Clubs were in use all along the line now.

Another surge, and this time the wall almost gave.

Owen looked up. The mounted force, sensing that this was its moment, began to ease its way forward.

One or two hardy spirits had already succeeded in scaling the railings. It did them no good, for they were immediately seized by the men waiting there and hustled away.

The Khedive would complain tomorrow of the invasion of his premises. But he would complain anyway.

Part of the police wall caved in. The crowd was no longer surging in unity but milling as people fought to keep their feet.

Owen's hand went up again.

A bugle sounded. The mounted force emerged from the side street and headed straight for the flank of the crowd. The crowd on that side broke.

The horses were halted by the sheer thickness of the crowd. The riders began to use their clubs.

Anther bugle sounded and a similar force crashed in on the other side.

The crowd wavered. People were beginning to run.

The pressure came off the wall of police at the railings and they began to move methodically forward, clubbing everyone in their way.

The two mounted detachments had maneuvered their way round so that they were pressing now not just from the flanks but from the front too.

The crowd was forced back.

Back again. The detachments regrouped and charged again, this time from the front.

The crowd was breaking up everywhere. The fighting was in little pockets now, except at one side of the square, where a mass of demonstrators was still struggling to reach the railings.

Owen rode over.

The fighting was at its fiercest here. All around the struggling mass of people men were lying, most of them students, judging from their clothes.

Other students came and helped them away.

The square was mostly clear now, but for this one large pocket. The foot police pulled back from general chasing and concentrated their efforts on this one large group.

The group suddenly split. Part of it, the larger part, was immediately engulfed by a sea of policemen.

The smaller part burst through the ring and headed straight for the railings. They threw themselves against the railings, shaking their fists and screaming threats and abuse.

If the Khedive was watching, he would have no doubt of the message.

The police rallied and plucked them one by one from the railings.

One or two of the most defiant climbed up the railings and for a long time hung there kicking their feet at the police below.

Owen urged his horse forward.

The police succeeded at last in dislodging them and hustled them away. Owen recognized two of them: Mahmoud and Georgiades.

CHAPTER TEN

"OK, OK, OK," said Paul soothingly. "He's a pain in the ass, I know. But it'll not be for much longer. The delegation has nearly finished its work. Another couple of weeks and they'll be back in London, Roper included."

"Every time we go anywhere he's bloody there and says something that sets her going."

"He won't next time. Not if it's in the next few days. He's out of Cairo."

"Where is he?"

"Oh Christ, I don't know. In the desert somewhere. He and Plumley. It's the best place for him."

"The only drawback is he comes back."

"When he comes back he'll only have a very few days. Then Cairo will be safe again."

Owen still felt aggrieved. However, he had been saying so to Paul for the past half-hour and thought it was probably time he stopped.

"Drink?"

He went off to the bar. By the time he came back Paul had thought of a diversion.

"The Old Man's very pleased about the demonstration. Went off well, didn't it?"

"Just about right," Owen admitted, thinking of Mahmoud and Georgiades.

"No one hurt. The damage contained. The Khedive not too much affronted. Excellent!"

"And all without the Army," said Owen pointedly.

"Oh yes, but the Army was the decisive factor, wasn't it? Or so I've been telling them. I mean, it wouldn't have gone off anything like so quietly if they hadn't known that the moment they stepped out of line, there was the Army, ready to pounce."

"Or so you've been telling them."

"Quite so. Anyway, it's much better to be told you're a hero than to have to demonstrate it."

Owen's mind reverted.

"You don't happen to know where exactly he's gone, do you?"

"Roper? I wouldn't have thought it was worth going to the lengths of tracking him down and killing him, if that's what you have in mind."

"No, no. But where he is, trouble usually is, and I'd like to be forewarned."

"Somewhere down in Mina."

"Not Hamada?"

"I think that's the name of the place."

"Funny."

"Why?"

Owen told him.

"I wouldn't have thought it meant anything. He's probably just got unfinished business there."

"Yes," said Owen, "and I'm beginning to wonder what that business is."

•   •   •

Mahmoud and Georgiades were held for twenty-four hours, like most of the others who had caused trouble at the demonstration, and then released. The Government did not bother to press any charges.

Georgiades was a bit of a hero among the students afterwards, though very modest.

Mahmoud had attracted attention too. The students had not really noticed him before because he wasn't attending the normal undergraduate course—he was, indeed, already a graduate—but just a few specialist courses to refresh his knowledge in the areas. However, Georgiades had had a chance to talk to him while they were in prison together and was able to tell the students something of his unfortunate background.

Apparently he'd fallen foul of the British. They'd not liked the way he'd tackled a case—had accused him of political bias, in fact, which was a bit rich, coming from them. They'd more or less insisted he be given a country posting.

That was the absolute kiss of death for any ambitious young official and Mahmoud had quite rightly objected. When they had overruled him, he'd walked out.

Now he was going to try and earn a living pleading in the Mixed Courts. But that was a bit specialist and he'd needed to brush up his knowledge of international law first. A law lecturer friend had suggested he apply for special dispensation to attend selected lectures and, somewhat to his surprise, it had been agreed.

The Dean of the Law School had, it seemed, been particularly sympathetic. Perhaps, a hundred years ago, he'd had his own troubles with the British. Anyway, he'd pushed the dispensation through virtually on his own say-so. The students hadn't thought he'd had it in him.

After their experience in prison together, Mahmoud and Georgiades kept in touch. They often went to a café together, along with other student friends, and talked law and politics.

Mahmoud, as a matter of fact, was pretty helpful on the law. He even managed to explain some of it to Georgiades. It was quite useful just listening in. You picked up something yourself.

On politics both of them were, not surprisingly, bitter.

Mahmoud, who obviously knew quite a lot about the law, pointed out that the British action at the demonstration had been extra-judicial and therefore inadmissible in constitutional terms. You couldn't quite follow all the points that he made—some of his arguments were definitely final-year stuff—but you could see how the way he'd been treated had really got to him.

Even Georgiades, who was a mild, uncritical sort of chap, seemed stirred up. The students, on reflection, put this down as a clear case of consciousness-raising.

One day someone introduced them to a sympathetic member of the staff of the Faculty. They got into the way of going to a café together after lectures.

He seemed really interested in what they had to say. Students were, he remarked, often closer to the issues of the day than staff were. There were others, too, who would be interested. He suggested one evening that they might like to go with him to a meeting of a debating club he was a member of.

They went, and certainly there were a lot of people who seemed to feel like them. The tone of the discussion was, well, pretty fierce. Mahmoud spoke really well. Georgiades was a bit lost.

Afterwards, they went on to another café with just a handful of the people who had been at the debate and continued the discussion.

Meanwhile, the constitutional crisis continued. Ali Osman was definitely back in favor. Sa'ad's brilliance at the demonstration hadn't quite convinced the Khedive. It had, in fact, alarmed him. Anyone who had such a masterful relationship to the mob was potentially dangerous. You wouldn't want to give him too much power.

Besides, Ali Osman had a way with money. He seemed able to conjure it up in vast quantities. The Khedive thought that a very desirable quality in a Minister; certainly one of his Ministers.

The massive demonstration had, however, one unlooked-for effect. It seemed for the moment to have bled off some of the Nationalist pressure. For several days afterwards the streets were relatively quiet.

There were no more cases of following and no more attacks.

That could, of course, be for other reasons. There was a huge police presence on the streets. Owen had retained some of the provincial police he had brought in for the demonstration and was using them very conspicuously in the city.

More to the point, perhaps, his agents were everywhere. Rewards, really large rewards, were advertised for information. Descriptions of men the police wanted to interview were widely circulated. The two men who had followed Jullians would hardly recognize themselves in the descriptions but perhaps it had made them wary, for as the days went by there was no further incident.

Owen knew it wouldn't last. But the longer it lasted, the more chance it gave him. For if the shadowy figures behind the attacks were really worried that their agents might be recognized, might they not be tempted to use someone new? Someone who had a grudge against the British, someone committed to the cause, someone who was obviously very, very bitter?

•   •   •

Fairclough, notable for perhaps the only time in his life, was becoming a bit of a bore. Owen could hear him at the far end of the bar regaling his cronies yet again.

"Hand of Allah," said Fairclough, "that's what I thought it was. You know, Fate picking me out. Just at random. But now I'm not so sure. I reckon they had me in their sights all the time. And do you know why?"

"It was the only way they could shut you up, Fairclough," suggested a passer-by, overhearing.

Fairclough ignored him.

"It was that salt business."

"Salt? I'm not quite with you, Fairclough," said one of the opposing team, bewildered. The bridge match had finished some time before and hosts were entertaining visitors afterwards.

Fairclough explained the duties on behalf of Customs and Excise which had taken him to Hamada.

"Salt's very important to the Arab," he said. "Take salt with them and you're their friend for life."

"Then why did they want to kill you, Fairclough?" asked the man who had passed by previously, now returning with a glass in each hand.

Fairclough let him go past.

"So all that salt at Hamada was a big temptation. There was a place up in the hills which was a collecting point for the whole area. Some deserted buildings—it had been a shrine once, I believe. In a good state of repair still. And, out of the way like that, Customs thought it wouldn't be perpetually reminding people of the stuff we'd taken away from them."

"Why didn't you just give it back?"

"Wouldn't do, old boy. Technically it was still contraband. It would be giving stuff which had been illegally acquired back to the people who had illegally acquired it."

"Yes, but just leaving it there—"

"A big temptation. As I said. The old Pasha down there was really worried about it. Had to keep the place flooded with armed men, so he told me. Otherwise the local brigands would have had the lot. Not to mention the gypsies. Bloody there in force, the day I went."

Fairclough put his glass down.

"Thanks. Yes, I will. Same again. Yes, the place was crawling with them. The old Pasha came down to me and said, 'Look, effendi. I've got to clear these beggars out.' Well, not quite in those words, but I knew what he meant. 'Would you mind coming tomorrow?'"

"It's always 'tomorrow' in Egypt," said one of the visitors, newly arrived from England and already an expert on the country. "Tomorrow, *bokra*," he said, eager to demonstrate his new command of the language.

"The bokra boys, that's right," Fairclough granted him. "Mind you, I must say he had a point. There were people everywhere and he couldn't let that go on. Had to clear them out somehow and I dare say he wasn't too keen to let me see how he did it. They're a bit rough and ready in the provinces. Still get the old *curbash* out, given half a chance. Thank you. Cheers."

His first swallow diminished the contents of the glass by about half. His face was already growing pinker.

"I said I'd give him an hour. And to give him his due, by the time I got back they were all gone. The gypsies, that was."

"Taking everything with them, I expect," said another of the visiting team, an older hand. "Including your trousers."

"Not in my case. Not this time at any rate," said Fairclough, with a loud laugh which ended in a hiccup.

"I still don't see the connection," said the literal-minded visitor who had questioned Fairclough first. "What's all this got to do with you being shot at in Cairo?"

"That's when they saw me, you see," Fairclough explained. "It's the only time I've been out of the office so it must have been then. And because salt's so fundamental with them, the image of me would have been fixed in their minds. The man who's come to take the salt from them. Fairclough. That's why they wanted to kill me."

"You were the Government to them."

"Well, yes," said Fairclough modestly, looking down into his beer, "I expect so."

"I still don't see what this has got to do with something that happened in Cairo," the literal-minded visitor maintained obstinately.

"Egypt's a big country," said the old hand wisely, "but a small place. Word gets around. Someone must have seen Fairclough down in Hamada and then seen him again in Cairo and passed the word on."

"*I* passed the word on," said the previous interrupter, going by yet again with empty glasses, "but the beggars bungled it."

• • •

Soraya denied it hotly.

"Certainly not," she said. "We hardly even noticed him. And if we had, he wouldn't have been worth mentioning."

She perched herself on Owen's knee. Owen automatically began to transfer his money, thought better, and divided it equally between her and him.

Soraya took it gracefully.

"Thank you," she said. "You can keep the rest as a gift from me."

They were in a night club near the big hotels. Owen had gone down to the Citadel without much hope and had been pleased and surprised to hear that Soraya was back in town. He had expected the gypsies to be still on one of their vast nomadic treks.

"They are," said his informant, "but Soraya has come back. She quarreled with her man down in Minya and came back alone."

She was as usual working the tourist area, which was where Owen had found her.

"Of course we take information," she said, snuggling her head against Owen's shoulder, "but no one's interested in information about a fat, funny little Englishman. And anyway we wouldn't know who to give it to. Not in Cairo. In Hamada we would, of course. In the provinces it's different."

"What sort of information do you take?"

"Messages for merchants. 'Meet Abdul Latfi at Bir Hamna with the camels,' that sort of thing. It's very important and so they pay us. That's the kind of information we're interested in."

"Why is it important?"

"Well, suppose you have a big merchant in Aleppo. He wants, say, a dozen slaves for the markets in Istanbul. The best place for slaves is the Sudan. Well, he sends an order down—"

"By you?"

"Not usually an order. There are standing arrangements. All we carry is messages about times."

"Times when the merchant's agents will pick up the slaves?"

"Yes. It has to be done secretly, of course, because the British get so excited about it. The traders usually pick a place outside a town—"

"In the hills outside Hamada, for instance?"

"Well, yes." Soraya pouted. "You're not really interested in me. You're only interested in your work."

Zeinab had been saying much the same thing. It wasn't true, really. There were lots of things he was interested in. Soraya, for a start.

"Not so," he protested, stroking the back of her neck.

Soraya sat up.

"We could go somewhere," she said, eyes gleaming.

Owen thought that perhaps it would be better if they did. They were beginning to attract attention. Private endearments in public were not a feature of the Muslim way of life, even in a seedy night club.

Afterwards, though, with Soraya nestling drowsily in his arms, his mind returned to his other interest.

"They told me at the Citadel that you had left your man," he said.

"Yes," said Soraya sleepily.

"Was that because you came to me at Hamada?"

"Yes," said Soraya. "No," she corrected herself, "it was because I didn't give him any money afterwards."

"I didn't give you any money."

"It was for love," said Soraya, sitting up suddenly, wide awake, eyes flashing. "We did it for love. That is what I told him. He hit me and I stabbed him. A Ghawazi girl does not take blows. Unless she wants to, of course. You can beat me if you like," she offered, slipping back into his arms.

"No, thanks. I am sorry, though, to come between you and your man."

"It's all right," said Soraya. "He'll come back. Or perhaps I'll go back to him."

Owen was relieved to hear that the stabbing had not been fatal.

"What were you down in Hamada for?" he asked. "Were you taking messages to Ali Osman?"

"There probably were messages," she said, "but that wasn't why we went to Hamada. We were going to take the guns down to Khamda."

"Guns?"

"Didn't I say? The slaves are not paid for in money, they're paid for in guns. Guns are always wanted in the Sudan."

"The Mahdi?"

"Isn't he dead?"

"Yes, but . . ." Owen wondered if he had stumbled on something. Ever since the Mahdi's forces had been broken by the British and the British had taken over running the country, it had been the constant fear of the Administration in Egypt that the Mahdi's supporters would regroup and rise again.

"Who are the guns for?" he asked.

"I don't know. Guns fetch a good price in the south."

He would have to look into this. If arms were getting through to some of the big tribes in the West, particularly the more independent ones around Darfur, that was something the Administration needed to know.

"The gypsies take the guns down to Khamda?"

"Yes."

"Why there?"

"That's where we meet the slavers."

"You trade the guns for the slaves?"

"We don't trade anything. We just carry the guns."

"Why do you have to call in at Hamada?"

"Because that's where the guns are. That's where we pick them up."

"You don't bring them down with you?"

"No. That would be too dangerous. The guns don't come that way anyway. They are landed at the coast, at Ras Gharib. Then they are brought across the desert to Hamada."

"What happens there?"

"They're just left there. There's a place in the hills."

"By a shrine?" asked Owen, light beginning to dawn.

"Yes. Up in the hills. Near where you found us."

Owen, his lips touching the nape of Soraya's neck, reflected. The arms trade and the slave trade were both illegal. Both, however, were widely practiced.

The slave trade was rooted deep in the culture of the area. For centuries Arab slave traders had come down from the north and for centuries the black villages of the south had supplied them with slaves. Khartoum, the capital of the Sudan, had been the great slave center of Africa until the British had arrived and put a stop to it.

Or thought they had. Slaving was now illegal in the British-governed Sudan but how could a handful of District and Police Commissioners, less than a hundred in all, police a million miles of desert? In the remoter areas slaving still thrived. And it was only too easy to bring slaves across the desert without going near a town, without coming within sight of human habitation, up and out of the Sudan and into the nearly equally remote southern and western parts of Egypt.

From there it was equally easy to ferry them across to the coast and ship them across the Red Sea to places where not only no questions would be asked but slaves were a normal feature of the economy.

Slaves were still in enormous demand throughout what remained of the Ottoman Empire. Black slaves from the Sudan fetched a particularly good price.

The arms trade was newer. It was, however, quite as profitable. To own a gun was the ambition of every desert Arab. It sounded, though, as if these guns were being purchased in bulk. It would be very interesting to know who by and what for.

Both trades were highly profitable. He wondered what the volume was.

"How often do the slavers come?" he asked.

"Four times a year. This time, however, there were too many guns to be shipped in one load. Another is coming."

"It is still to come?"

"Yes."

"When is it due to come?"

"Any day now."

"At Hamada?"

"At Hamada."

"Do you know . . .?"

But Soraya's mind had moved on to other things.

•   •   •

The students were on the streets again.

"Something we could have done without right now," said McPhee, preparing to go out with a detachment to quiet them down.

"It was bound to come," said Owen, taking it with what to McPhee was surprising equanimity. "Things have been too quiet."

Ever since he had returned from Hamada there seemed to have been an uncanny lull. The huge demonstration in front of the Abdin Palace had drawn off a lot of the anti-Government energy and the number of sporadic local outbreaks of violence had fallen sharply.

Even—and this was surprising—the reports of following had dwindled to a trickle. What instances there were seemed attributable more to game-playing youths than to genuine terrorists.

"You've got them scared," said the loyal McPhee.

Nikos had a different view.

"Those two were the only ones who could make bombs," he said. "When they blew themselves up there was no one else Rashid could go to."

"That doesn't explain the followings," Owen pointed out.

"Nine-tenths of them were imaginary anyway," said Nikos.

The lull, for whatever reason, was welcome. But now it seemed to have ended. And the British had only themselves to blame.

What had brought the students again on to the streets was the evident determination of the British to pursue Mahmoud for the prominent part he had played in the Abdin demonstration. They had, apparently, demanded his expulsion from the Law School.

"Victimization!" declared the student with the tribal scars whom Owen had remarked previously, pounding his fist on the café table.

"Victimization!" his friends round the table echoed.

"Victimization!" said Georgiades, a little late, but then he was always a bit slow to cotton on.

"We must resist!" declared the scarred student passionately. "Give way now and they will trample our liberties forever!"

"Resist!"

"Resist!"

The cries rose to the plastered ceiling of the café. The newspapered patrons of the café, however, among them Owen, read on with indifference.

"Let us march on the Citadel!"

"Let us march on the Palace!"

"Let us lie down in front of the English Barracks and tell them they can shoot us if they wish but Mahmoud must be reinstated!"

"Yes! Yes!"

There was a general thumping on tables.

"What's up?" asked the proprietor of the café.

"We are going to march on the Barracks."

"Good. You wouldn't like to start as soon as possible, would you?"

The students rose indignantly and trooped out. Outside, they hesitated for a moment.

"Oughtn't we to go to the Dean's first?" asked Georgiades. "I mean, we don't know yet that Mahmoud has actually been expelled."

The students thought that a good idea and set off to march to the Dean's office, gathering support as they went. By the time they reached it, their numbers had swollen to such an extent that they filled the small square in front of the School offices.

They stood there for some time, shaking fists and chanting slogans, until at last someone came down to ask what they wanted.

They demanded Mahmoud's reinstatement.

"He hasn't been expelled yet," said the emissary. "The Dean is still making up his mind."

"He oughtn't even to be considering it," declared the student with the scars, who had constituted himself the students'leader.

"He's got to consider it," said the emissary. "He's received a direct request from the Minister of Education."

This didn't please the students at all and there was pandemonium in the square for the rest of the morning, which ended only when the students learned that the Dean, and everybody else, had gone home for lunch, using a back door.

There were no windows for them to break and they had to content themselves with hurling stones at the heavy wooden shutters.

The Dean's decision was announced the following day. He had previously gained considerable respect, even from the students, by his willingness to bend procedures and admit Mahmoud as a special case to certain lectures. Now he lost it all by bowing to British pressure.

He had reluctantly reached the conclusion, he said, that it was in the best interests of the Law School for the special arrangements made for Mahmoud to be terminated. Mahmoud would therefore be debarred from attending further lectures.

The students rose in fury and marched in a body first to the Dean's office, where they threw stones for several hours, and then on in a mass procession to the Abdin Palace, where they demonstrated until it was dark.

The situation seemed so ugly that the Army put itself on full alert. Doubtless it was knowledge of this, and the fact, of course, that it was dark, that finally induced the students to go home.

The Khedive delivered a formal protest to the Consul-General both about the injustice to his subjects and about the

Civil Administration's tolerance of violence and disorder on his very doorstep.

The protests continued for some time, although not on quite the same scale. They were substantial enough, however, to force the Administration into a misguided concession. In a blatant attempt to appease the students the authorities released from prison a former student, one Elbawi, who had been convicted of an attempt on the life of one of the royal family.

This did not please either the Khedive, who made another formal protest to the Consul-General, or the students, who saw it as an attempt to fob them off with something which ought to have been conceded long ago anyway.

Elbawi himself had the right attitude. He declared himself innocent of anything other than fighting for justice. That struggle must go on. The injustice presently being done to Mahmoud was merely another in the long series of injustices which characterized British rule in Egypt, and he called on the students to resist it as he himself had tried to resist a previous injustice.

The students thought it a pretty good speech, a brave one, too, in view of the fact that the British must be keeping their eye on him and would certainly have no hesitation in clapping him back in prison if he showed any sign of stepping out of line.

There was very keen interest, to say the least, when Elbawi submitted an application to be readmitted to the Law School and allowed to complete the course of studies interrupted by his imprisonment. Student feeling ran high. The Dean, no doubt aware of that, wisely accepted Elbawi as a student, thus repairing some of the damage caused by his previous action.

Elbawi was reinstalled as a student and took up his place immediately. On his first morning the students carried him triumphantly around the square outside the Dean's office. Elbawi made a tremendous speech, rather like his first one.

After that, though, he settled down quietly as a student. He did not even join in the processions and demonstrations the students were now organizing every day. The students were surprised at first but then on reflection understood that in the circumstances the poor chap could hardly be expected to do anything else. He had probably been told that any sign of public dissent would see him back in prison.

What he was prepared to do, however, was address private meetings. Over the next few days he addressed dozens of these, in cafés, in lecture rooms, in students' lodgings.

For the most part he spoke about his time in prison. He spoke with surprising restraint, quietly, objectively, as if he were describing what had happened to someone else. But on occasion, and especially when he was describing the time he had spent cutting stone in the quarries at Tura, he could not keep the bitterness from breaking through.

You felt that though for the moment there was nothing much he could do, at some point in the future, given half a chance, he would want to strike back.

The one who was really bitter, though, and understand-ably, was Mahmoud. As he said, the British kicked you out of Government service and then when you tried to find a job not in Government service they kicked you out of that too, or at least stopped you from earning a living at it. They had you either way.

And that was how it would always be, he went on, while the British were in control. It was Mahmoud today, he told the students; it would be them tomorrow. The only way out was to resist now, to drive the British back into the sea, as he put it.

The students cheered heavily at that. Mahmoud was so right. That was the only way out.

Georgiades, who had been pretty close to Mahmoud at one time, when they had been in prison together, but who now seemed to have drifted a bit apart, wanted to know how ex-actly they were going to manage that. He thought it would be pretty difficult to drive the British into the sea.

Some of the students were rather impatient with him, the one with scars particularly. Others, however, who knew he meant well, pointed out that the wave of student protest, which was still pretty small at the moment, would mount higher and higher until it became a great tide which would sweep the British away.

That seemed to satisfy Georgiades. You only had to point these things out to him.

The wave of student protest, though not yet of gigantic proportions, was washing around with sufficient vigor to alarm the Army. They made it clear to the Consul-General that they felt things were getting out of hand and that it was only a matter of time before they would have to be called in.

The Mamur Zapt, however, seemed to be taking it all very calmly.

• • •

He was, though, having trouble on another front.

"Hamada?" said Zeinab incredulously. "Again?"

"Something has come up."

"It's that girl!"

"Nonsense. She's in Cairo."

"So you know!" pounced Zeinab. "You've been seeing her."

Owen lost this one, too.

• • •

This time he went by the desert, leaving the boat at Faza, where a tracker was waiting for him with camels. They rode through the night and reached the hills above Hamada just before dawn.

The tracker hid the camels among the rocks and then they climbed on foot up the stony slopes, the sun coming up behind them as they walked, lighting the ground with a strange unearthly light.

He was cold and stiff after his ride. In the desert at night the temperature plunged down towards freezing point. He had wrapped himself in Bedawin robes but now was glad to stretch and exercise himself. The sun gradually became warmer on his back.

They curved around the hillside into the darkness again and emerged on a little ledge which looked down into a valley. The valley ran back up into the hills and halfway up; as the sun reached around the hill and lit up the lower slopes, he saw a low, white-walled building.

One of the trackers touched him on the shoulder and pointed. A little beyond the shrine, low in a hollow, so low that you could hardly see it, was another building. It was built of the same mud bricks as the shrine but, without the white stucco of the shrine, blended inconspicuously into the rock.

"The Place of Salt," said the tracker.

"That is where the arms were taken?"

The tracker nodded.

The consignment had arrived two days before. There had been twenty baggage camels in the caravan, all heavily loaded. They had come in the afternoon when the world was at siesta and it had taken until nightfall to unload them.

The men who had come with them spent the night on the rocks in front of the Place of Salt, huddled for warmth around a solitary campfire made from dried camel dung. There was, of course, no wood, either in the hills or in the desert below. In the morning the men had left, taking the baggage camels with them.

The men in the Place of Salt had worked on for most of the morning, stacking the arms more securely, probably covering them with bags of salt. They had left too.

"We watched all day. There are no guards."

Owen looked down at the two buildings just beginning to emerge from the shadows. The sun, creeping up the slopes, began to touch the shrine and turn the whiteness red.

"Then let us go down," he said.

The doors were barred with heavy wooden bolts but not padlocked. The trackers drove the bolts out with the butts of their rifles.

Inside, all was dark and it took a moment or two for Owen's eyes to get used to it. All around the floor, stacked against the walls, bales were lying covered with heavy sacks. He pushed one of the sacks aside with his foot. The bale underneath was solid and heavy. A tracker cut it open with his dagger. A little trickle of powder ran out, white and crystalline.

The tracker tasted it on his finger.

"Salt," he said.

They moved the bale away. Underneath was another bale, less bulky, less solid, more angular. The tracker cut it open. He put in his hand and pulled out a rifle.

The trackers, interested in such things, took it over to the door where the sunlight fell through and examined it appreciatively.

It was new and oily. Owen looked over their shoulders. German made.

He called the trackers back and began to work through the rest of the bales. He wanted to see if there was anything beside rifles.

They had gone about two-thirds of the way along one of the walls when the trackers stopped and looked at each other. Two of them went over to the door and looked out.

"Someone is coming."

They slipped back into cover, one each side of the door. Gently one of them eased the door to.

The other trackers covered the door with their guns.

Whoever it was was approaching on foot. There seemed to be only one.

He came up to the building and gave a grunt of surprise as he saw the open door. Unsuspecting, though, he pushed it open and stepped inside.

One of the trackers caught him deftly around the neck. The other pinioned his arm by his side.

"What the hell is this?" said Roper.

Chapter Eleven

Never been here before in my life," said Roper. "Don't know a thing about it."

"Just wandered in off the desert?"

"That's right."

"Out early, weren't you?"

"It's cooler this time of day."

"Surveying?"

"What else?"

"That's what I'm asking you. What else?"

"Look, what's all the excitement about? I'm out surveying as usual. I see this building, I come over to take a look. What's wrong about that?"

"You take a look in all the buildings you see, do you?"

"Out here there aren't many buildings—there aren't *any* buildings. So when I see one, I take a look."

"Plumley with you?"

"Not this morning."

"Where is he?"

"About four miles back. Making himself a cup of tea."

One of the trackers slipped out.

"Bring him here," said Owen.

"Don't worry," Roper said to the tracker. "You'll find him all right. I haven't killed him." He turned back to Owen. "Look, what the hell is this?"

"I thought you'd finished in these parts?"

"We have, really. Just checking on something."

"What?"

"The presence of crystalline deposits."

"Salt?"

Roper's eyes flickered for a moment. "I dare say there's salt in these hills," he said, "but that isn't what I was looking for."

"You could show me the deposits?"

"Glad to. Plumley could, too."

"Does he know you're here?"

Again the slight flicker. "We don't always tell each other where we're going."

"Or what you're doing?"

"We divide the work between us. It's a big area."

"Anyone else come with you?"

"Who were you thinking of?"

"Guide, escort?"

"We've got a couple of Bedawin with us. They're out hunting."

"For hare?" Owen said skeptically. He suddenly remembered something.

Roper shrugged.

"Not much else, is there? Might see a gazelle, I suppose, but it's unlikely. Hare would do. A couple for the pot would be nice."

"Add to the breakfast?"

"That's right. Look, it's quite normal for Bedawin to go hunting."

"You didn't feel like going with them?"

"Surveying's my business," said Roper, "my only business."

"You don't know what's in this building?"

Roper pushed a sack aside with his foot.

"Artillery," he said, "or so it looks."

"You don't know anything about it?"

"Why should I?"

"I thought you might have brought it here."

Roper glanced up and down the room.

"Looks a lot for me to carry," he said drily. "Of course, I could have asked Plumley to help."

"Oh, some friends could have done the actual carrying," said Owen. "I wasn't thinking of that."

"Oh? What *were* you thinking of?"

Owen was silent. It had all happened a bit too quickly. He hadn't had time to prepare his questions, to think them through, as he usually liked to do.

Roper was looking at him with amusement.

"I don't think you've got anything on me," he said.

The trouble was, he was right. OK, it was suspicious him coming in like that. But his answers were all plausible, or at least sufficiently so as not to leave Owen much immediate purchase.

Except that the arms were here and Roper was here, and Owen was reluctant to believe that was just coincidence.

"Can I go, sir?" said Roper, with mock politeness.

"No," said Owen, and walked out of the Place of Salt into the morning brightness. He stood for a moment, looking down the slopes, past the shrine, almost dazzling in the early sun, and out across the desert. Far away there were some little dots which were moving towards him.

"No," he said, turning back to Roper, who was still standing pinioned at the door. "No, there's a thing or two I want to check."

Deliberately he walked away. He needed time to think. In a few moments Plumley would come and he would have either to release Roper or charge him. That would depend, had to depend, on what Plumley said. And on what questions Owen asked him.

One of the trackers came out of the Place of Salt and walked off through the rocks to where Roper's camel was standing hobbled. He stood beside it for a moment silently. Then he walked away and began to wander up and down apparently aimlessly.

Owen sat down on a rock. It struck surprisingly chill and he got up again and began to walk up and down for warmth. The sun now had flooded the valley with light but it was a light without heat. On the rocks there were a few genuine crystals of frost.

The dots on the desert had become people. Plumley he could tell at once. There were two Bedawin with him, as well as Owen's tracker.

He watched them come up the slopes towards him.

"Hello?" said Plumley, making his camel kneel so that he could dismount. "What's the problem?"

"No problem particularly," said Owen. "Just a question or two."

He led Plumley off to one side where they could not be heard and indeed not seen from the Place of Salt. He did not want Roper calling out.

"I'm surprised to see you down in these parts," he said. "I thought you'd finished here?"

"We have, more or less. There are just one or two things we wanted to look at again."

"You wanted to look at? Or Roper wanted to look at?"

"Roper, I suppose. Though it's of interest to both of us."

"He was the one who suggested coming back?"

"I suppose so, yes."

"What was it he particularly wanted to look at?"

"Rock formations. Layers of quartz."

"Crystalline deposits?"

"Yes. Probably. I say . . ." Plumley hesitated. "Nothing's happened to him, has it?"

"No, no."

"I mean, I would blame myself—"

"No, no. He's all right."

"Perhaps I shouldn't have let him go by himself."

"I'm surprised he didn't take one of the Bedawin."

"He didn't want to. I suggested it. But he said it would be all right. And of course he knows his way around. Almost as well as I do."

"He's not been here before? Apart from with you?"

"No, no. He knows his way around generally, I mean."

"You've been out in the desert, I take it?"

"Yes."

"Seen anyone?"

"A few nomads."

"A caravan?"

"No." Plumley hesitated. "Met someone from one, though. It was out at Falya. There's a little bit of an oasis. Well, hardly an oasis. Just a tree, really, but it's one of those hollowed-out baobabs the nomads keep filled with water. Anyway, we met a rider there. He said he was with a caravan."

"Did he talk to Roper?"

"Roper doesn't speak Arabic."

"You spoke for him?"

"Yes, yes. I suppose you could say that."

"Can you tell me what was said?"

Plumley looked at him with a worried expression on his face.

"Is anything—" He stopped, shrugged his shoulders, then started again. "I don't remember, really. Nothing much. One thing, though, one thing that stuck in my mind because it surprised me. The man from the caravan spoke first."

"Sorry," said Owen. "I don't quite—?"

"He was the one who started the conversation. He said, Tell the foreigner that—'"

"That?"

"Well, that's the bit that surprised me. That phrase. What I had to tell Roper was pretty ordinary. It was just that phrase that struck me. As if he was passing a message. As if he was expected to pass a message."

"What was the message?"

"Nothing much. 'The goods have been delivered.' Something like that."

"That'll do," said Owen.

He told Plumley to wait where he was and then went back to the Place of Salt.

The solitary tracker was still wandering up and down. He came across to Owen.

"The foreigner lies," he said. "He said he had not been to the Place of Salt before."

"But you know he has been?"

"That is what the tracks say."

"Are you sure it was him and not just the camel?"

The tracker led him over to some rocks. There was a shallow pool of sand beside them in which some indistinct marks were faintly visible.

"This is where he left his camel. It is the same prints, you see."

"He didn't make them this time?"

"No." The tracker was positive.

"How do you know that he was on it?"

"Well," said the tracker, "that's easy. You can see the way he rides. It's not the way a Bedawin would ride, not with the weight like that. And then you see, this is where he made the camel kneel. A proper rider wouldn't do it like that. And, here, this is not an Arab foot. You can follow it, you see. It goes right to the Place of Salt."

"Thank you, Abou," said Owen. "Once again you show that you are a tracker among trackers."

The man bowed his head with pleasure.

Owen went back to Plumley.

"Have there been any other early morning expeditions?" he asked. "I was wondering whether Roper could have come here before?"

Plumley thought it over.

"Yes," he said finally. "Two days ago. He went off by himself and came back about noon. But—"

"Thank you," said Owen, and turned to go.

Plumley walked a little way with him.

"What's it about?" he asked quietly.

"Guns," said Owen. "There's a big shipment of guns over there."

Plumley nodded, then dropped back, thinking. Owen went on into the Place of Salt.

Roper looked up at him.

"Well?" he said.

"I think you're going to have to tell me another story," said Owen.

"Oh?" said Roper. "Why is that?"

"Because the other one wasn't true."

"It sounded all right to me."

"You knew the guns were there," said Owen, "because the man had told you."

"What man was this?"

"The man at the Falya oasis. Where the baobab tree was."

"You've been talking to someone," said Roper.

"Yes."

"He misheard," said Roper. "It's easy when you don't speak the language properly."

"Plumley speaks the language pretty well."

"Oh, sure. It's a legal point I'm making."

"There's another thing. You said you hadn't been here before."

"That's right."

"I think you have."

"Don't remember it. I'm sure I'd remember going to a place like this."

"Two days ago."

"Two days ago?" Roper frowned. "I certainly went out by myself. But that was surveying. And a long way from here."

"Then what was your track doing here?"

"Oh," said Roper. "I see." He looked at the tracker. "Clever boy!" He shook his head, almost regretfully. "I don't think it will do, though," he said. "Not in a court of law. A bit flimsy."

"Out here it isn't. A tracker's word is enough to hang a man on."

"But would it be heard out here?"

One of the most spectacular injustices of the Egyptian legal system was that part of it known as the Capitulations, a system of privileges conceded to foreigners. These privileges included immunity from direct taxation and immunity from the Egyptian law.

No European or American could be punished unless it could be proved that he had committed an offense, not against Egyptian law, but against the law of his country. Proof of transgression against the law of his own country—whatever that was, and nationality was pretty elastic in Cairo—was required before a charge could be laid at all. And even if a charge was accepted the alleged offender would have to be tried by his own Consular Court.

"I think we'd find a way of making sure it was," said Owen, with more confidence than he actually felt.

"You see," said Roper, "I'm a bit of a special case. It's not just the delegation. It's the interests behind the delegation. They're big, you see. They're in the City, the London City, and they're big."

"Are they behind the arms shipment too?" asked Owen.

"Oh," said Roper, "what a suggestion! I'm shocked. You've really shocked me, Owen. Have you no faith in your own countrymen? A bloody agent of the Crown, too. For the time being, I mean."

"I think I'll be holding you after all," said Owen. "Definitely."

· · ·

"You can't," said Paul flatly.

"Why not?"

"To start with, he's applied for bail, and there's no way the judge can refuse it."

"To hell with the judge. I'm the Mamur Zapt, aren't I?"

"Not for long, if you go on at this rate."

"I can hold anybody who's a threat to order."

"You can hold anybody normal. Roper isn't normal. He's a member of a visiting delegation. Also, he has powerful friends."

"I should be holding them as well."

"Quite so. But if they're so powerful that back in London the Prime Minister doesn't want to know, and here in Egypt the Consul-General thinks he'd better keep quiet, and the Khedive probably sees nothing wrong anyway, who does this chap Owen think he is?"

"I'm not going to let him get away with it."

"Well you haven't let him get away with it," said Paul reasonably. "You've seized the arms, you've stopped the deal from going ahead—"

"But that so-and-so's getting off scot-free."

Paul shrugged. "Most so-and-sos in that line of business *do*."

"Are you saying I've just got to let him go? Take him down to the Gezira and buy him a drink or something?"

"Let him buy you one. He'd like to. He's got a great respect for you, Gareth. He says you're the only straight policeman he's ever met. And to come across him in Cairo! He's had a great shock, Gareth. I think he probably needs a drink."

"Paul, you're not taking this seriously."

"I am. I am. Seriously enough to counsel you to distinguish your interests from those of mankind and pursue the former, just this once."

"It's a sellout!"

"Look, Gareth, this is really a sideshow. Aren't you spending too much time on it? I thought your main business at the moment was supposed to be preventing a major conflagration from developing in Cairo?"

"These arms will start a conflagration in the Sudan."

"Then we'll be able to send the Army to put it out. That seems an excellent idea. It's a long way away and they'll be gone for months. The more I think about it the more I like it."

"If it's a choice between stopping a war in the Sudan and stopping a few terrorist attacks in Cairo, which is the more important?"

"It depends from whose point of view you're seeing it. If you could stop people from taking pot shots at us as we're going to work, I, personally, would regard that as a great achievement, Gareth."

He regarded Owen compassionately.

"Tell you what: you can stop the war if you like. I mean, after you've put out the conflagration in Cairo. Only leave Roper alone. He's too hot for you. There are other people in this, surely? Why don't you go for them?"

•   •   •

"You should have let me kill him in the first place," said Soraya, stretching out on the cushions. "I could still do it, you know," she offered.

"Thank you. That won't be necessary."

"I would do it for love. To show how much I love you."

"You can show me in other ways."

"That too," Soraya granted.

Afterwards, she said drowsily: "It might be better if you put me in your harem. Ghawazi girls do not usually join harems, but I would make an exception in your case."

"Thank you. I foresee difficulties, however."

"What difficulties?"

Owen hesitated. "I am not sure there would be room," he said.

Soraya looked puzzled. "I do not understand," she said. "Is your house not big enough?"

"No, no. It's just that, well, my harem is already occupied."

"Surely you have room for one more? How many wives have you got?" asked Soraya, interested.

"Well, it's not so much a question . . . Actually, there's only one. But I don't think she'd like it."

"We would fight," said Soraya. "That is proper among wives."

"I don't think it would be very peaceful."

"Well, no," said Soraya. "But there would be lots of passion."

"I think I've got plenty of that already."

"Your wife is very passionate? Then we would get on," said Soraya.

"I don't think so."

"She would be jealous, of course. But that would make her all the more passionate. Me too. It is good for there to be rivals in a harem."

"I am not sure that I could cope. Thank you very much. It would be very nice, I am sure, but—"

"You do not love me!" Soraya sat up, eyes fiery.

"Of course I love you!"

He attempted to pull her down. She shook him off indignantly.

"No! You love her, you do not love me. I am nothing to you, she is all. I will kill her!"

"For Christ's sake!"

He grabbed hold of her by the shoulders and forced her back upon the cushions.

"Just cool down a moment—"

For a moment Soraya stared furiously up at him. Then her eyes closed.

"That is better," she said.

•   •   •

"Does Ali Osman know about the guns?" Owen asked.

"Of course. He is the person who arranges it all."

"What do you mean, 'arranges it all'?"

"He brings the two sides together. The traders let him know when they are coming up. He then lets the merchants in the north know. They send the guns down and Ali Osman arranges for the two sides to meet. Sometimes he has to store the guns."

"In the Place of Salt?"

"Yes."

"What about the slaves?"

"They are held in an oasis to the south. It is bad for them to be held there too long as it is hard to hide people. It is better to store the guns."

"And Ali Osman takes a cut, presumably?"

"It is a good business," said Soraya enviously. "Both sides pay well."

Strangely, Zeinab's reaction was not dissimilar from Soraya's.

"Leave it to me," she said immediately when Owen told her about his difficulties.

"Leave what to you?"

"Roper. I will have him killed."

"Just a minute—"

"My father will supply me with assassins. There will be no difficulty."

"I am sure there won't. However—"

"You needn't worry. No one will know. I can see you have to keep out of it. You are always telling me about these Liberal MPs in England. Perhaps," said Zeinab reflectively, "I should have them killed too."

"There are too many. Someone would be sure to notice."

"Of course, it would be difficult at such a distance. Perhaps you could invite them all over here to a feast. Then we could poison them all."

"No, no, no, no."

"Or perhaps you could invite them to Paris!" Zeinab's eyes sparkled. Complete Francophile, as so many of the upper-class Egyptians were, Paris was the center of her cultural universe. "I could arrange for the Zouaves to massacre them in the Champs-Elysées."

She laughed merrily on seeing Owen's face.

"Perhaps, on the whole, it would be better to stick to our first plan. I will go round and speak to my father at once."

"No you don't. You stay here. And leave Roper alone. I'll look after him."

"Will you fight him?"

"In a manner of speaking," said Owen.

•   •   •

"Congratulations, Pasha!" said Owen.

Ali Osman smiled graciously.

"Thank you," he said. "But what precisely," he asked cautiously, "are you congratulating me on?"

"Your new-found success with the Khedive."

The Pasha waved a plump forefinger at him. "You are anticipating, my friend. Just a little. But you are anticipating."

"It has not been announced yet?"

"No. Unless," said Ali Osman with sudden eagerness, "you have heard something that I have not?"

"No. But it is so much in the air—"

Ali Osman sat back on his cushions, a little disappointed.

"I am assured it is a matter of hours," he said.

"To have come back to this extent after so many setbacks!"

"Well," said Ali Osman modestly, "a statesman is resilient if nothing else."

"When I remember how it was when I first came to see you—"

"After I had been so brutally attacked," said Ali Osman, shuddering at the memory.

"And your rivals seemed so advantageously placed! Well, I congratulate you on such a turnabout."

"Experience," said Ali Osman, "experience is what tells in the end."

"Indeed. It is experience which tells you at just what point it is timely to deploy the money."

"Well, I wouldn't put it quite like that," Ali Osman protested. "You are taking too cynical a view."

"I am sure it was the winning factor. Especially with the Khedive."

"Let us say that," said Ali Osman, smiling broadly, "after we have won."

"What puzzles me, though, Pasha, is how it was possible to find such a considerable sum at that point in the campaign? Surely even your great resources had been strained by so protracted a battle?"

"An immense drain. The money some people spend!"

"Then how?"

"Friends. Friends rallied around. One is not without support. Particularly when people saw how things were going. When they saw some of the possibilities they shuddered, positively shuddered. And then they said: 'Let us go for the man we know.'" Ali Osman's eyes twinkled. "The devil we know."

Owen chuckled sympathetically.

"It is a tribute to your personality, Pasha, that so many suddenly realized that you were the man they could trust."

"Well . . ." Ali Osman waved a deprecating hand.

"No doubt the money from the traders helped."

"Traders?"

"The slave-traders. And, of course, the arms merchants. What puzzles me, though, as I said before, was the timing. Surely it was not coincidence? And was not the arms shipment an unusually large one? Two separate deliveries? I feel the coincidence must have been prompted. And therefore, Pasha, I offer my congratulations."

Ali Osman was silent. The bonhomie leaked out as from a punctured balloon, leaving a very sharp, concentrated, bird-like man behind: not a friendly sparrowlike bird but a big, formidable, predatory hawklike bird.

"Your meaning is not altogether clear," said Ali Osman.

"The money," Owen explained. "That is where you got it from. The merchants paid you and the slavers paid you. A lot."

"Even if they had," said Ali Osman, "the commission on such exchange hardly amounts to a fortune."

"No. And that was another thing that puzzled me. But then I thought: these men have an interest in continuing trade. In perhaps expanding it. What better guarantee of the right conditions than a Prime Minister in office? Might not a loan have been offered? A large one, long-term, repayable—well, let us not say *repayable*, let us say *discountable* in terms of your future support?"

"My friends rallied around, as I was saying, and offered such a loan. It is not unusual."

"These were your friends?"

"Hardly. Slave-trading, as I am sure you know, is illegal in Egypt. The arms trade is, well, confined to the British."

"I think I must ask you for the names of your friends."

"I would be glad to oblige. I must first, however, check that my friends are willing for their names to be produced.

You see, there are some eminent British names among them. Well-known firms, famous in the City."

"Represented on the delegation, perhaps?"

"Why," said Ali Osman, beaming, "you have understood!"

• • •

The wave of student anger over the dismissal of Mahmoud rose to a great height, quivered ominously—there were several noisy protests in front of the Abdin Palace, which provoked more angry letters from the Khedive—and then, surprisingly, subsided.

It was nothing to do with Owen. It seemed to happen all of its own accord. One moment the students were rampant in the streets. The next they were quietly going about their lectures, books tucked dutifully under their arms. It was as if they had suddenly lost interest.

"Can't understand it," said Georgiades. "I woke up and went in one morning and it was as if they had all switched off."

"Students are like that," said Owen. "One morning something is of absolutely overwhelming importance to them. The next they have forgotten about it entirely."

"I felt it a bit myself," Georgiades admitted. "When I got in and everybody was talking about something else, all that protest stuff suddenly seemed a long time ago. I quite enjoyed talking about something else. Still, I hadn't forgotten about it entirely, the way they had."

"Ah well, you see, they're young."

"And I'm old. That's what my wife keeps telling me. Still, I'll tell you one thing. It's a good life being a student. You go in to a few classes, you sit around talking for hours, it takes a long time before it matters that you don't work. I think I could settle for being a student."

"Of course you don't get paid if you're a student."

"For once," said Georgiades, "I seem to have the best of both worlds."

The small radical faction had broken up. For some days there had been increasing tension between the moderates, of whom Georgiades was perhaps representative, and a tiny extremist fragment grouped around Mahmoud.

The moderates had eventually walked out in disgust from one of the meetings, bearing Georgiades with them, a little bewildered by it all, poor fellow, but ever obliging.

That left the extremists in even greater isolation. They drifted away from the Law School altogether and were seen just occasionally huddled in cafés. One or two came back after a while. Mahmoud seemed to have dropped out of things altogether.

• • •

Owen, sitting in his room, was feeling aggrieved.

He had gone to Paul hoping that Paul would help him nail Roper and Paul had more or less told him to forget about it. That was bad enough. Worse, though, Paul had suggested that there were bound to be other people involved and that he might go for them instead.

But when he had done so, when he had started putting his hands round Ali Osman's throat, Ali Osman had promptly played the same trick as Roper!

It was unfair. Well, no, it wasn't exactly unfair, because Egyptians should certainly be able to play the same cards as Europeans; but what stuck in Owen's gullet was that anyone should be able to play the cards at all.

He didn't believe that anyone should be allowed to place themselves beyond the reach of the law.

Certainly not Roper.

And, while he was thinking about it, certainly not Ali Osman.

It was unfair, yes, dash it, it was unfair, that he, Owen, should have put so much time into it, only for it all to come to nothing.

Paul had said that it was just a sideshow. Well, maybe it was, but it was an important sideshow. Running guns into an area like the Sudan where they might be used to start a war *was* important, not something you could disregard just like that.

And so was the slave trade. The British had thought they had eradicated that and here it was, going on as if the British had never existed, and Ali Osman making a bloody living out of it, no, more than a living, enough to bloody tip the national political scales! And *that* took real money.

Owen, chair tipped back on its rear legs, shoulders resting against the wall, feet on his desk, coffee in his hand, felt aggrieved.

Gradually, though, a sense of proportion began to reassert itself; loath though he was to admit it, Paul had been right. The gunrunning, the slave traffic too, was really a sideshow. Important though it was—and he certainly ought to do something about it—it was not as important as what was going on in Cairo, which was, after all, his main job.

Paul was right. What had Ali Osman got to do with students throwing bombs in Cairo?

Except that—he *did* have something to do with it.

Two of those students throwing bombs—not one, *two*, on two separate occasions—had come from the Pasha's estate at Hamada.

That could not be coincidence.

The front legs of Owen's chair came down with a crash.

Ali Osman *did* have something to do with the bombing!

Owen had gone down to Hamada not knowing who the local Pasha was, knowing only that a bomb had exploded there and killed its bearers, and wondering if the roots of the similar explosion in the café, which had killed another boy from Hamada, might somehow lie in the village.

When he had learned that Ali Osman was the local Pasha he had been surprised but had thought nothing of it.

His attention had been on the estate. What was it there, he had asked himself, which had led to local boys on two separate occasions, considerably separated by time, to become involved with extremist groups in the city?

He had thought initially that perhaps there was some group of zealots there, maybe even a conscious group of radicals. The thought had not survived his visit to Hamada. The villages were ordinary, sleepy, not very zealous about anything so far as he could see, and the very reverse of radical.

Could there then be, he had asked himself, some one person who had influenced the boys, someone in a position to influence them, a schoolteacher perhaps? But the schoolteacher at Hamada had not been that sort of person, nor did there appear to be any other person in the villages who could fit the bill. There was no one there sophisticated enough, knowledgeable enough, political enough, to be involved in terrorist politics in Cairo.

Except Ali Osman himself.

And Ali Osman *was* sophisticated, *was* knowledgeable and *was* most definitely in politics, right up to the hilt.

But *terrorist* politics? Weren't they opposed to everything Ali Osman stood for?

Well, were they? What did Ali Osman stand for?

That, surely, was abundantly clear; he stood for himself. His sights were on the highest position in the country, after the Khedive, and he had made it plain, very plain now that Owen came to think about it, that he would stop at nothing to get there.

Discount the mask of foolishness. The man Owen had talked to the previous day had been very far from a fool and had toughness and determination to go with his sharpness.

A man who dealt in slaves and guns might well be prepared to deal in terrorism also—if it suited him.

If he could use it for his own purposes.

In the labyrinthine web which was Egyptian politics Ali Osman might have spotted some advantage to be gained by playing the terrorist card; not in the obvious way that Sa'ad was playing the Nationalist card but more deviously, more secretly, an insider's way, out to outflank the interloper from outside the old, charmed circle.

But if he had, if he had decided to play the terrorist card, he would play it for all it was worth. The man who exchanged guns for slaves was not someone who was going to be held back by scruple: scruple about, for instance, the lives of students, whether they came from his own estate or somewhere else.

The two boys from Hamada had been just weapons.

But they were not weapons to be used by Ali Osman himself, not directly, that was. They were weapons to be placed in the hands of others.

Rashid's, for instance.

CHAPTER TWELVE

I know you," said the man. "You are the Mamur Zapt."

"And I know you," said Owen. "You are Ali Osman's man. And you came to me once bringing a message from him."

"That is true," agreed the man, pleased to be remembered.

They had met under the trees beside the souk, where many of the servants of the great houses went after they had made purchases for their masters, to sit and drink tea and talk.

Owen dropped into a sympathetic squat beside the man.

"I remember too," he said, "that although you were in the Pasha's house at Hamada, that was not where you came from in the first place."

"I am a Sudani."

"From Dongola."

The man was surprised, and pleased.

"Yes," he said, "from Dongola."

"Are there many Sudanis in the Pasha's household?"

"Quite a few."

"Slaves?"

"Not all of us. Some of us were born in the Pasha's house. Though of course our parents were slaves."

"And you?"

"I came up as a child in one of the great caravans."

"So you have been in the Pasha's service a long time." Owen looked at him. "Twenty years?"

"And a little more. But it was not at first this Pasha. It was his father."

"The caravans have, then, been coming for a long time?"

"Oh yes. Since as long as my father could remember."

"Is your father still at Hamada?"

"No. He died many years ago."

"But your wife is at Hamada," said Owen, "and your children. I remember."

"You remember well," said the man.

"I remember you saying that it was a long time since you had seen them."

"Four years," said the man, with a sigh.

"The children will be growing up."

"The eldest is already working in the fields."

"Do you want him to work in the fields?"

"I would prefer him to work in the house. And perhaps he will one day."

"He may follow his father," said Owen. "That is the way it should be."

"I have hopes."

Owen sipped his tea, the black, bitter tea of the servants.

"If I had a boy at Hamada, though," he said, as if considering, "I would be worried."

"Why so?"

"In my work I have met boys from Hamada. They are dead."

The man went perfectly still.

"Be easy. It does not happen to all the boys from Hamada. Only to some."

"Why does it happen to some?"

"It happens to some who are chosen by the Pasha. And that is what troubles me."

"I have not heard of it."

"I think you have. You were at Hamada, were you not, when the two boys were killed by the bomb?"

"Only one was from the village."

"And you were here in the city when the second boy was killed. Again with a bomb."

"I did hear of it."

"Again from Hamada. Why is it," asked Owen, "that boys from Hamada are killed by bombs?"

"Each time there was another with them. And they were not from Hamada."

"Nor did they come from the same place. What is special about boys from Hamada that they are made to be killed by bombs?"

"There is nothing special about boys from Hamada."

"What is special about Hamada, then, that two of its sons, on two separate occasions, are killed by bombs?"

"There is nothing special about Hamada either," said the man, troubled.

"Then there is something else that is special," said Owen, "and I want to know what it is."

"That is why you have come to me?"

"You are a father," said Owen, "of a boy at Hamada."

The man stared down at the dust in front of him. He stared for a long time. At last he lifted his head.

"I would help," he said, "if I could. But I cannot think of anything."

"Perhaps it is not at Hamada," said Owen. "Perhaps it is when the boys come up to the city. Who meets them?"

"They come to the Pasha's house."

"And then what happens?"

"They are given food and a place for the night. The next day they are sent to the Great School."

"Who sends them? Who tells them what they are to do?"

"Mohammed. But it is not Mohammed you are looking for. He does as he is told."

"And who tells him?"

"I do not know. Word comes."

"Who does it come from?"

"The Pasha's people. The people who handle such things."

"Who are these people?"

"They are from outside. They are not in the Great House."

"They are at the School?"

"No, no. They are the people who handle the Pasha's business."

"Do you know their names?"

The man was silent.

"You told me," said Owen, "when we spoke before, that it was you the Pasha sent when there were messages of importance. Have you been sent with messages to these?"

"I have," the man said reluctantly.

"You would not tell me what the messages were, would you?" said Owen. "Because you are the Pasha's servant and one he trusts."

"You are right. I would not tell you."

"I shall not, then, ask you. But I shall ask you the names of the Pasha's people, because if you do not tell me, there are others who will."

"I shall not tell you."

"Very well. Tell me this, though. Think of those boys and tell me this: did the Pasha ever send you to someone at the School of Law? Someone named Rashid?"

The man hesitated. He hesitated for a long time.

"He sent me to no one at the School of Law."

"Think of those boys; and think of your son."

"He sent me to no one at the School of Law. But—"

"Yes?"

The man's eyes met his.

"I am the Pasha's man. And I am loyal to him. I would tell you nothing. But I think of those boys. So I will tell you. The Pasha sent me to no one at the School of Law. But he did send me to people called Rashid."

"They are a firm of lawyers," said Nikos. "They act for the Pasha in legal matters."

"Other matters too?"

"General affairs. They are in a sense his business agents."

"So they would handle things like fixing up a place at the School of Engineering for a boy the Pasha was interested in?"

"That's right."

"And our Rashid is part of them?"

"A cousin. He's the bright one of the family."

"The other ones must be pretty bright."

"Once a family has made the breakthrough they look after the next generation. Rashid—our Rashid—is one of the next generation. It was his uncle who got them established as lawyers."

"When did they take on the Pasha's business?"

"Well, that was it, you see. That's what got them started in the first place. Rashid the elder was a boy on the Pasha's estate, and obviously a bright boy. The Pasha sent him up to be educated."

"I thought they all went to the School of Engineering?"

"That's *this* Pasha. I'm talking about this Pasha's father."

"I see. They did things differently then."

"You only need a limited number of lawyers."

"Especially as they tend to get dangerous ideas."

"Not Rashid the First. He steered clear of anything like that. He was too busy making money and consolidating his position. Besides, he wasn't, strictly speaking, a free agent. Although he was a qualified lawyer, he was still the Pasha's man."

"Slaves?"

"Don't think so. Fellahin, rather. Much the same, I suppose. Mother a slave, perhaps. All the Rashids have a touch of black in them. But they've been in the Pasha's service for generations. And when the elder Rashid set up as a lawyer, he was still in the Pasha's service. Handled all his business and only his business."

"What's the position now?"

"Pretty much the same. The firm is bigger now, of course. He's got his sons in it, two of them, and a nephew or two. It looks after them all. They do pretty nicely."

"And they're still the Pasha's men?"

"Yes."

"What about our Rashid?"

"He's the independent one. He's the only one to strike off on his own."

"How independent is he?"

"I don't know. He certainly keeps in touch with the firm. Maybe he does a little business on the side for them. A lecturer doesn't make much money."

"That's not quite what I was asking."

"What were you asking?"

"Is he still the Pasha's man?"

"Ah!" said Nikos. "That's the question!"

•   •   •

Mahmoud rang.

"I've been approached," he said.

And put the phone down.

•   •   •

"It is you again," said the man.

"It is me again," Owen agreed.

The man had finished at the souk and was on his way home. Owen dropped in beside him.

"It is important," he said, "or I would not come."

The man did not reply. He looked ahead of him as if he were calculating how far he had to go.

"What is it you want to know?"

"I have found the Rashids, and that was helpful. I wish to ask you about one particular Rashid, though."

Owen described him.

The man shook his head. "I have not seen such a man," he said.

"He is at the Law School. You have not taken a message to him?"

"I have taken no messages to the Law School."

"He lives in the Sharia Geheinat. Have you taken messages to him there?"

"No," said the man.

"You serve your master," said Owen, "and you serve him well. And that is right. But you are also a father. Remember why I ask these questions."

The man inclined his head in acknowledgment. Then he looked Owen in the face.

"I have answered you truly," he said.

Now it was Owen's turn to bow his head in acknowledgment. He reflected for a moment.

"You answer truly the questions I ask," he said, "but you do not answer the questions I do not ask."

"That would be difficult."

"Not if you knew the big question, the question that lies at the bottom."

"What is that question?"

"It is about Ali Osman and this Rashid I spoke of. Do they know each other? Have they met? Is Rashid Ali Osman's man?"

"That is not one question but three. However, I think I understand you."

He was silent for a moment, thinking.

"I am loyal to the Pasha, so I will answer only the questions you ask. However, I remember why you ask them. So I will say to you that you ask the wrong questions. Does the mountain go to Mohammed?"

Owen thought hard. They turned off the main road and up behind some houses, where the hard dust of the street gave way to soft sand.

The sand pulled at their feet and slowed them down. The man seemed content to dawdle. Owen realized he was being given his chance.

"The Pasha has not sent to him," he said slowly. "Has he sent to the Pasha?"

"Not sent."

"Been, then? Has he been to the Pasha?"

"He has come to the Pasha. Many times recently."

"Thank you," said Owen. "That is what I needed to know." He hesitated. "And can you tell me further what was said when he came to the Pasha?"

"I cannot. For they spoke alone."

They were beginning now to pass along the backs of some tall Mameluke houses. Owen guessed that one of the houses was Ali Osman's. His guess was confirmed, for the man suddenly stopped and said: "We are approaching my master's house. It is better if you are not seen with me."

Owen thanked him and prepared to take his leave. They shook hands warmly. Then, as the man was about to turn away, Owen said: "You have not answered my last question."

"What was your last question?"

"Is Rashid Ali Osman's man?"

"That," said the man, "is something you must answer for yourself."

•　　•　　•

"They are a respected firm of lawyers," said Nikos.

"They are the Pasha's people. You said it yourself."

"Yes, but that doesn't mean to say they'd get involved in something like this."

"Not if he asked them? Told them?"

"No. I think they'd draw the line."

"Would Ali Osman keep them if they drew the line?"

"I don't think it would come to that. He's too astute to ask them to do something they might object to. They're too useful to him as it is. Respectable."

"So he would ask somebody else?"

"Well—"

"Rashid?"

"It is odd that he should be seeing Ali Osman separately," Nikos admitted.

"I'd like to know if he was seeing him on their business."

"That would be hard to find out."

"You could try the clerks."

"I would try the clerks. But they tend to be all family in a firm like that, and loyal."

"You could try them."

"It's a risk."

"Take the risk."

• • •

"I've been approached," said Elbawi.

"Good!" said Owen with satisfaction.

"Well, yes. I suppose so. I was hoping they wouldn't."

"It's what we let you out for."

"I know. All the same . . ."

"Who approached you?"

"A man named Hawzi. I've seen him about the place before. He sort of hangs about the Law School. He came up to me as I was going home. We went to a café."

"You knew it was going to be this?"

"Guessed it. He said there were people who were very angry at the way I had been wronged and wished to help me. They had raised some money and wanted to give it to me."

"In return for—?"

"No, no. Just give it. A sort of, well, testimonial. If I was willing to accept it he would bring it the following day. That was today."

"And he did?"

"Yes."

"You've got the money?"

Elbawi took a small bag out from under his shirt.

"How much?"

"I've not counted it."

"And that was it? He just gave you the money?"

"No," said Elbawi. "That wasn't all. He said the money was just to help me. But there was more to it. They wanted to hit back, to take revenge for what I had suffered. As a matter of justice, so to speak. They were going to do that anyway, quite separately. But they thought I might like to be involved."

"Let's get this straight. *They* were going to take revenge. *You* were going to do the dirty work?"

"No. I was just going to play a minor part. I would be in the crowd. There would be arabeahs coming along. When a certain one came along I was to give a signal."

"That all?"

"As far as I was concerned, yes."

"Do you know what was going to happen then?"

"The arabeah would slow down to go up the hill—this was all going to happen at the Citadel—and as it slowed, someone would step out of the crowd and fire. There would be two men, one on each side."

"Two men," said Owen.

"That's right. He didn't say anything about them, though."

"No matter," said Owen.

"Then I was to go home."

"OK. Well, all that's very useful. You'll be able to show us the place where you are to stand, presumably?"

"Yes."

"Fine. And when is all this going to happen?"

"Tomorrow. Just before sunset. There is to be a small gathering to celebrate the Massacre of the Mamelukes. Symbolic, you see. The end of an old regime. The bit I'm concerned with is going to be symbolic too."

"How many are going to be at this gathering?"

"Only about a dozen. Less than twenty. They want to keep it selective, you see. Only some of the Pashas, those with political ambitions."

"Pashas?"

"Yes. It's to be an intimate gathering, you see, the chosen few. Only it has to be in public because they want everybody to know they're the chosen few."

"Have they actually been chosen?"

"Not as far as I know. The whole thing is really intended as a hint to the Khedive that they should be chosen."

"And it's Pashas? All Pashas?" asked Owen, puzzled.

"Yes."

"No one else?"

"No."

"Then who—who is the one who is going to be attacked?"

"Ali Osman."

"Ali Osman?" said Owen incredulously. "But that's—that's ridiculous!"

• • •

"Yes," said Mahmoud, "they have told me. Ali Osman."

"Ali Osman *Pasha?*"

"That's right. He's one of the old party hacks."

"I know who he is. I'm just—surprised."

"Why are you surprised? I would have thought he was quite a natural target for the terrorists. Identified with the old regime, friend of the Khedive, feudal landlord, known to be corrupt and harsh. I would have said he was just the sort of target you might expect."

"Well, yes, it's just that I was, well, working along different lines."

He told Mahmoud about Hamada and about the guns and the slaves.

"Slave traffic?" said Mahmoud, his face darkening. He was both a liberal and a firm believer in law as the basis of a just society. "I thought that had been abolished."

"I thought so too. But he's in it in a big way."

"Why haven't you arrested him?"

Owen started to explain, then stopped. Mahmoud was a Nationalist, too, and he wasn't likely to take kindly to the view that it was undesirable to move against Ali Osman because of the strength of the British interests he had lined up behind him.

Especially in the present circumstances.

"I'm trying to get it right," Owen said weakly, "politically right, I mean."

Mahmoud nodded. He was Cairene enough to know that things had to be politically right before you could do them.

"I'll get him," Owen promised, "but I want to let things run as they are just for the moment."

"Of course!" said Mahmoud enthusiastically. "You want to find out who his associates are. Pull in the whole lot of them."

"That's right. And there's another thing too. Something that particularly interested me. It might interest you. One of his associates is Rashid."

"Rashid? My Rashid?"

Owen nodded. "Your Rashid."

"But—but that can't be."

"That's what I thought. When you told me that Ali Osman was going to be the next target."

•   •   •

They were sitting outside a café in one of the small, crowded streets near the Bab el Wezir. Above them towered the famous rock, on the brow of which stood the Citadel.

Much of Saladin's marvelous castle was now in ruins. The stateliest part of it, Joseph's Hall, had been blown up in 1824 to make room for a still more fabulous building, the mosque of Mehemet Ali, with its Arabian Nights-like domes and minarets. Nowadays, too, it shared the space with the headquarters of the British Artillery stationed in Egypt, located in the deserted palace of a former Khedive.

Four conquerors, then, and each in his time had passed away, leaving only a building behind them.

Except, of course, the British.

A place of myth. And the most potent of the myths was the Massacre of the Mamelukes.

One day in March 1811, Mehemet Ali invited the Mamelukes, the princes who had ruled Egypt for over five hundred years, to a reception in the Citadel and, when it was over, suggested they ride in state through the city, escorted by his troops.

As the Mamelukes proceeded between the two lines of the Pasha's troops down the steep lane, hemmed in by rock and rampart, which leads from the Bab el Wastani to the Bab el Azab, the troops fell on them and killed them. One only, according to legend, escaped.

There was an added potency in the myth. By the time their dynasty came to an end, the Mamelukes had declined greatly from the warrior caste they had originally been. They had become decadent and corrupt—as decadent and corrupt, might it be said, as the Khedives and Pashas who had succeeded them? And might it not be their turn to be swept away as brutally and dramatically as the Mamelukes had been by Mehemet Ali?

Owen, aware of the power of myth and symbol to stir the Islamic mind, felt uneasy. The attack was intended to be symbolic, Elbawi had said. Owen was as much concerned about the symbol as about the attack itself.

"Obviously we're not going to let it happen," he said. "We'll have our people there and they'll pick up the men as soon as they spot them. No hanging around this time. We're not going to make *that* mistake again. At least we'll have the killers out of the way. But, of course, the one we're really after is Rashid. And that's where you come in."

"He's really clever," said Mahmoud. "He never does anything himself. He always works through other people."

"That's why this is so important. If he really does want to speak to you in person."

"That's what the message was."

"I can't quite see—I mean, why should he approach you now, when he's already set something up?"

"Perhaps he's thinking ahead to the next one."

"Yes. Or perhaps—" Owen suddenly sat up—"perhaps there's another part to this one. Something we don't know about yet."

"Someone else to be killed?"

"Another Pasha, perhaps. Someone besides Ali Osman. I'll have a look at the party and see who else is to be there."

Mahmoud finished his coffee.

"Of course," he said, "it may not be a case of some*one* else."

"What do you mean?"

"It might be more than one. Have you forgotten that Rashid has a predilection for bombs?"

•   •   •

Mahmoud left first. Owen sat on at the table drinking another cup of coffee. The café was well away from the Law School and from the Bab el Khalk and there was little chance of their being recognized. All the same it was as well to be careful.

Owen felt a hand on his shoulder. A small hand.

Soraya slipped into the chair vacated by Mahmoud.

"Your friend has gone. You can talk to me now."

"What are you doing here?" said Owen, surprised.

"I live here," said Soraya, pointing along the street. "Would you like to come home with me?"

Owen had forgotten that this was the area of the gypsies.

"That would be very nice," he said. "However, I am working."

"In the café? You are like my man. He sits in the café drinking tea when he should be stealing."

"Are you and your man together again?"

"Sort of," said Soraya vaguely.

The owner of the café came out, looked at Soraya sternly, and Owen questioningly, then shrugged his shoulders and went back inside.

Soraya beamed and drank some of Owen's coffee.

"Your friend looked nice, too," she said. "Nicer than your other friend."

"Roper, you mean? That is certainly true."

"Is he married?"

"Mahmoud? No."

"It is time he was," said Soraya censoriously. "You too."

"I dare say we'll get around to it sometime."

"Among my people," said Soraya pointedly, "it is the custom to marry young."

"Are you married?"

"I dare say I'll get around to it. One day."

•   •   •

"To do this to me!" said Ali Osman, upset. "Rashid!"

"He was your man, wasn't he?"

"Up to a point."

"Up to what point?"

"Does that matter?" asked Ali Osman. "Obviously not to the point when it would stop him from killing me."

"Yes, it does matter. He did things for you. What things?"

"Oh, various bits of business."

"Liaison with illegal Nationalist groups?"

"Well, yes, you might say that."

"Getting them to follow public servants? So that you could create an atmosphere of crisis which you could turn to political advantage?"

"My dear fellow!" said Ali Osman, staring. "What can you mean?"

"To shoot at Fairclough?"

"Certainly not!" said Ali Osman firmly. "The idea!"

"To throw bombs?"

"The one in the café was left, wasn't it?"

"The one at Nuri was thrown."

"I had nothing to do with either."

"But Rashid did."

"If he did," said Ali Osman earnestly, "that was nothing to do with me."

"He was your man, wasn't he?"

"Not in this. Not in this," said Ali Osman fervently.

"My question was," said Owen, "up to what point?"

Ali Osman sat silent for a long time, looking at Owen seriously. At last he said: "I shall have to tell you, shan't I?"

"Yes."

The Pasha was silent for a moment or two longer. Then he pulled himself together.

"Since you obviously know the answer already," he said, "I will tell you. Rashid is the nephew of Haround Rashid, my lawyer. The Rashids are good people, have worked for me for a long time. Entirely trustworthy. Except for Narouz Rashid."

"Narouz Rashid is the one at the Law School?"

"Yes. The bright one of the family. And the most untrustworthy. Mark that, my dear fellow! The two go together. Education is a bad thing and should be confined to those too stupid to benefit from it. That is why I only send dull boys up to Cairo to be educated. That is why—"

"Yes, yes. Did you send Narouz Rashid to be educated?"

"No. The Rashid family had more or less left my estate. They had set themselves up independently in Cairo. That was even before I inherited. Of course, they still worked for us, were still heavily dependent on us. But by then they could pay for their own education."

"And they all went to the Law School?"

"It is, after all, the only place. If you want to become a lawyer."

"And Narouz?"

"Went there too. Paid for by his grandfather. A clever boy, as I said. Too clever by half. He had ideas of his own. 'Haround,' I said, 'this boy is dangerous. He will end up by getting you all in trouble. Take my advice and get rid of him.' Well, of course, they did. Very sensibly."

"Let us get this straight," said Owen. "You make them get rid of him; and yet he now works for you?"

"On commission. On occasional commission. You don't make much money as a lecturer at the Law School. I bear him no ill will."

"The question is," said Owen, "does he bear you ill-will?"

Ali Osman regarded him thoughtfully. "It would appear so," he said, "wouldn't it?"

"Tell me about the commissions."

Ali Osman spread his hands and shrugged.

"Very well," he said, "if you must know. Narouz Rashid has links with a wide variety of Nationalist groups. The sort of groups that are not officially part of the Nationalist Party. The sort of groups that the Nationalist Party likes to steer clear of. At a time like this such groups can be useful. They will cause trouble on the streets. If you pay them."

"And you were paying them?"

"Rashid was paying them. I was merely providing the money."

"And what exactly were you paying them for?"

"He was paying them," corrected Ali Osman. "I was providing the money. What I wanted was trouble in the streets.

You know, at public meetings and processions and demonstrations. Not too much, naturally. Just enough to worry the
Khedive. And to embarrass the Nationalists."

"And that was as far as it was to go?"

Ali Osman looked at him soberly. "That, I swear, was as
far as it was to go."

Owen thought it over.

"The other," said Ali Osman, "was something he added
for himself."

Owen was still thinking. He felt half inclined to believe
Ali Osman. The other half, however, said that here was
someone who would cheerfully use others for his own advantage and would not be too particular about what happened to anyone who got in his way.

"Very well," he said, "I shall put you to the test. You will
go to the Citadel exactly as arranged. You will carry on as if
you knew nothing. My men will be in the crowd. You will
have nothing to fear."

"I certainly hope so," said Ali Osman.

"And if we pick up those two men I shall perhaps be disposed to take a lenient view of your actions. Some of them,"
he added, remembering the slave-trading and gunrunning.

Ali Osman bowed his head in acquiescence.

"And Rashid?"

"There, too. I shall need your help."

Ali Osman smiled thinly. "It will be given," he said, "with
the very greatest of pleasure."

•   •   •

Mahmoud rang.

"I've seen him," he said.

"Rashid?"

"Yes."

"What did he say?"

"He asked me to throw a bomb. At the group of Pashas
which would assemble in the Citadel."

"He actually asked you? Straight out?"

"Yes."

"Then we've got him," said Owen exultantly.

"Don't pick him up just on my say-so. He could always claim he hadn't meant it. Been testing me or something. Wait till I'm actually given the bomb."

"When will that be?"

"At the Citadel."

"Someone will give it you?"

"Yes. Elbawi."

"Elbawi!"

"Yes. He doesn't know yet. He thinks he's just there to give a signal when Ali Osman's arabeah arrives. Just before he sets out he'll be given a package to deliver."

"Will Rashid be there?"

"In person, you mean? I don't know."

"I'll put someone on him. We want to know where he is so that we'll be able to pick him up immediately."

"Someone good."

"Someone very good," said Owen.

He thought for a moment.

"Is the shooting still going to go ahead?"

"Ali Osman? Yes. But that's just a decoy. They are going to see that his arabeah gets delayed so that he arrives last. The others will all have assembled. They will hear the shots and then when everyone is rushing around I will be able to get close and throw the bomb. But I throw the bomb anyway."

"Are there any other permutations?"

"Not as far as I know," said Mahmoud.

•　　　•　　　•

Owen made his dispositions carefully. There would be handpicked men in the crowd, four of them, two for each gunman. They had been given descriptions of the gunmen and had rehearsed all morning. Now they were walking up and down the street which led up to the Citadel, familiarizing themselves with the street, getting used to operating in a crowd.

There were other men, too, only they would be held back. Owen didn't want them getting in the way. They were there in case things went wrong. Once Ali Osman's arabeah had gone by they would move quietly into the streets, not sealing them off—Owen didn't want the gunmen to panic and try shooting their way out, not when there were ordinary people about—but ready to intercept as they tried to escape if things went wrong in the main street.

Owen would join them just before things started to happen. He did not want to go down before as that would increase the chance of someone seeing him and recognizing him. He stayed in his office, quietly checking arrangements, especially those for disposing of the bomb afterwards. He wanted no accidents.

He was just able to set off for the Citadel when the phone rang.

The voice was so agitated that at first he could not tell who it was. Then he realized: Elbawi.

"They've found out!"

"What have they found out?" said Owen with sinking heart.

"About Mahmoud."

"Tell me."

"That he's—he's working for you. They are going to kill him."

"I'll get on to him right away."

"He's at the Citadel."

"I know."

"That's where it will happen. After he's thrown the bomb."

"He's not going to throw any bomb."

"I know. But he'll be there. They'll find him. And even if he doesn't throw the bomb they'll kill him."

"Who are 'they'? Do you know?"

"The two men."

"The ones who are going to kill Ali Osman?"

"Yes. But they're not going to kill Ali Osman now. They are going straight for Mahmoud. You've got to stop him before he gets there."

"I can't. He's already gone."

There was a silence. And then the voice said shakily: "The two men. They've—they've already gone too."

CHAPTER THIRTEEN

Owen couldn't find Mahmoud.

There on the terrace of the mosque of Mehemet Ali were the Pashas, a little group talking quietly among themselves, pausing occasionally to look out over the marvelous view at their feet, old Cairo with its hundred minarets, the broad, gleaming sweep of the Nile, the Pyramids dyed to royal purple by the advancing sunset.

The group was almost complete now, waiting only for Ali Osman. Owen saw Nuri glancing impatiently at his watch. The arabeah was obviously late. That part of the terrorists' arrangements at least was going to plan.

Mahmoud must be somewhere about. But where the hell was he?

He wouldn't be too far away because he had to be near enough to be able to throw the bomb. Mahmoud, stickler for accuracy that he was, had insisted on carrying out his role to the letter. That was, he had said, the only way to make sure that things happened the way they were meant to happen. Rashid would certainly have planted an observer in the crowd and if he, Mahmoud, deviated from the plan, this might alert them and cause them to deviate too.

But where the hell was he? Owen had circled all around the terrace and he wasn't there. He had tried the neighboring En-Nasir, a ruined mosque with a forest of pillars, all good for hiding behind, but Mahmoud was nowhere to be found.

He walked back to the Bab el Azab gate and stood for a moment looking down at the crumbling steps which fell down to the houses below, and then up at the steep ramparts which hemmed the gate in.

The Bab el Azab was where the Pashas' act of remembrance would actually take place. It was there that Mehemet Ali's troops had waited for his signal to fall on the Beys and massacre them. The gate had seen the end of an old regime. It was hoped—by the assembled Pashas—that this symbolic gathering would see the beginning of a new.

Owen climbed up onto the ramparts to get a better view. A hundred yards away he could see Georgiades moving among the pillars of the En-Nasir. He could see others of his men. But no Mahmoud.

He climbed down off the ramparts and walked across to Georgiades.

"I'm going down into the street. Handle things up here, will you?"

"They'll be moving soon," said Georgiades. The Pashas were beginning to stir, giving up hope of Ali Osman's arrival.

"Keep looking," said Owen.

He started walking down the street. He was looking for the two gunmen as well as for Mahmoud. He tried to recall their image to his mind, that brief glimpse he had had of them at the start of all this.

At the bottom of the street he saw Elbawi. His face was grey and miserable and he leaned shattered against a wall. He looked up dumbly as Owen arrived.

"Have you seen him?"

"Yes," said Elbawi.

"Did you tell him?"

"No," said Elbawi wretchedly. "I—I couldn't."

"Why the hell not?"

"He just reached out and took the bomb."

"Bomb!"

"I had it. They gave it to me and I took it up the street. You told me I was to do exactly as had been arranged!"

"OK, OK. But why the hell didn't you speak to Mahmoud?"

"He was behind me. He just reached past me and took it out of my hands. I looked up and he was gone."

"When was this?"

"A quarter of an hour ago."

"Bloody hell."

Owen wheeled away and hurried back up the street. It had become more crowded.

Another thought struck him. Suppose Mahmoud was actually carrying the bomb when they reached him? Suppose it exploded as he fell in a crowded street?

He saw one of his marksmen.

"What the hell are you doing? I thought you were supposed to be by the Pasha?"

The man pointed.

A little further up the street, completely hemmed in by people, was Ali Osman.

"You've got to be *near* him!" Owen exploded.

"Hassan and Abdul are near him. Mahboub and I stand back a little that we may watch."

His eyes were scanning the crowd continuously. It made good sense.

"OK," said Owen. "Keep going."

He followed Ali Osman up the street. The little knot surrounding the Pasha seemed to have come to a halt. There were cries of "Make way for the Pasha!"

Owen squeezed past along the wall. He hadn't envisaged it being as crowded as this. There was nothing he could do, however. He had to leave it to his marksmen.

And Ali Osman did not really matter.

As he passed an open doorway someone pulled at his arm. He spun around. It was Soraya. She drew him through the door.

"Not now," snapped Owen.

Soraya pouted.

"It is never now with you," she said. "What is wrong with you?"

"I have to find a man. Quickly!"

"Men can wait."

"This one will be killed."

"Who is he? The fat Pasha?"

"No. My friend."

"If it is your friend the Englishman, why worry?"

"It is not my friend the Englishman. It is the Egyptian, Mahmoud."

"The one I saw with you yesterday? The nice one?"

"Yes." He pulled himself away.

"I have seen him."

"Mahmoud?"

"Yes."

"When?"

"Ten minutes ago."

He caught hold of her. "Where? Where did you see him?"

"Climbing up the steps by the Bab el Azab."

"Climbing up the steps?"

"Yes."

"But I was there then!"

Soraya shrugged. "I saw him."

"That must have been just after I'd left."

"Do you want me to find him?"

"Yes. Tell him his life is in danger. They have found out."

In an instant the small form was gone. Soraya, used to slipping through crowds, and knowing the street, found gaps where the bulkier Owen could find none. He pushed his way up laboriously. All the time he was looking for the gunmen.

Where the hell was Mahmoud? And why the hell had he got the bomb with him?

A thought struck him, a stupid thought, which he dismissed at once but which would not go away.

Why did Mahmoud have the bomb with him? Because he meant to use it.

Ridiculous! Stupid! Mahmoud was his friend, on his side, responsible, loyal.

But a Nationalist.

And he *had* been wronged. It wasn't just pretense. He *had* fallen foul of the British authorities, he had been publicly dismissed from a case. Those in the know knew it wasn't quite like that. But . . .

Ridiculous. The man's life was in danger because he had put it at risk. Because he felt it was his duty.

Ridiculous. Shameful, to think such a thing. Owen reproached himself.

He was nearly at the top of the street now. Ahead of him, yes, outlined against the beautiful twilit sky, he could see the little group of Pashas gathering at the Bab el Azab.

They were looking down the street. One of them suddenly began to wave a hand. Then they all began waving, beckoning. Ali Osman! They must have seen Ali Osman.

There was a shout behind him.

Where the hell was Mahmoud? And where the hell were the two gunmen?

Immediately in front of him there was a sudden commotion. An onion-seller's stall had been upset by the swirl of the crowd, the stall had collapsed and the onions spilt all over the street.

The onion seller rushed out into the crowd to recover his wares. Sundry small boys, street urchins, rushed out to pilfer. Neighboring stall-holders and shopkeepers rushed out to prevent them. The upward movement of the crowd came to a halt.

Owen found himself stumbling over onions. He bent down and put his hand against the wall to recover his balance. A slight gap opened in front of him.

And then he saw.

A little way ahead, moving purposefully up the street, two men, one on one side of the street, one on the other. They were in shirt and trousers and there was nothing to distinguish them from many others in the crowd. Except that they were familiar.

He had seen them before, once briefly, when he had looked back up the street and caught, just for a second, a glimpse of the men who had been following; a second time, more clearly, much, much more clearly, when they had been following Jullians.

He pushed a stooping stall-holder out of the way and forced a passage along the wall, behind the stalls, pushing the stall-holders firmly aside. He came clear of the crowd and stepped out into the street and fell in behind the men.

They were almost at the top of the street now. Above, the ground flattened out and became the Citadel plateau.

There was the Bab el Azab. And there, coming towards it, was the little group of Pashas, joined now by Ali Osman.

And there, standing quietly to one side, looking aimlessly out over the vista below, right next to the edge of the rock, beside the steep fall, was Mahmoud.

The two men in front paused slightly, exchanged glances, and then moved quickly on.

Owen had brought his gun with him this time. He took it out.

The men ducked suddenly behind a wall. Owen thought for a moment that they had seen him. He slipped into a doorway and then, as nothing happened, slid cautiously along to where they had disappeared.

There was a step down to a drain and then a deep gadwall, a ditch used for carrying water, ran along beside the wall.

The two men had dropped down into the ditch and were creeping along it. As Owen watched, they stopped, straightened up and took out their guns.

Owen fired first.

One of the men spun around and fell back against the side of the gadwall. The other turned. Owen saw for a moment a frenzied face.

And then the face simply disappeared. It was as if a giant hand had reached into the gadwall and plucked it out.

And then, as Owen watched, the second man disappeared. This time there could be no doubt about it. A hand *had* reached in and—plucked him out!

Owen ran up the gadwall, put his hand on the wall, and scrambled out.

There was a little group of people in front of him. One he recognized at once: Mahmoud. Beside him was the slight slip of a figure that was Soraya. On the ground were two men, both still. And towering over them were two outlandish figures that seemed slightly familiar, Berbers from the south.

One of them was holding something in his hand.

They saw Owen and beamed.

"Effendi!" they greeted him. "You spoiled it!"

"Spoiled what?"

He recognized them now: Nuri Pasha's ruffian body-guards.

"The fighting. We saw them coming and would have fought with them. But then you fired!"

"Fortunately you did not kill them."

"So we did."

"What's that you're holding?"

The man looked down at his hands sheepishly. He showed the thing to Owen. A head.

"It seems to have come off," he said.

•   •   •

The gypsy girl had reached Mahmoud. Warned by her, he had looked up and seen the two men as they were pulling out their guns.

"I dropped flat and missed the next bit," he said. "When I looked up there was a melée going on at the edge of the gad-wall. By the time I got there it was all over."

"They were good," said Soraya appreciatively. "Nuri picks his men well."

"I looked for you before," Owen said to Mahmoud. "Where were you?"

"I took the package from Elbawi," said Mahmoud. "It really was a bomb. I didn't know what to do with it. I couldn't find your man," he said to Owen. "I knew I had to get rid of it. I couldn't just carry it around. Not in a crowd. So I went down the steps from the Bab el Azab and crawled around the rock and stuffed it into a crevice. It took longer than I thought."

"What about the reward?" said Soraya. "I found him, didn't I?"

Owen took out his wallet.

"Not *that!*" said Soraya scathingly.

•　　　•　　　•

Rashid needed to be dealt with first.

He had not come, as Owen had half-expected he would, to the Citadel. Owen sent a man to his lodging. The agent he had posted there said that Rashid was still inside.

"He has been there all day," he reported, when Owen and Mahmoud arrived. "He did not go to the Law School today."

"Are you sure he's there?" asked Owen. He began to feel misgivings.

"He was there last night," said the agent. "I saw him."

"He may not be there now," said Owen. "This is the way he would have come out."

"Unless he used a back way."

"It is not easy to use the back way. And then, why should he?"

"We'll soon see."

He posted his men to cut off any attempt at escape. Then he and Mahmoud went into the block of flats, climbed up to the third floor and found Rashid's door.

Mahmoud tried it gently. It was locked.

Owen called up two huge constables. They stood back from the door, braced themselves and looked at Owen expectantly.

"One moment," said Owen.

He tried the door of the adjoining flat. It opened at once and he went in. A surprised man looked up at him.

"The Mamur Zapt," said Owen.

He went across to the window. There was no glass, just heavy wooden shutters. He pushed them open.

"Stand here," he directed one of his men. "That's his window. See if he tries to get out."

He went back into the corridor.

"OK," he said to the two large constables.

They threw their weight against the door. It held for a moment and then burst open, spilling them inside.

Mahmoud and Owen ran in.

The room was empty but there was a door leading to an inner room. Mahmoud threw it open.

Rashid was lying on the bed. There was blood all over it.

"Throat cut," said Mahmoud. He looked at Rashid's hand and then under the bed. "No weapon."

"Someone else," said Owen.

The shutters were open. Owen went across and looked out.

"Roof, I should think," he said.

Rashid's jacket was hanging over the back of a chair. Mahmoud put his hand into the inside pocket.

"Wallet still there."

"Not money, then."

"No."

Georgiades came in from the corridor. He saw the body and stopped.

"Hello!" he said. "What's this?"

He walked across and looked at it dispassionately.

"Professional job, I'd say."

He turned away and began to search the room meticulously.

"Yes," said Mahmoud. "I'd say that too."

He took up a position in the center of the room, directly in front of the bed, and began to look systematically about him.

"Yes," he said, after a moment. "That's what I would say. Clean, simple cut from left to right done from behind by someone who knew how to do it. No sign of struggle, all over in a moment, very expert. Professional, as you say. And that I find a little puzzling."

"Why?" asked Owen.

"No sign of struggle, door locked. Rashid must have let him in. Why, I ask myself, would Rashid let someone like that into his room?"

"Because he wanted to employ them."

"A throat-cutter? Guman, yes; a potential thrower of bombs, yes. But a throat-cutter? That's not the way political assassination works. At least, not in Cairo. I don't think Rashid knew he was a throat-cutter and I don't think he meant to employ him. I think he let him in because he came from somebody else. Somebody important."

"Yes," said Owen. "That's where I was, too."

• • •

"What if I did?" said Ali Osman. "Does it matter?"

"Yes," said Owen. "You can't take the law into your own hands."

"The hand of the law is not always entirely consistent in Egypt," said Ali Osman. "It's much better to settle these things on a personal basis."

"So you did send him?"

"As I said, the law is not always consistent. You cannot count on it seeing things the way you do. The injustices that can come about, my friend! And so I think we should leave the matter in doubt. You should be satisfied that Rashid is dead. I, well, when a man has attempted to kill me, I—" Ali Osman smiled like a hungry wolf—"would not expect him to live long."

• • •

"The trouble is," said Owen, "that unless we find the actual killer and get him to confess, there's not much we can do."

"I take it the Parquet are looking into it?" said Paul.

"Yes. The case has been put in the hands of one Mohammed Bishari. Mahmoud says it is bound to take a long time."

"Is that entirely an accident, would you think?"

"I would think some of Ali Osman's gun-running money has found its way into the Parquet."

"Well," said Paul, "it's not strictly your business any longer, is it? The terrorist attacks have stopped, the Army is safe on the streets, God's in his heaven and all's right with the world."

"I wouldn't say that. The Khedive still hasn't made up his bloody mind and Ali Osman still think's he's going to be the next Prime Minister."

"It's between him and Sa'ad."

"In that case it's likely to be Ali Osman. Unless we can stop him. Can't you get the Government to do something about the gunrunning?"

"No. It needs someone more powerful at home. Powerful in Whitehall."

"Does it?" said Owen thoughtfully.

•　　　•　　　•

"Good God!" said the Army. "Gunrunning!"

"I'm afraid so. Regular caravans. Shipments in bulk."

"Bloody hell!"

"And all going to the south as far as we can tell."

"The Sudan? Hmm, that's dangerous. We could have another war on our hands."

"That's what I thought."

"The Khalifa's dead, of course, but there's bound to be someone else they could rally to."

"Pretty tricky down there."

"Like tinder, old man. All it needs is a spark."

"And guns."

"By Christ, yes. And guns!"

"Thought I'd better tell you."

"Absolutely right, old man. Absolutely right."

"The trouble is, I can't touch him. Too powerful. Powerful friends—" Owen dropped his voice—"back at home. We need someone on our side. Someone who can speak up for us. Powerful voice. Whitehall."

"You can rely on us. On to it right away. Oh, and, Owen—well done! Damned smart work!"

•   •   •

And so Ali Osman fell from power. The efficient political machine of the Army—efficient at politics if nothing else— had gone to work, whispering in the clubs, arguing in the corridors, questioning in the House.

Was it true that the Khedive was proposing to appoint a notorious slave-dealer as his Prime Minister? Nonconformist souls in the Government's ranks rose in wrath.

And a gunrunner to boot? Some Nonconformist souls pursed their lips and muttered "Business." Others, the pacifist conscience of the party, recoiled.

Arming the south? That meant war. Sound Conservative heads wagged. Had our Army's glorious conquests gone for nothing? Was the Mahdi to march again? The rot must be stopped.

The delegation made an early return to London. Its report was unaccountably long in appearing and when it did appear its recommendations were innocuous. There were, alas, fewer opportunities of commercial benefit than had been supposed.

Roper appeared some time later in South Africa.

The Minister sent a telegram to the Consul-General. The Consul-General had a word in the Khedive's ear. And Ali Osman retired speedily to his estate, this time, if not quite permanently, at least for several years. The Mamur Zapt made a point of ensuring that his years of retirement were not interrupted by further commercial considerations.

The Pasha took his banishment hard. "It is so uncivilized down here, *mon cher*," he complained in a letter to Owen, "and so uncomfortable. Cannot you intercede for me? You know I have always been a supporter of the Khedive, and of the British, of course. And, after all, didn't I do you a favor?"

• • •

One day Soraya claimed her desserts.

She came up to him as he was waiting outside the Continental Hotel.

Unfortunately, Zeinab came down the steps just at that moment.